Honeymoon with Death

A Second Sons Inquiry Agency Regency Mystery

Featuring Prudence Barnard Gaunt and Knighton Gaunt

By

Amy Corwin

Summary

On their honeymoon trip through Europe, Prudence and Knighton join a small group of travelers to see the triple falls on the river Velino in Italy when tragedy strikes. Their carriage breaks down on a remote road, they are accosted by bandits, and escape only to find one of the travelers dead the next morning in a ravine near the bandits' ambush location. The mystery deepens when they discover the victim is wearing another traveler's cloak.

To make matters worse, the inn they are forced to stay in is reputed to be haunted.

As Knighton and Pru investigate, they discover the other passengers of the coach were not the strangers they seemed. Revenge, envy, and frustrated love vie as motives, and Knighton is pushed to desperation when Pru is kidnapped. He must use every ounce of logic and intelligence to find the killer and free his wife before there is another death on the road to Rome.

Facebook and Newsletter Connection

Connect with Amy Corwin and "like" her page on Facebook at http://www.facebook.com/AuthorAmyCorwin for fun news and book teasers.

Sign up for her newsletter for information about new releases, book sales, and freebies here or through her Facebook page.

Copyright

This is a work of fiction. Names, characters, places, incidents either are the product of the author's imagination or are used fictitiously. Any resemblance to actual persons, living or dead, business establishments, events or locales, is entirely coincidental.

Honeymoon with Death

COPYRIGHT © 2015 by Amy G. Padgett

Contact information: contact@amycorwin.com

Cover Art by Amy G. Padgett
Publisher: Fireside Mysteries
Editorial Services provided by: Vince Dickinson

Publishing History
First Edition, 2015

Chapter One

October 11, 1819 – The Umbria region, central Italy

Pru closed her eyes and clung to the ancient coach's strap, trying to catch even a small breath of the cool air that occasionally puffed out from under the leather curtain. They should never have sent her maid and her husband's valet on to Rome in their own carriage to secure rooms for them during the busy season approaching Christmas. While the notion seemed practical, and they thought they would enjoy the company of the six other travelers, this had not proved to be the case.

The carriage swayed and rattled. The entire world seemed to jerk and spun. Back and forth—jolt—bounce and a wallowing lurch forward as the vehicle rattled over the ruts in the winding, hilly road. Her grip tightened as she listened to the worrisome creak of the leather suspension straps supporting the carriage, the clatter of the wooden wheels, and the constant clopping of horse hooves. The roads through the hills were treacherous. A mistake by the coachman or bolting horses would send them hurtling into the rocky ravines that fissured the ancient hills around them.

Thoughts about the dangerous road did nothing to take her mind off of her queasiness. The vehicle rumbled onward, and nothing granted her even a moment's relief.

If only she could roll up the curtain and get some fresh air, perhaps the motion wouldn't bother her so much. Any hint of coolness would surely settle her stomach. Even as she took a long breath, Mrs. Ruberry, the woman next to her, shifted. Onions, garlic, and the heavy odor of stale perfume filled the confined space. The smells hinted unpleasantly at the greasy sausages Mrs. Ruberry had consumed during their last stop.

Pru turned her head, but couldn't avoid the memory of that meat, glistening and spitting fat as Mrs. Ruberry bit

1

into it. Her stomach clenched and rolled. She clutched at the strap even more desperately as her skin prickled with icy sweat.

She would not be ill—she simply would not!

Only another day. Two at most. The coachman refused to travel after dusk due to the ruffians infesting the area, but he said they might even reach Terni today if they were lucky. Once there, they could break with their traveling party and send for their own coach.

She smiled resolutely when her husband leaned forward and caught her free hand. He gave her fingers an encouraging squeeze, and she tightened her hold on him, grateful for the distraction. When she gazed into his eyes, so warm with sympathy, the answering flutter in her stomach made her feel better.

Three months... She could hardly believe they had been married over three months now, despite the fact that they were traveling through Europe on their honeymoon. She still felt as excited and nervous as the day they had stood in church and recited their vows. His loving glance and slow, lopsided smile continued to make her feel breathless and deliciously self-consciousness.

He made her feel beautiful and desirable.

Prudence Barnard Gaunt. Mrs. Knighton Gaunt, wife. Just thinking of her new name filled her to bursting with joy.

"How are you feeling?" Knighton asked, stroking her hand. His warm fingers temporarily soothed her.

Finally, she caught a blessed gust of cool, pine-scented air that managed to puff out from under the curtain.

"Well enough." If only the carriage would stop bouncing and lurching over the bumpy road.

She flushed at her words. They felt like a lie, but she refused to admit she wanted to get out of the carriage and just sit in the fresh air for a few minutes. There had been more than enough tiresome discussions about travel sickness and its cure. She had never experienced such illnesses before and loathed the weakness it implied.

The strangest thing was that she had not felt queasy before, even on their rough passage over the English Channel. She had thought she was immune to such things until the last few days.

Knighton smiled and gave her hand another squeeze as he mouthed the word, "Liar." He understood her so well—he'd guessed that despite her assurances, she still felt a trifle delicate.

If only the coach would stop swaying from side to side.

Or that Mrs. Ruberry would have washed off her perfume that morning instead of adding more. And that she hadn't eaten quite so many garlic sausages and onions.

Just the thought of the greasy dishes made Pru's stomach revolt. She pressed her fingers against her lips and swallowed hastily.

Without advising the four other occupants, her husband rolled up the curtain next to Pru and fastened the leather flap with two ties. A flood of fall air brushed her cheeks and trickled through the smooth dark hair framing her face. The fresh air smelled sweet and clean, and she could almost taste the sunshine illuminating the green hills around them in dramatic sweeps of light and shadow. She turned to stare out of the window and breathe deeply, grateful for the invigorating, slightly astringent scent of sun-warmed pines. Her tender stomach settled immediately, and she relaxed, resting her head against the squabs as she studied the scenery.

Stretches of oak woods were broken here and there by deep green, needle-leafed Aleppo pines that cast the occasional, deep shadow over the winding road with their gnarled branches. The deciduous trees had mostly lost their leaves, although a few brown and sere remnants clung to the ends of their fragile branches. A few olive trees dotted areas adjacent to wide fields, the signs of small villages nestled in the valleys between the rolling hills.

Amy Corwin

"What have you done?" Mrs. Ruberry cried suddenly, awaking from her brief nap. She clutched at her collar as if choking before she tried to reach around Pru to pull the shade down.

Knighton blocked her with his arm. "My wife needs some air," he said in a calm voice.

"Air? Are you mad? I have never heard of such a ridiculous notion. Cover that window immediately. You will make us all ill—have you no consideration for the rest of us?" She shivered and rubbed her wool-clad arms, releasing another acrid cloud of garlic, onions, and stale perfume. She poked Pru in the side as she jerked around and gave her a hard look.

"I am sorry, but if we could leave it open just a few minutes, I would appreciate it." Pru leaned as far away from the woman's elbow as possible, clinging to the curved side of the coach.

"A few minutes? A few minutes is all that is needed to bring sickness to all of us." Mrs. Ruberry flung a heavy arm around the thin shoulders of the girl she chaperoned. "I am responsible for this young lady and cannot present her ill to her cousins in Rome because of your lack of manners. One would think you, and your husband," she cast an angry look at Knighton, "would have enough consideration for others to ask before doing anything so foolish. It is absolutely reprehensible. Please have the goodness to think of the others in this conveyance and close that window immediately, Mr. Gaunt, or you shall force me to ask the driver to bring this carriage to a halt."

Oh, please, not another delay. Pru glanced beseechingly at her husband. She was well past the ability to reason with Mrs. Ruberry.

Over the last two days, the woman had complained and berated everyone in the coach for one reason or another. Just an hour ago, the driver threatened to force all of them out of his coach and go on without them if they couldn't keep her from yelling at him about his handling of his horses. It had taken all the patience Pru and Knighton

4

could muster to convince him to ignore the ill-tempered woman and carry on.

No one was exempt from her oft-scathing criticism, and the only lucky ones were the two men who rode on the roof behind the driver.

"Oh, Mrs. Ruberry, *please*. You are embarrassing me," Miss Catherine Demaretti, the young woman next to her, said in an agonized voice." Why must you always make such a fuss over everything? I, for one, would like to look out the windows. I would like to see where we are going." The girl rolled her eyes in such a hoydenish, arrogant manner that it confirmed Pru's previous suspicion that Miss Demaretti might be at least partially responsible for her chaperone's uncertain temper.

Not that Mrs. Ruberry needed much to set her off on another tirade.

"You had best hold your tongue, young lady, and do as you are told," Mrs. Ruberry replied sharply. "When I was your age, young people did not address their elders in such a fashion. I warn you right now that your cousins in Rome will not tolerate such behavior. Ladies in Rome are proper and respectful."

"How would you know? You have never been to Rome." Miss Demaretti tilted up her chin and set her mouth in a mulish line.

"I *know*, never you fear. So you just sit there and be quiet until you are spoken to," Mrs. Ruberry said.

Miss Demaretti gave her chaperone an angry glance, but she didn't reply. At least she seemed to have enough delicacy of feeling to avoid a prolonged argument in public, and Pru was profoundly grateful for that small mercy.

Disagreements always made her uncomfortable, and for some reason, such fights between relative strangers seemed even worse. Perhaps because she didn't know the participants well enough to know how shrewish they might become.

She let out a long sigh. Maybe it wouldn't be such a catastrophe if the coachman did abandon them all on the side of the road and drive on without them. At least Pru and her husband could free themselves from the rest of the increasingly unhappy party of travelers.

Then, just as she was beginning to enjoy the journey through the lovely countryside, one of the other men in the carriage, Lieutenant Fisher, pulled out a pipe and leather pouch of tobacco. Smoke soon wreathed the head of the gentleman sitting next to her husband. Between that and the overpowering muskiness of Mrs. Ruberry's perfume, Pru could hardly speak for fear of being ill.

The light breeze coming through her small window was suddenly insufficient. The close confines of the coach, and the insistence by the other passengers that the other leather curtains covering the windows remain closed to protect them from the cool breezes of October made her seriously consider requesting a perch on top of the carriage.

Only the knowledge that her husband might object to her assuming such a precarious position kept her silent. And she didn't want to abandon her handsome husband to the other travelers.

Her husband... She still had difficulties believing it was finally true.

After so many years alone, she'd given up hope of finding love, or even companionship. Now, she could hardly believe that she had both. As she gazed at the sharp lines of his face, the strength of his chin, and the ironical arch of his dark eyebrows, she caught her breath with the overwhelming rush of love. He was not perfect, but he understood her. No other man who would ask her sincerely for her opinion and actually listen to her reply. That alone made her cherish their close relationship.

When she caught the amused glance of the middle-aged, pipe-smoking lieutenant sitting on Knighton's right, she dropped her gaze to her hands. Her fingers clasped together tightly in her lap, and she worked to wipe her fatuous—and she knew it had to be quite fatuous after staring so fixedly at her husband—smile off her face. She detested the thought that the other passengers could see her emotions stamped clearly upon her face. Despite her age of eight-and-twenty, she must look like the silliest, dewy-eyed girl, newly married and completely besotted by her husband.

One would think she could control her emotions better.

She'd never been one to show her emotions and disliked the thought of such silliness. She was a mature woman, and the thought that she'd been caught staring in bemusement at Knighton by a virtual stranger made her warm with humiliation. After three months, she ought to be quite *blasé,* instead of giddy every time she caught Knighton's dark gaze.

"Well? Are you going to close that window or not?" Mrs. Ruberry prodded her again with her elbow.

Pru, noting how her husband's mouth tightened, hastily untied the shade and let the curtain drop. Although she made a show of tying it down at the far bottom corner, she left the corner nearest her undone, hoping to get a bit of air now and again without Mrs. Ruberry noticing.

"Thank you, Mrs. Gaunt." Mrs. Ruberry examined her boldly, her blue eyes avid with curiosity. "You will thank me later for insisting. You are already too pale, and indeed look halfway ill already. Perhaps you suffer from travel sickness, my dear?" She leaned closer to her, the odor of garlic wafting around them as she gave Pru's arm an awkward pat. Her gaze flicked to Knighton and then back. "Or something else. It must be a terrible thing to have such a weakness. I knew a lady once who suffered so terribly that she could not even catch sight of a conveyance of any kind in the street before she was quite ill. Of course, I have never been ill a day in my life, but I have always been so sensitive to the weaknesses of others that I am quite known for it. Why many say that my mere presence is as good as a tonic to bring them back to perfect health. Well, never mind if you feel weak." She fumbled in her reticule, her elbows poking and bruising Pru uncomfortably before she pulled out a twist of brown paper. She handed the packet to Pru. "Here, you take this. 'Tis nothing but a bit of mint, but I daresay you may find it soothing."

What she would find even more soothing was the chance to escape the close confines of the coach and ride on the roof, regardless of the propriety of the action.

When Pru didn't immediately take the twist of paper, the woman pushed it into her hands. "Truly, it will make you feel ever so much better, and 'tis better than uncovering the windows." She gave an elaborate shiver that managed to bruise Pru's side yet again. "That nasty, cold air will bring illness to all of us. You will see, mark my words. Now you just chew on a bit of mint when you need to. I should have brought some lozenges, but I am so rarely ill, you see, that I did not think to do so."

"Thank you, Mrs. Ruberry." Pru tucked the small herb packet into her own reticule. The thought of chewing on dried mint brought forth such a strong urge to empty her stomach that she could only clamp her mouth shut and sit rigidly for half a minute until she brought her reaction under control.

"You are very welcomed, my dear." She crossed her left arm over her right and awkwardly patted Pru's wrist again. "We must all help each other, must we not? If you need ought else, you must not hesitate to ask." She followed up this statement by switching her hands and gesturing to the girl on her left. "As you know, I am accompanying Miss Demaretti to visit her cousins in Rome. Will you be going on to Rome, as well, Mrs. Gaunt? Or do you plan another excursion before arriving in that great city? I hope so, as it will be much nicer if we can maintain our friendship in Rome. I do so enjoy viewing the scenery and monuments in the company of my friends and acquaintances—it is much more amusing and gratifying to share similar and sympathetic opinions. Don't you find it so?"

8

The thought of sightseeing around Rome in the company of Mrs. Ruberry made Pru's nausea return with a vengeance. "We go to Terni, of course," Pru replied, nodding at Knighton as a flutter of pride at being his wife tickled her. "After that, I am unsure of our plans."

"Oh, you must go on to Rome with us. We will be fellow travelers, then," Mrs. Ruberry said. "I am relieved to discover our traveling companions are so delightful, my dear, though it is a pity that you are plagued with the traveling sickness. These old, swaying coaches cannot be comfortable for you, I'm sure. Though of course, I do not mind such things, myself. I am always quite comfortable when I travel. Many have remarked upon it, indeed."

Their conveyance swayed and wallowed like an overloaded galleon battered by thundering waves.

Pru swallowed and clenched her jaw. Only a few more hours.

She nodded, swallowing rapidly as she fumbled for the tie holding the leather curtain in place. Her husband, noting her distress, quickly untied the curtain and rolled it back up.

"Oh, you must not do that again! You will make your wife sick—can you not see that she is ill already?" Mrs. Ruberry asked in a strident voice. She reached around Pru and tried to pull the leather shade back down. When Knighton frowned at her, she subsided back into her seat with a frown wrinkling her coarse features. "Mark my words, that air will be the death of us all."

Pru marked her words, but gulped in the fresh, cool air anyway, thankful to get the taste of perfume, garlic, and tobacco smoke out of her mouth. The breeze carried the sharp, clean tang of autumn, brightened with the scents of cedar and pine, and her unsettled stomach once more eased.

She could not go on with the curtain covering the window no matter how much Mrs. Ruberry protested.

"I'd like to keep the window open, if you don't mind," Pru replied. "I've never been in this part of the world and would like to see what lies around us."

"Nothing but a few scraggly trees and rocks, my dear." Blue eyes all too sharp, Mrs. Ruberry flashed a knowing, and remarkably hard gaze over Pru's face. "If you're feeling ill, it'ud be much better for all of us if you were to take another pinch of that mint: I have my charge here," she patted Miss Demaretti's arm again, "to consider."

"Oh, do be quiet, Ruberry," Miss Demaretti said, frowning petulantly at her chaperone. "I'd rather have the windows open, as well. There is little enough to do, and I'm tired of playing cards and sleeping."

"Then we must certainly have the windows open." Captain Marshall, the young man sitting across from Miss Demaretti, rolled up and fastened the leather curtains on the two windows on their side of the elderly coach. "I must say, I approve of your decision, Miss Demaretti. Dashed uncomfortable traveling in the dark like fish packed in a barrel of salt."

The girl's lashes fluttered as she cast her gaze down demurely to her hands clasped in her lap. A soft smile curved her Cupid's bow mouth as she said, "Thank you Captain Marshall. That is truly kind of you."

"At your service, Miss." He nodded, a lock of wavy, blond hair falling into his blue eyes. "I doubt a bit of fresh air will be the death of us, eh?" When Mrs. Ruberry glowered at him after this optimistic and ironic reiteration of her own statement, and he pushed the hair off his forehead in a nervous gesture and reseated his hat as he added hastily, "Though of course, it would be quite different if it were night, Mrs. Ruberry. Quite different." His gaze flicked between Mrs. Ruberry and her charge as he seemed to twitch nervously, and his words grew increasingly chaotic. "Night air and whatnot... I'm sure no one would want that."

"Indeed," Mrs. Ruberry cut in sharply, putting an end to his rambling. She cast a frowning glance at Pru's window, and the color drained from her face. "Oh, no!" she screeched and pointed a shaking finger at the window. "That driver will kill us all!"

Pru glanced out. Her heart jumped into her mouth. "Oh, my!"

Instead of the ground and gentle hills, the sky and a few treetops filled the view as the carriage bounced and jerked along the edge of the road skirting a sharp ravine. She prayed that their coachman was as expert as he claimed.

Lieutenant Fisher, sitting between Captain Marshall and Pru's husband, glanced at the scenery and continued to smoke as if perfectly content with their precarious position.

"Beautiful day," Lieutenant Fisher commented. "Remarkably clear skies."

"Clear skies?" Mrs. Ruberry repeated, shaking with indignation. "Have you no regard for our safety?"

"I should think we are safe enough," Lieutenant Fisher said. "No need for concern."

"Perhaps you should glance out of the window again, sir," Mrs. Ruberry responded.

Pru, watching the exchange, wondered if she should ask Knighton to bring out his deck of cards again to make everyone forget their concerns. In truth though, she hesitated because she'd grown sick of endless games, and she knew it would not guarantee an end to the tension between the members of their ill-assorted party.

Unfortunately for Captain Marshall, no one could miss his partiality toward Miss Demaretti, or Mrs. Ruberry's disapproval of that attraction. What surprised Pru was that of the other men, only Mr. Hethering thus far had seem inclined to compete with the captain for Miss Demaretti's attention. Mr. Hethering, one of the men on the roof, had been diligent in finding opportunities to cut out Captain Marshall and enjoy Miss Demaretti's lively company during their brief carriage stops.

And it was no wonder since Miss Demaretti had a beautiful, round face with rosy, plump cheeks, sparkling brown eyes, and thick brown curls that many men might admire. When she wished, she could be a delightful and surprisingly well-informed companion. It was unfortunate, however, that Mrs. Ruberry's remarks often brought Miss Demaretti's childishly petulant disposition to view.

Thankfully, as the young lady was only sixteen, she might still develop a character to match her angelic face. Or perhaps not. Miss Demaretti cast a black look at her chaperone, pursed her bow mouth for a moment, and then tilted her chin up in preparation to speak.

Before the girl could utter a word, however, a loud crack shuddered through the coach. The vehicle lurched to the right and then tilted abruptly. Pru would have fallen to the floor if she had not caught her husband's strong, outstretched hand. Mrs. Ruberry was thrown forward and only the lieutenant's outstretched hands kept her from landing in his lap.

Through the open windows next to Pru, a terrifying view of a mountainside scattered with sharp rocks, ravines, and dark pine trees slanted down toward a misty valley below. It was a dizzying and frightening sight as they teetered on the very edge of a long drop down to scattered boulders and rubble.

"I'm falling!" Miss Demaretti screamed as she cast a frightened glance out Pru's window and threw her arms around Mrs. Ruberry. "We must escape, Violet, the carriage is slipping—I can feel us falling!"

"No one is going to fall," Knighton said curtly as he fumbled with the carriage's only door next to Pru.

When he opened it, the door swung out loosely over the abyss, showing only a narrow edge of the road immediately under the carriage. A bare six inches of ground lay between them and disaster.

Pru hooked her right arm through the window to keep from falling out and held on to Mrs. Ruberry's shoulder with her left. "Is there any room to climb out?" Her voice sounded breathless, and she sucked in a sharp gasp when there was another crack.

Her breath caught in her throat. The carriage tilted alarmingly toward the ravine, top-heavy as it was with baggage. She could hear thumps and slithering from the roof as the two men who had been forced to rid atop due to the already overcrowded interior scrambled to hold on.

"Yes," her husband grunted as he caught the edge of the door for support before leaning out a few inches. "There is just enough room if we are careful. You men, shift your weight toward the opposite side when I climb out. I will assist the ladies to exit first." He glanced apologetically at Pru.

She nodded quickly, knowing what he needed from her. "I'll help Miss Demaretti and Mrs. Ruberry and then follow them."

Knighton depended upon her to keep her head and help the others. If only she felt as calm as he sounded. She turned her head away from the window, ignoring the pull of the terrifying ravine. Her weight, combined with that of the other men, would provide stabilization while Miss Demaretti and the somewhat portly Mrs. Ruberry scrambled out.

The carriage shook. Rocks cascaded down the mountainside, dislodged by the carriage. The coachman spoke sharply to the horses in an attempt to control the frightened animals. Every movement made the coach shudder and created another cascade of rubble.

Knighton as he climbed out and clung to the door and coach fender. The two other men quickly slid toward the opposite side as the conveyance trembled and groaned.

A few rocks from the verge rolled over the edge, clicking and rattling their way down the hill. The noise went on and on, and they all froze, listening with tense faces until the sounds of the tumbling stones faded away.

13

"Come, Miss Demaretti, you must go first." Pru stretched her arm across the trembling body of Mrs. Ruberry to catch hold of Miss Demaretti's wrist.

"Careful!" Mrs. Ruberry's shrill voice cut through the tension, immobilizing the others in the coach. "You'll send us all down the mountain to our deaths!" She twisted as if to push her way past Pru's arm, but when she caught her glance, the older woman thrust her hand against her charge's back and literally pushed her toward the door.

"Excuse me, Miss," Captain Marshall said apologetically as he braced Miss Demaretti with his hands around her waist and lifted her through the door. He held on to her until Knighton caught her and eased her around the rear of the coach to the road.

The conveyance swayed as the weight shifted, and another shower of stones bounced over the side.

In a state of panic, Mrs. Ruberry climbed past Pru, elbowing her aside and nearly kicking her in the face in her haste to follow the girl out. Knighton caught her and ignored her wild words as he swung her around the fender and pushed her onto the road next to Miss Demaretti.

Without the plump woman's weight, the coach wallowed and lurched, sending more and more rocks down into the ravine. The narrow edge of the road crumbled under the broken wheel. The coach leaned further over the ravine. The horses, restive and terrified by the sounds, snorted and whinnied, jerking the conveyance even more, despite the driver's attempts to calm them and keep the vehicle stable.

Pru squeezed her eyes shut. Despite her efforts to remain calm, her mind feverishly flashed terrifying images of the coach tilting over the edge. Tumbling and crashing against the rocks, they would be smashed into pieces and scattered over the scree at the base, like so many crushed porcelain dolls amidst the wooden debris of the coach. She clutched one of the leather straps as the conveyance shifted again.

"You're next, Mrs. Gaunt." Lieutenant Fisher gripped Pru's arm to steady her as she stuck her head out of the door.

Knighton stood precariously next to the carriage steps. He gripped her around the waist and before she could say anything, he lifted her out and wrapped his arms around her. He literally carried her to safety.

When her feet touched solid ground, he briefly pressed his face against her neck. "Thank God," he murmured into her hair. When he let her go, his eyes sought hers before he said, "Make sure the other women are unharmed."

Pru stepped out of the way quickly to let him attend to the delicate operation of getting the other men out before anything happened to upset the coach and send it hurtling into the valley below. The carriage lurched as Lieutenant Fisher climbed out, leaving Captain Marshall alone inside.

The motion jarred loose a larger rock. The boulder crashed against other outcroppings, causing a small landslide as it bounced and tore through the trees below the road.

<u>Chapter Two</u>

Unable to help herself, Pru grabbed the hem of her husband's dark blue wool jacket to hold him back from the edge. The carriage swayed precariously, inches away from the steep hillside, as the coachman tried to control the frantic horses. His young assistant leapt down and ran forward to grip the halter of one of the lead horses, trying to guide the four prancing horses away from the edge. If they panicked, they could be dragged over the rocks along with the coach.

The coachman's voice was harsh with panic as he commanded his assistant to keep the animals calm, oblivious to the horses' twitching ears and fresh terror each time he called out.

To her relief, Captain Marshall climbed out at last and scrambled over the narrow ledge of the road with the void spread out behind him. He gripped Knighton's shoulder with one hand to swing around the fender of the coach, laughing with relief when he could finally walk on solid ground several yards away from the abrupt descent to the ravine.

Pru yanked her husband back as well and threw her arms around him, heart pounding. The coach swayed and creaked, but did not go over, despite the broken wheel and ominous listing toward the hillside.

Grinning and eyes bright, Knighton hugged her tightly and did not release her, even when he lifted his head to ask sharply, "Is everyone safe?"

"*Si.* So it appears," the laconic driver answered, flicking quick glances behind him to the passengers clustered together on the road. "Three ladies and five gentlemen, *si.*"

"What about your coach boy?" The tension did not leave Knighton's body at the coachman's answer.

Apparently he had been so preoccupied with getting the others to safety that he had not seen the boy run forward to the lead pair of horses.

16

Pru could feel hard knots of muscles as she pressed her left cheek against her husband's chest, listening to the reassuring thud of his heart. What would she have done if she'd lost him? If he'd tumbled down the hill with the coach and screaming horses? The thought sent such a flutter of panic through her that her hands tightened on him.

"That one." The coachman leaned over to spit on the ground. "*Si, signore.* Nimble as a monkey." He laughed. "First one to climb off, you see."

Out of the corner of her eye, Pru saw the youngster step away from the horses and wave, grinning and flushed with excitement. He appeared to be thrilled by the entire adventure, though they were far from out of danger.

He jumped up on the fender to peer over and pointed excitedly. "Broke a wheel, *signore*. Nearly went over, *si?*"

Knighton released Pru and grabbed the boy's thin jacket, pulling him away from the coach. "Stay off until we move it away from the edge."

"It won't go over, *signore*." The boy wiped his nose on his sleeve before running a clearly expert eye over the vehicle. "We have driven closer to the edge than that. It is a yard or more, *si?*"

He clearly had no sense of distance for they were closer to six inches than a yard from the edge.

"So you say, you scamp," Mrs. Ruberry stepped forward, dull red anger flushing her cheeks. "This is your fault, Coachman. You nearly murdered us all!" She pointed a shaking hand at the driver. "I've said all along that you would kill us all, have I not? You clearly know nothing of horses or hired conveyances. This is nothing short of disgraceful! You should never have been allowed to drive this coach. If I had known we would be subjected to such unskilled driving I would never have allowed Miss Demaretti," she flung an arm around the girl, ignoring her furious scowl, "to place one foot inside that dreadful coach. Not one foot, do you hear me?"

"The Pope in Rome—he can hear you," the driver mumbled, his brows jutting over his eyes. He stared at Mrs. Ruberry's garish, plaid skirts as he continued to speak, saying a few choice bits in his native *patois* that made Pru blush. Her knowledge of foreign languages was limited, but not quite limited enough for her to avoid comprehending that he was not complimenting Mrs. Ruberry or her parents.

When he failed to respond with the appropriate shame, Mrs. Ruberry released Miss Demaretti and stepped closer, her hands fisted at her sides. "Well? Have you no excuse? You should recompense us all for this dreadful journey. I daresay we are lost as well. Do you even know where we are?"

"*Si,* certainly better than the signora," he snarled back.

"Perhaps we should consider what we are to do. What did you say your name was, driver?" Knighton stepped between the two combatants just as Mrs. Ruberry raised her skirts with one hand and stepped up on the front wheel closest to the coachman, as if to climb up and drag him down from his perch.

"Albert Charron, signore," he said grudgingly, though his black eyes never left Mrs. Ruberry's face. He was a short, heavily-muscled man with wide, sloping shoulders and grizzled hair that looked like he regularly slept in the stables with his horses.

Pru stifled an inappropriate giggle when she heard his name. His slouching, ill-tempered appearance was remarkably similar to her imagined figure Charon, of Greek mythology fame, who ferried dead souls to Hades. With a shiver she realized that had they not been so fortunate and escaped from the carriage so expeditiously, his resemblance to the mythological Charon would have been even more similar.

"The carriage wheel is broken." Knighton glanced up at the darkening sky, his brows drawing together. A low line of crimson lit the edge of the western sky, leaving night to paint the rest a dark, soft blue. "Where is the nearest village?"

"Benerosa" Charron climbed down heavily and walked around the carriage to stare at the rear, right-hand wheel. "*Si*, Benerosa is nearest. A mile, maybe more. We will not make it tonight."

"If we assist the ladies, it is not too far to walk." Captain Marshall stepped forward, resetting his beaver hat at a rakish angle on his head. He nodded at Miss Demaretti before addressing the coachman. "We will send back assistance, of course. Should be on our way again tomorrow, come mid-morning, I should imagine. Once the wheel is repaired and all that."

"Imagine what you want, signore. There is no going forward until this wheel is replaced. Who can say when that will be?" Charron kicked the offending wheel, dislodging one of the spokes and stood back hurriedly as the carriage rocked.

"Captain Marshall is correct." Knighton eyed the coach. "We will assist you to move the carriage away from the edge, and then we should take what we need for the night. We will send assistance back to you when we reach Benerosa."

"Send assistance? *Mio Dio.* Do you think I wait here? At night? Do you forget the *banditi?*" Charron stared at him as if he had suddenly started raving.

"No. We are well aware of the dangers. But we can't leave the coach unattended," Knighton confirmed in a calm voice. "And as that is your responsibility, I am sure you will wish to remain and ensure the safety of the vehicle and your horses."

"I will stay—nothing scares me!" The boy raised his thin arm and flapped his hand for attention. "I will sleep in the coach and fight off any *banditi*. You will see when you come with the new wheel."

"There. That settles it, signore." Charron moved forward to run an expert hand over one of the horse's flanks. "He will remain, you see. Though I think I must take these beauties with me."

"You are not leaving a boy out here alone," Knighton said.

"Luc takes care of himself," Charron answered.

Luc glanced from Charron to Knighton. "I stay. Honest, I'm not afraid, signore."

"No, you can't. Not here and certainly not alone." As he spoke, Knighton lifted his head and tilted it to one side as if listening.

Pru turned slightly to peer through the gathering darkness at the gray ribbon of the road. In the distance, she could hear the slow, tired clippity-clop of horses' hooves. When she put a hand on her husband's forearm, she felt him grow rigid with tension.

"Are any of you men armed?" He picked up his greatcoat from the fender of the carriage where he'd deposited it, before he helped the other travelers to descend. He patted the heavy wool until he found what he was searching for in one of the pockets. With a light hum of satisfaction he removed a pistol.

"Of course," Lieutenant Fisher and Captain Marshall responded simultaneously as they hurriedly patted their coats and pulled flintlock handguns from various hidden locations.

A moment later, Mr. Hethering also grunted a positive response and suiting his terse reply to action, he pulled out a key and fumbled with a long box. After a few minutes, he extracted a pistol and hurriedly loaded it with a ball from the case.

"Are you ready, Mr. Hethering?" Knighton asked in clipped, impatient tones.

Hethering nodded.

It seemed most of the men felt the need for weapons during their travels. The Napoleonic Wars might be over, but they had been warned several times by various officials and border guards that there were thieves and brigands taking advantage of the unwary, particularly in some of the less populous environs of Rome.

Hence Charron's reluctance to travel after dusk.

"It may be nothing, just a few travelers like ourselves. But a show of arms may be useful." Knighton winked reassuringly at Pru. "It wouldn't do to be entirely casual after dark in these hills."

By the time all the men had retrieved their weapons and checked their loads, Knighton had moved to stand a few yards in front of the coach. He'd barely assumed the forward position before the slumped forms of three horsemen plodded into view.

The horses appeared as weary as their riders. The animals' heads hung low as they slowly neared the coach, small rocks clattering under their hooves. The men riding the horses had bent heads and rounded shoulders, and at first, appeared too tired to even notice the stranded travelers.

Twenty yards away from Knighton, they stopped. The man slightly in the lead straightened and raised his hand as if signaling the others to halt, though they already had. The horses seemed grateful to stop, and their heads hung even lower.

Although all three men were bundled in heavy cloaks, with scarves wrapped around their lower faces, and hats pulled low over their foreheads, Pru felt a sudden rush of dread. The fact that their faces were mostly hidden seemed to bode ill, as if they feared they would be recognized. A palpable tension filled the area around the three men, and she flicked quick glances first at the hillside rising above the road on the left, and then at the ravine on their right.

There was no place to go except along the rutted road.

These men were dangerous. She had no doubt of it. And they were trapped. Tired as the strangers obviously were, the three men on horseback could easily catch anyone who tried to run and herd them to wherever they wanted them.

"Good evening," Knighton flung the words out in a calm challenge.

"*Buona sera*—good evening." The lead man leaned forward slightly, his head moving slightly as he studied the coach and small group of passengers. "But it seems this evening is not so good for you, *si?*"

"Are you from Benerosa? Our coach has broken a wheel. We would appreciate some assistance," Knighton said.

"Ah, most assuredly. And with ladies, *si,* assistance would be most needed."

"Will you go back to Benerosa and send help? A coach, perhaps, or a wheel if one is available." Captain Marshall stepped forward to stand a few feet behind and to the left of Knighton.

The cheerfulness of the young man's voice grated on Pru's taut nerves. Couldn't he see that these men were dangerous? That they were not simple villagers on their way home? She'd spent years learning to recognize the emotions of others, and there was a hardness in these riders that she could sense, a suppressed violence that warned her they would be lucky if the horsemen left them alive and in peace. She didn't trust the strangers' awful, assessing silence. This situation would turn into a terrible tragedy if they were not all extremely cautious.

Her throat tightened when she realized her husband stood virtually alone between the horsemen and the passengers, exposed. He would be the first target. Her heart pounded so hard she could feel it in her constricted throat. As she wavered in dread, she put a hand against the side of the coach to steady herself.

The ground under her feet seemed to tilt toward the sharp edge of the ravine. The rocks and dark clumps of fir trees—glimpsed hazily through the black distance—seemed to pull at her. The dizziness increased, buzzing in her ears.

She couldn't faint—she'd never fainted in her life. What was wrong with her?

Somehow, the question seemed so rational that it steadied her, although her mouth filled with a bitter taste. She swallowed hastily, straining to pay attention to her husband and the men blocking the road.

"Ah, it is unfortunate you misunderstand." The rider in front chuckled. "We are not from Benerosa." He clicked his tongue and his horse clopped forward a few steps until the animal's nose was only a yard from Knighton's shoulder. "We cannot send back the help you seek. But the ladies, *si*, we can be of some small assistance perhaps to them. We take them with us, *si*? They are three and we are three. They must ride with us. Then they do not have to walk all the way to Benerosa in the night."

"No." Knighton grabbed the reins of the horse and turned the animal's head to the side. A quick slap on the powerful neck, and the horse moved into the gap between the carriage and the mountainside before the rider could bring it to a halt. Her husband raised his pistol, letting one last ray of crimson light illuminate the dull metal, before he motioned to the other men to show their weapons. "Despite your kind offer, I think the ladies had best stay with us. We are traveling together, and I'm sure you will agree that it is best to remain together as a group. After all, there are bandits in the area, or so we have heard. Perhaps that is why you travel with companions, yourself?"

The leader threw his head back and laughed harder. He slapped one thick thigh and twisted back, leaning over his horse's rump to stare at Knighton. "*Si*. That is why we travel together—for mutual protection." He pressed his right hand over his chest in an overly theatric gesture. "And why we must insist that the ladies may be better in our care."

Even the optimistic Captain Marshall had apparently begun to suspect the three men might not be as helpful as he hoped. He strode back to stand in front of Miss Demaretti and far enough away from Knighton to give himself a clear shot. Lieutenant Fisher imitated him and stood a few feet to the left, giving him a clear view of the two men on horses a few yards away on the road. Their actions were so quietly methodical, so calm, that it suggested they had not been as much on the sidelines as one might hope during the war with Napoleon.

Another hot burst of liquid filled Pru's mouth as her stomach twisted. Before she could control the urge, she turned and braced her arm on the fender of the carriage as she retched helplessly in long, painful bursts. When she finally straightened, her face was wet with perspiration. She dug into her reticule and retrieved the small packet of mint Mrs. Ruberry had thrust into her hand, thankful now for the clean taste of the herb.

"Oh, my dear, one would think you could find a more appropriate time and place for that." Mrs. Ruberry pressed her gloved fingers over her own plump mouth as she gagged. "I could never tolerate sickness of any kind. It is simply too bad that you lack self-control." Thankfully, she had the good sense to stay where she was instead of moving closer to Pru. She put an arm around Miss Demaretti and pulled her closer. "Are you faint, too, my dear?"

Miss Demaretti shook her head, frowned, and elbowed her away.

"Pru?" Knighton called, over his shoulder as he faced the apparent leader of the horsemen.

"I am fine." Pru stuffed another wilted mint leaf into her mouth, wishing the herbs were fresher.

"Travel sickness," Mrs. Ruberry said. "Mark my words. Some simply cannot manage the travails of a long journey."

"I have traveled a great deal and have not been ill before. Perhaps what I ate did not agree with me." Pru leaned against the carriage, her limbs weak and shaking. It couldn't be travel sickness. They weren't traveling in the swaying carriage now and hadn't been for several minutes, and all she had had to eat that day was a slice of bread and some tea.

The only other notion that explained her illness was even worse. She refused to countenance the idea that she might simply be reacting to the tension in the air like any other weak, frightened woman.

She'd never been so silly in her life and refused to start now.

"This is your wife, *si*? Pru—*bravo*. But she is ill, too ill to ride. Perhaps the other ladies though—they do not wish to walk this road in the dark?" The lead horseman gestured toward Mrs. Ruberry and Miss Demaretti. His gaze lingered on the young woman, sweeping up and down her crimson cloak with its fine ermine trim. He clearly realized that such clothing meant the girl was well-off, if not rich, and his quickened interest was plain in his alert tension. "Certainly this girl is too young, too delicate, for such a thing."

Mrs. Ruberry's arm tightened around the girl, and for the first time since she'd met the socially maladroit Violet Ruberry, Pru thought that Catherine Demaretti's parents may have chosen her guardian for the long trip overseas well. Mrs. Ruberry did not want for courage, no matter what other qualities she might lack.

"A brisk walk will not harm any of us," Pru said in as strong a voice as she could manage. "We thank you for your concern, but I believe we will proceed as a group, as my husband suggested."

"Will you then leave all your trinkets and valuables here, unattended?" The horseman clicked his tongue. "Most assuredly you would find all gone in the morning."

"You will find that we are prepared to guard our belongings with sufficient vigor to ensure their safety," Lieutenant Fisher said using his pistol to point to the carriage.

"But if you guard the carriage, who will guard the ladies? There are three of us, *signore*, tired though we are." The leader gestured at the two other riders. "And who is to say if there may not be three *banditi,* or more, nearby? Though you are five, you have only four armed men, or am I mistaken?" He chuckled. Clearly he was a man who was easily amused. "We do not count the boy. Or the driver, of course."

Luc jerked forward, scowling, as if to object to being so casually dismissed. However, Mr. Hethering stopped him with a firm hand on the boy's thin shoulder.

"There are enough of us," Knighton replied sharply. "And although I thank you for your concern for our welfare, we must not delay you any longer, as you not going to Benerosa."

There was a moment of breathless silence as the three riders seemed to consider this statement.

Then the leader nodded once. "*Si. Buona sera.* I wish you well on your travels." He clicked his tongue and gently kicked his heels against his horse's flanks. The horse pushed past Mr. Hethering and the ladies, followed closely by the other two horsemen.

Pru held her breath until the last horse, flicking its long white tail, eased around the disabled carriage and disappeared into the shadows of the road.

As she watched them go she thought they would be fortunate, indeed, if that was truly the last they saw of the trio.

Chapter Three

Tension knotting his shoulders, Knighton waited until the three men disappeared down the road to slide his pistol back into the pocket of his coat. The horsemen rode in the direction from which the coach had come and soon disappeared into the intensifying gloom. When the hollow sound of the horses' hooves faded, he turned to his wife.

"Pru, how are you—are you well?" He strode over to her and lifted her head, studying her pale face.

In the entire time he had known her, she had never been ill or showed any sign of poor health. The fact that she had been sick now was almost more frightening than the brigands they had just met.

"Yes. I am quite well." Her voice was clear and strong, but when he looked into her troubled eyes, he didn't believe her.

"There is no need to be brave. You are clearly not well." He looked around and noticed a large boulder by the side of the road. With an impatient gesture, he shrugged out of his coat and placed it around her shoulders before leading her to the rock. "Sit here and rest. We need to move the carriage away from the edge of the road before we decide what to do."

She opened her mouth as if to demur, but as she stared at him, her expression softened. With a rueful smile, she shook her head. "I never thought you would be such a bully when I married you. I hope you have not deceived me."

"Perhaps you are too easily deluded," he said lightly as he brushed off the surface of the rock and waited until she seated herself. "It is the only explanation for your willingness to accept me as your husband. At any rate, stay here where you are safe. I won't be long." He waited with one hand on her shoulder until he felt her relax within the warm depths of his coat before he walked away. A thoughtful frown creased his face.

His wife's frail health worried him. She had been trying to hide her illness for several days, and he had been watching her with growing concern, waiting for her to explain it away. When he suggested they end their honeymoon trip and return to England—before arranging to join this party of travelers to see Terni and the triple cascade on the river Velino—she had firmly refused and laughed at his concern.

Despite that, her wan face and lack of appetite made him anxious. He feared she thought him overbearing and too protective of her, but he did not want to lose her now, not when he had finally found her.

And beyond his own fears, what about Pru? How could she enjoy their travels if she grew ill and unable to eat? Today she had eaten only a few crusts of dry bread, a slender piece of some local cheese, and a few pickles. She could not go on like that; she was already too thin. He flatly refused to risk her health simply to view a few tumbled-down buildings, random statues, and a manmade waterfall.

"Men!" Knighton called, striding back to the coach. "One of us must keep watch while the rest move this carriage away from the edge." He cast a quick, assessing glance over the men standing in a rough half-circle around him. "Mr. Hethering, you are armed. Would you kindly keep watch? I don't trust those horsemen—"

"Horsemen—*banditi*." Charron, the coachman, interrupted with a snort. "Their leader meant to murder us all. You are fortunate he was too tired to bother."

"You recognized him?" Knighton asked. The heavyset driver had thus far appeared reluctant to do anything that might possibly be of assistance to any of the travelers so his burst of garrulousness was somewhat surprising. And although Knighton wasn't overly impressed with Violet Ruberry's mental capacity, after the last couple of days, he'd been prepared to admit that she might not have been far wrong when she accused the driver of sheer incompetence.

"He is well-known around these parts." Charron puffed out his chest and rubbed the side of his nose as if thinking.

However, to Knighton, it was obvious that what their driver was considering was how to make the most of everyone's attention. The muscles in Knighton's jaw tightened. He'd be damned before he'd prod the coachman to tell them the name of the robber.

One of the men who had occupied the roof of the carriage had less self-control and took the driver's bait.

The passenger lifted his hat long enough to run a curiously small hand over his short, salt-and-pepper hair, and asked, "Well? Who was he, then?"

"Calls himself a Captain. Me, I do not believe such a thing." He spat on the ground again and chuckled. "Captain Pasquino Nacchio. The signore was never a Captain, unless Napoleon made him one when he ruled the region." He shrugged. "But who is to say? Captain or not, most travelers here have reason to fear his attentions."

"Interesting though that may be," Knighton said dryly, "we would be foolish to linger here."

"What do you propose?" The passenger with the graying hair asked. Mr. Henry Savage, if Knighton remembered correctly.

"As I said, we must move the coach to a safer position. Then, half of our party can go to the village for assistance. Benerosa is the name of it, I believe, Mr. Savage."

"That is what I understood our charming coachman to say, as well." As a cool breeze swept down the road, Savage touched the brim of his hat and held it in a peculiarly precise movement. He was a slight man with a neat, black moustache, brown eyes with a network of wrinkles around them, and very delicate—almost feminine—hands and feet. Although he appeared to be about forty, he might easily be mistaken for a stripling, if one didn't look too closely at his face or graying hair. "Perhaps we should light some additional lamps? I would

29

dislike it immensely if we were to shift the carriage right down the hillside." He nodded to Hethering, who had perched on the roof along with him, and motioned for the boy to scramble up and retrieve the spare lantern the coachman had strapped to the side of his seat.

George Hethering strode closer. He was well-built, but still several inches shorter than to Knighton's six feet five. He stepped to the coach and held up a hand to take the now-lighted lamp Luc held. "Climb up and take the reins, Charron, my man. It shouldn't take much to shift this abominable vehicle a few feet. Just a bit of sweat and swearing, eh?" After a quick glance around, he set the lamp a few yards up the road where there was room to leave the carriage without depositing it in the center of the road.

Hethering shrugged out of his jacket and pulled off his top hat, revealing black hair with a streak of pure white running through the forelock on the left side. He appeared fit and full of good humor, though Knighton detected a certain shiftiness in his blue eyes that warned him that Hethering might be one of those gentlemen who lived by his wits, generally to the detriment of anyone foolish enough to trust him.

The other two gentlemen who had been inside the carriage with Knighton and the ladies, Lieutenant Fisher and Captain Marshall, joined them by the tilting coach and, despite the rapidly cooling autumn air, removed their jackets in preparation to assist.

When Charron began to climb back up to his seat, Knighton called to him, "Let the boy drive. He's lighter, and we can use your back, Charron."

"My back? Is it not bad enough as it is? Bouncing over these roads like water in a hot pan, *si,* but always it is Charron do this, Charron do that." His heavy, dark brows jutted out in a deep scowl as he glanced over his shoulder at Knighton.

"I regret the necessity, then," Knighton replied smoothly before gesturing to the boy, who was grinning widely and already sitting in the high seat with the reins in his thin hands. "Good man, Luc. You won't have to drive far. Just keep the horses steady."

"Signor Charron?" Luc asked in a hesitant voice, seeking the permission of the coachman.

"*Si, si.* Go. The gentleman knows my business as well as his, *si?*" Charron stepped to the rear of the vehicle and faced Knighton with his fists on his hips.

Ignoring the coachman's smoldering temper, Knighton arranged the men around the rear of the carriage while he took the most precarious position at the shattered wheel. The conveyance tilted dangerously toward the sharp incline, even though the rim of the wheel was at least six inches from the edge of the road. Knighton gripped the fender and moved gingerly around it, the leather soles of his boots slipping on the rocks as he maneuvered to brace himself and lift the coach.

"Ready?" He put his shoulder against the body of the coach and gripped the remnant of the wheel to lever it up off the ground.

The men grunted their readiness and heaved. The heavy coach groaned and lurched forward a foot. Before Knighton could adjust his position, the wheel slipped out of his grasp. His boots skidded out from under him as if oiled. He landed on his knees with a jerk, and it took a moment after he staggered to his feet to feel the warm trickle of blood down his right shin. A three-inch slash in his black trousers revealed a nasty gash. The cut started to burn, but he didn't have time to worry about it.

The other men grunted and heaved, unaware of his fall. The coach juddered and shook a few yards, heading at an angle toward the opposite side of the road. He dashed after it in time to prop up the right side before the entire carriage swayed too far over to be righted. His back and arms protested as he gripped the end of the axle. Sweat stung his eyes, but he stumbled forward a few more feet, breathing in short pants.

"Halt!" he gasped. "Stop the horses."

Luc's sharp ears caught his command and, thankfully, he pulled back on the reins and kicked the brake lever into place. The sound of grinding wood bounced off the rocky mountainside on their left before the exhausted men released the carriage and staggered back. The remains of the broken wheel shattered completely, sending shards of wood flying like shrapnel into the shadows. The carriage canted sharply and the right end of the rear axle dug into the ground before the coach settled with a groan.

Luckily, despite aching arms and backs, no one appeared seriously injured.

"Knighton!" Pru called, partially rising when he approached her. "Your limb—you are bleeding!"

"Just a scratch." He caught her and, ignoring the stares of the other passengers, hugged her against him, taking a long, deep breath. The rich fragrance of fresh lavender from her smooth, dark hair, laced with the warm scent he always associated with Pru, eased his tension. He nuzzled her softness before he reluctantly let her go and studied her face.

Night had well and truly fallen around them. The road had faded into a track of pale gray amidst the blackness. The last quarter of the moon gilded the rocks and the pale faces of the travelers with silver. Pru looked otherworldly in the poor light, her dark hair and clothes blending into the shadows around them and leaving only her face visible.

When she dragged his jacket off and attempted to wrap it around him, he laughed and got it away from her before draping it back over her shoulders. His shirt was damp, and he was so overheated from his exertions that streamers of mist flowed off his linen-clad arms.

"Keep it. It will keep you warm," he said. "You must stay here with the other ladies. Will you be all right waiting with them?"

She caught at his hands and held them in a tight grip. "Stay with us—you are injured. Let the other men go without you."

"Surely you don't think I'm that poor a specimen that a small scratch would stop me?"

"Of course not." Her mouth curved into a brave smile, but her lips trembled with the effort. "Must you go?"

"No need." Mr. Savage came up behind them and halted a yard away. To Knighton's surprise, the dapper little man had already put his jacket and hat back on and appeared as neat and clean as ever. Not even one bead of sweat dared to trickle down the side of his sharp-featured face. "If I am not mistaken, you are armed, are you not, Mr. Gaunt?"

"Yes, however—"

"Very good. It would be best not to separate you from your wife, then, while she is so clearly indisposed. So you will stay here. Mr. Charron and Captain Marshall have also volunteered to stay and guard the ladies. The rest of us will make our way to this village Charron mentioned."

"Benerosa." Knighton nodded thoughtfully. If he stayed, he could keep his wife safe.

"Indeed. Benerosa." Savage grimaced as if the very name brought up images of damp beds, fleas, and drafty rooms. "I had hoped we would reach Terni, but I suppose that is too much to hope for tonight. In any event, we shall endeavor to locate a wagon or other transport for hire and will return as soon as possible."

"A wheel," Charron interrupted. "We must have a wheel to continue to Terni."

"Obviously." Savage shrugged. "We will do what we can."

"My coach." Charron eyed the ancient vehicle as if seeing it for the first time. His gaze lingered on the heavy trunks strapped to the back. "I would go, but..."

"You may certainly stay here if you wish," Savage replied with apparent unconcern as he turned. "It is entirely your choice. I am relatively sure we can locate this village, Benerosa, without your assistance."

"There is no returning without a wheel." Charron grabbed Savage's shoulder, but the smaller man shook his meaty hand off and brushed his coat where the coachman had touched him.

"We certainly shall return, with a wagon, to fetch the ladies and secure our baggage. Your wretched conveyance is hardly our concern." Savage strode away while Charron shook his fist and swore at his back.

"Calm yourself, Charron," Knighton said. "We will repair your coach as soon as possible. For now, it is imperative that we watch for the return of your Captain Nacchio and do what we can to ensure the comfort of our fellow travelers."

Charron flicked a black look at Knighton and eyed his crippled carriage, muttering imprecations under his breath as the other men organized themselves and started down the road in the direction the coach had been going. Lieutenant Fisher took the lead and strode confidently until they all disappeared into the darkness.

"If you're looking for something to do, Charron, you and Luc can unload the trunks. It will be easier to replace the wheel if it is not so heavily loaded," Knighton said.

The activity would keep them warm and occupied. It might also preclude any panic over the thought of being stranded on a little-used road with brigands infesting the area.

Shrugging, Charron turned and stamped back to his coach. However, instead of unstrapping the trunks and baggage, he seemed intent on studying the rocks at the side of the road.

"You heard him, you lazy sot!" Mrs. Ruberry eyed the coachman. Her mouth curved down in disgust. "Those rocks aren't likely to get up and walk away, no matter how much you stare at them. Why can't you do as you ought and unload our bags? I, for one, have no intention of leaving my belongings to be pawed through by that dreadful robber. Do as Mr. Gaunt said and unload our things *immediately!*"

"*Mio Dio!* Harridan!" He turned to face her, his ugly mouth twisting. "I may have to drive you, but orders from the likes of you? No. This I do not take. If you want your trunk, you may get it down." He bowed to her with a flourish. "You are welcomed to it."

"You will do as you're told or face the consequences." Mrs. Ruberry's eyes flashed coldly in the moonlight. The gray light made her coarse features even harsher, with deep lines running from her nose to her wide mouth and giving her the haggard appearance of an aging actress heavily made up for the part of a shrewish fishwife.

Knighton felt Pru shift uncomfortably next to him, and he felt a flash of sympathy. He was not the only one who loathed emotional scenes. She disliked them just as intensely, and he was reluctant to cause her any more discomfort.

"Mrs. Ruberry, perhaps you'd like me to retrieve one of the carriage blankets to arrange a place for Miss Demaretti and you to rest. It may be an hour or more before the men return," he said. "So there is little reason to remain standing in the road."

"Quite sensible, I'm sure. This night air can't be good for any of us." Mrs. Ruberry nodded, the huge plumes on her bonnet bobbing with the movement. "Thank you." She put an arm around Miss Demaretti and led the girl to the side of the road, near the rock where Pru had previously been sitting.

"Allow me, Miss Demaretti. I am happy to oblige," Captain Marshall interrupted hastily when Knighton took a step toward the tilting carriage.

Miss Demaretti stopped to cast a smile in the young man's direction, peering slyly up at him through her dark lashes. "You are so thoughtful, Captain Marshall. I feel so overwhelmed, that I hardly know what to do."

"Of course—frightful turn of events—shouldn't wonder at it." Awkward phrases tumbled out of Marshall's mouth as he flushed and first stepped toward the coach and then, appearing to forget what he was about, stepping back toward Miss Demaretti.

The girl bit her lower lip as she watched his confusion, clearly trying not to laugh.

"The blankets are in the coach," Knighton reminded him.

Captain Marshall stared at him, eyes wide with surprise, before he straightened and adjusted his cravat nervously. "Right. In the coach. Won't be a minute, Miss Demaretti. And Mrs. Ruberry, of course." He touched the brim of his hat in a quick acknowledgement of the girl's disapproving companion. Not that his gesture mollified the older woman in the least.

If anything, Mrs. Ruberry's expression hardened further. "Well, get on with it, then. If we are to depend upon you for protection, I fear we will be sadly let down." She waved him off and put an arm around the girl's waist to draw her further away from the captain.

Marshall leaned through the window and drew out several blankets, which he handed to Mrs. Ruberry with a hastily sketched bow before he joined the men standing by the coach. To avoid any more unpleasant conversations, Knighton, Captain Marshall, and Charron unloaded the coach, stacking the trunks, boxes, and other baggage next to the ladies. When they had finished, Charron unhooked the horses, and in a rare gesture of affection and responsibility, he curried them with an old brush he kept under his seat and walked the animals up and down the road to keep the horses from growing too cold.

The chill in the air intensified as they sat on the rocks, and long tendrils of mist curled over the gray road, leaving damp patches behind. The horses' backs steamed, and all of them, men, women and animals alike, puffed out small clouds of foggy air as they breathed.

Head bowed, Knighton watched his wife with concern. She huddled within his coat, drawing up the lapels as protection against the cold. The weather was far from freezing, but the damp air made the cold penetrating and uncomfortable.

He rested his hip against the rock where his wife sat and put an arm around her in an effort to warm her. She shivered and snuggled closer, a gesture which met with mixed success as her silk bonnet scraped across his face every time she moved.

"It should not be long," he murmured in between blowing out small puffs of air to keep the feathers adorning her hat out of his mouth.

"Do you think those men will come back?" Pru asked after a moment.

There was no point in pretending he didn't understand which men she meant. "It is possible."

"They gave up too easily."

"Yes. But their horses were tired, and I suspect they were, as well. They were probably more interested in a warm supper and a fire on the hearth than they were us." If they had been unarmed and easier prey, the three bandits might have shown a bit more determination. As it was, they may have shown enough resistance to dissuade them.

"And once they eat?"

He laughed and tightened his arm around her. "By that time, we shall be gone. No need to worry over misfortunes that will never occur."

"I suppose you are correct. I just wish we had never encountered them at all. I wish they didn't know anything about us." She flicked a quick glance at Miss Demaretti. "That girl's cloak with the ermine trim makes her appear wealthy—I am afraid that might convince them to come back."

"Our flintlocks should give them pause, no matter how attractive they found the thought of Miss Demaretti's fortune." He picked a fluffy piece of feather out of his mouth and adjusted the plume on his wife's hat to avoid eating it.

Glancing up, Knighton noticed that Miss Demaretti was sitting on a rug, miserably pulling her cloak more tightly around her throat. Mrs. Ruberry stood a few feet away in front of Charron, her face livid, clearly resuming their argument. At least she was making an effort to berate him quietly as their words did not carry to Knighton's ears.

Charron didn't look any happier than Mrs. Ruberry did. He scowled at her and shook his fist in the direction of Benerosa. Perhaps she blamed him for stranding them on the road, or thought he ought to have gone with the others.

Knighton straightened, feeling tired and sore from moving the coach. What on earth could they be arguing about, now? The combatants ought to have enough sense to calm down and remember where they were so they could maintain their vigilance. The last thing they needed was to give the brigands the opportunity to attack them while they were distracted by incessant quarreling.

Thankfully, the captain maintained a watch, pacing up and down the road and pausing to listen each time at the furthest extent of his patrol. Despite that, it wouldn't do to leave the young man as the sole watchman. Knighton knew, despite what he had told Pru, that the bandits had probably been watching them and would have seen the other men depart.

With a great deal of reluctance he stood, immediately missing his wife's warmth when a stiff, damp breeze whipped through his waistcoat and linen shirt.

He'd barely taken two steps before he saw Charron fist his hands and thrust his head toward Mrs. Ruberry.

"Miracle? *Mio dio,* no one has strangled you yet, *si? That* is the miracle, my fine *signora.*" Charron spat on the ground a mere inch from the toe of Mrs. Ruberry's half-boots. "Bah. There is no reasoning with a woman, particularly the English."

"How dare you, you insolent beast!" Mrs. Ruberry screamed back at him.

"Mrs. Ruberry," Knighton interrupted her. "Miss Demaretti requires your assistance."

When the woman turned her head to face him, her mottled face and hard eyes made him halt. She looked like the merest word would unleash a torrent of wrath, ill-deserved or not. When he looked at her in silence, she clamped her mouth shut. Slowly her heightened color and breathing returned to normal.

"I shall come at once," she said at last. She took a deep breath, but apparently couldn't resist flicking one more black look at the coachman before spinning around on one heel and walking stiffly toward her charge.

"*Puttana*," Charron swore softly and shook his fist at Mrs. Ruberry's back. "If she is married, I am a herder of swine. Who would have a one such as that?"

"Perhaps it would be better if you avoided each other in the future," Knighton suggested quietly. "And I would appreciate it if you would watch your language in front of the ladies."

Charron shrugged. "Me? I am the model of control, but that one... You see—you know. And how, I ask you, did that young lady come to be in the care of such a one? She is a fine lady, but that old one—no." He shook his shaggy head. "Something is wrong, mark me well, my fine signore. No good will come from that one."

"Stay away from her, Charron, and you won't have to worry about it." Knighton was about to return to Pru when he heard the sound of horses hooves in the distance.

The rocky mountainside and damp air made the noises echo strangely, bouncing from one boulder to the other and disguising both proximity and direction. Despite the tension tightening his chest, he calmly retrieved his pistol and went to the center of the road. He checked the flintlock as he listened to the sound of horses growing louder.

"Who is it? Can you see?" Pru glided to his side, her head swiveling as she glanced first in one direction and then the other.

"Not yet." He relaxed and faced the road leading to Benerosa as the creak of wagon wheels became discernable. "I believe our carriage approaches, my love."

"Are you sure?" Pru asked, one gloved hand clutching his sleeve.

"I believe we will both discover the answer in less than a minute." He peered through the mist, hoping that he wasn't being unduly, and uncharacteristically, optimistic.

The predicted minute seemed to stretch on interminably as they all faced the darkness coiling over the road.

Chapter Four

When the first horseman trotted into view, Pru smiled up at her husband and let out a long breath of relief. "Thank goodness. I don't believe I could have managed another hour perched upon that boulder after riding all day in Mr. Charron's coach."

Before Knighton could respond, Mr. Hethering rode forward on a plodding horse that looked as if it had just been wrested from its comfortable stall and resented it mightily. The shaggy, gray animal kept shaking its head, biting the bit, and pulling against the bridle in stubborn attempts to pull the reins out of Hethering's hands and presumably return home.

Behind him, a team of large draft horses appeared, eerily haloed by the mist settling over the road. The animals pulled a long wagon driven by Lieutenant Fisher. When she didn't see anyone else sitting on the bench next to the lieutenant, Pru watched for another rider. Strangely, the fussy and exceedingly precise Mr. Savage had apparently decided not to accompany them on the return journey.

Somehow, his absence failed to surprise her.

Her husband waved at Hethering, and Pru turned to find Captain Marshall helping Miss Demaretti to her feet. The girl seemed to trip on the hem of her dark green traveling dress, and with a gallant flourish, the captain put an arm around her trim waist to steady her. Pru smiled as the girl glanced up at him and laughed, but the girl's flirtation came to an abrupt end when Mrs. Ruberry looked their way.

The older woman strode over to them, the leather soles of her boots clacking against the stones and her face twisted like a gargoyle's in the wavering light from the nearby lamp.

"Catherine! Come here. No need to bother Captain Marshall and take him away from his duty." Mrs. Ruberry stared into the darkness behind the young man as she spoke.

Pru stiffened and looked in the same direction, wondering if the woman had seen or heard something beyond the pair. Nothing appeared on the road except swirls of silver-gray fog, but Pru still felt the prickling of uneasiness.

"Those men may return," Mrs. Ruberry continued. "I'm sure we would all feel safer if you continued to watch the road until we left, Captain Marshall. It is, after all, why you stayed here with us."

Captain Marshall's cheeks reddened at the older woman's rebuke. Pru almost felt sorry for him when she saw the disappointment clearly printed on his face. His wide mouth drooped, but he did his best to cover his reaction by stooping to pick up the rug Miss Demaretti had dropped.

He folded it awkwardly before handing it to Mrs. Ruberry. "Yes, Mrs. Ruberry. Don't worry—you have nothing to fear. I will keep watch. No harm shall come to you."

"See that your words are not as empty as a man's promise usually is." She grabbed Miss Demaretti's elbow and dragged her toward the wagon as the captain watched them go, a small V wrinkling the skin between his brows.

Miss Demaretti flung one last glance and coquettish smile over her shoulder at him before drawing her ermine-trimmed cloak more firmly around her neck and running a few steps to keep up with her chaperone.

The young lady would certainly lead Captain Marshall on a merry dance if he tried to fix his interest with her. He was no match for a young lady who could flirt so successfully right under the nose of her chaperone. Pru feared his efforts were doomed to failure in any event.

The girl was wealthy, and although the fact that Marshall was a captain at such a young age meant that he was at least well-off enough to purchase his commission, it was doubtful that her parents would wish for such an alliance. Second or third sons joined the military, not the heirs to the family fortune. No doubt, her parents planned to match their lovely daughter with an heir. Preferably a titled one. After all, it was the hope of all wealthy parents with only a few exceptions.

In fact, Pru had wondered since meeting the girl if she had been sent to Rome to avoid just such a *mésalliance*. Miss Demaretti would not be the first girl sent to cousins in a foreign country to make her forget an unfortunate infatuation.

And it wouldn't be the first time that a girl sent away thusly managed to contract an even more unsuitable alliance while traveling into exile.

"Luc, you lazy rascal! Load the trunks into the wagon." Charron cuffed the boy, who was stroking one of the horses, and knocked the cap off his head.

Pru stiffened. Did he have to be so oafish? Her dislike for the brutish driver increased as the boy immediately ducked his head and ran to the trunks. He tried his best to drag the nearest one down the road, but though his skinny arms shook with the effort, he could not move it more than an inch or two.

"Let the boy guide the horses and help turn the wagon around," Knighton interrupted when Charron scowled and started toward the lad. "There's little enough room on the road to move the vehicle. I'm sure Lieutenant Fisher would appreciate the assistance. The men can load the wagon once it's turned around, and Luc can assist the ladies to arrange themselves in the conveyance."

"He does as I tell him," Charron shot back. "He's a lazy ne'er-do-well and as strong as any man when he is not idling."

The statement was clearly ridiculous given the boy's young age and matchstick arms and legs, but the coachman clearly disliked have his orders countermanded in front of others. He scowled at Knighton, but when he caught his bland look, Charron clamped his mouth shut. The muscles in his jaw worked furiously, however he didn't argue.

As it turned out, maneuvering the long wagon on the narrow road was more difficult than it initially appeared. Once again, her husband, along with Hethering and the coachman, had to stand on the rocky slope to keep the rear wheels of the wagon from going over the edge and dragging the rest of the vehicle and the terrified horses into the ravine below.

After several minutes of grunts, muffled swearing, and tense wrestling, they finally got the wagon pointing in the correct direction. They were loading the trunks onto the bed when Pru thought she heard the soft sound of horses in the distance. She turned back to peer into the blackness draping the road and tilted her head to listen.

Knighton was busy arranging boxes, but Captain Marshall was nearby, checking the carriage for overlooked items. He continued to work, apparently oblivious to the muted noises.

"Captain, there are horsemen approaching." She touched his arm to get his attention.

"Are you sure?" He looked distracted as he climbed onto the fender to survey the roof of the coach, searching for remaining items. The slight edge of annoyance in his tone made her wonder if he thought her a hysterical woman who twitched nervously every time the wind rustled a few leaves.

Well, he did not know her and was still young enough to make such mistakes.

"Yes. I hear several horses quite clearly," she called up to him.

He glanced down at her and then over to the other men who were putting the last of the bandboxes and portmanteaus into the wagon. Knighton happened to look up and caught her gaze. In imitation of her posture, he cocked his head, apparently listening. His face grew serious and tension stiffened his neck as he jumped down from the wagon. He patted Luc's shoulder as he passed him and strode back a few yards. Luc watched him, an alert expression on his round face. When nothing happened, the boy finished unhitching the carriage horses and walked them over to the wagon to tie their reins to one of the railings at the rear of the vehicle.

"Help the women into the wagon, Hethering. Then you, Luc, and Charron start back to town with the women." Knighton stood in the center of the road, shoulders squared. "We have company coming. I would rather they not find anyone here who might entice them with dreams of a rich ransom."

"Anyone can be ransomed," Lieutenant Fisher pointed out rather unhelpfully. The tightness around his eyes and mouth betrayed his irritation. Perhaps he resented Knighton taking charge the way he had, although no one else had attempted to face the situation.

Someone had to take charge.

Under the circumstances, Pru was relieved that her level-headed husband had been the one to step into the gap. Although her judgment might not be entirely fair, the other men seemed less decisive or capable of the decisiveness and quick actions required to protect them all.

When she looked back at her husband, she saw him studying the hillside and the road as if searching for a tactical advantage or the potential for ambush. His dark brows bunched together over his proud nose as he evaluated their position and the wagon that remained stationary in the middle of the road.

"While it is undoubtedly true, Lieutenant Fisher, that anyone can be kidnapped, I believe bandits prefer the wealthy and weak. So let us not unnecessarily tempt them. If you would, please mount Hethering's horse and arm yourself. It would be best if at least one of us were mounted."

"Very well," Lieutenant Fisher replied through thin lips and strode over to the small nag Hethering had tied to one of the coach's front wheels.

"Captain Marshall should go with us," Miss Demaretti called over her shoulder. "To protect us."

"You will be safe enough with the other men, Miss Demaretti. It's not that far to the safety of the village." Knighton barely glanced at her. All his attention was on the misty road in front of him.

"But—" The girl flung a pettish glance at Pru, as if she expected assistance in convincing Knighton.

"You will see him soon enough," Pru cut her off. And without more ado, she turned Miss Demaretti around and pushed both her and Mrs. Ruberry toward the wagon. "Right now, we need to climb into this vehicle and leave as quickly as possible."

Charron and Luc were already sitting on the single plank seat behind the horses. Hethering frowned, but Pru waved off any advice he might consider giving them, determined to avoid any more delays or arguments. They didn't have time to indulge in such things. The rattling sounds of shod horses' hooves cantering along the rocky road was getting louder by the second.

"There is room in the back, next to the trunks. You can sit on one of the smaller boxes if you wish," Pru said, her hand on the older woman's arm.

When Mrs. Ruberry awkwardly tried to climb up, Pru threw caution to the wind and pushed her up from behind. Mrs. Ruberry gasped at the indignity and protested vehemently, but Pru ignored her and climbed up after her, wedging herself between two large trunks. Miss Demaretti followed quickly with surprising agility.

Mr. Hethering barely had to time to scramble up beside Luc before Charron flicked the reins. The wagon lurched once, twice, and then began to rattle down the road into the moon-silvered mist.

Pru strained to keep her husband in sight as long as possible, but the lieutenant, mounted on the shaggy beast Hethering had brought back, moved to the center of the road behind them and cut off her view.

* * *

The horsemen approached, the sounds of their mounts' hooves pounding louder and sharper. Dark shapes appeared on the road, only to dissolve again as thicker banks of fog cascaded down the mountainside and veiled the lane between the trees. Even the mist failed to hide the black silhouettes for long, though. Three horses cantered into view, their riders swathed in heavy, dark cloaks and hats. Behind them, Knighton saw two others.

Five.

So the bandit—Captain Nacchio, if Charron guessed his identity correctly—had improved his odds by bringing two more men. Knighton assessed them quickly, recognizing the center man riding slightly in front of the other four as Nacchio.

"Halt! Stay where you are," Knighton called, raising his left hand. At least the hammering of his heart hadn't made the pistol in his right hand waver. Over his shoulder, he flung quiet words to the two men behind him, "Steady. Remain calm. Let us avoid a fight if we can." When the horses slowed, he faced the riders and yelled in a commanding voice, "The others have gone. There is nothing here to interest you any longer."

Behind him, he heard the clatter of hooves indicating an excited horse wheeling around. Fisher forced his horse forward, bringing the animal up on Knighton's right side.

"Fisher—no. There is no need to challenge them," Knighton said, his voice raw with anger. "Go back to cover the road behind us."

Ignoring him, the lieutenant raised his pistol and squeezed off a warning shot. The explosion made his horse rear and dance on its hind legs, clearly unused to gunfire. Fisher nearly lost his flintlock as he struggled one-handedly to maintain control over the panicking horse.

Knighton stared tensely at the strangers, waiting for them to return fire. A minute clicked by, and all five horsemen were still mounted and apparently uninjured.

Damn him. Fisher had missed, either deliberately or due to poor aim.

In contrast to his jittery horse, the brigands' mounts plodded forward, inured to the explosive sounds of warfare.

Their self-control was more frightening than a quick volley of shots, for it seemed to betray evidence of a clear plan of attack.

The center rider—Nacchio—raised his pistol. As he did so, the other men flung back their cloaks and aimed weapons as well. Three held rifles, and the man on Nacchio's left held a heavy flintlock pistol. All were aimed at Knighton.

There would be no stopping them, now. The bandits had the numbers and the advantage of their more accurate rifles. Once they disposed of the men facing them, they'd be free to catch up with the wagon.

They could kidnap the women—and Pru—at their leisure.

And there was no question that Captain Nacchio had indeed noticed Miss Demaretti with her rich, ermine-trimmed red cloak and her traveling companion. Nothing could have signaled wealth more clearly, and the young girl would surely be worth a fine ransom.

A cold tremor rippled down Knighton's back. If he were killed, what would become of Pru?

"That's torn it," Captain Marshall said in a low voice on Knighton's left. He faced away from Knighton to present his right side, the thinnest possible target, to the riders. "The fool shot above their heads. Warning, I suppose."

Knighton cast a rapid glance over his shoulder at Fisher. The man had gotten his horse under control and was hunched over his flintlock, obviously working to reload it.

Just as Fisher raised his head, another shot rang out. Fisher lost control of his horse this time. The animal reared up on its hind legs and whinnied in terror. Rolling its eyes, the horse stamped, wheeled, and bolted down the road toward Benerosa, desperate for the security of its secure stall in the stable.

While the brigands were distracted, Knighton ran forward and grabbed the bridle of Nacchio's horse. He pointed his pistol at the captain's heart. "Stop—no more shooting! End this now or you will die, Captain Nacchio."

The captain stared down at him, his eyes glinting in the moonlight. "What name is this you use?"

"Your name, I presume."

"Ah, I see. Notoriety. It is not always desirable to be so well-known, *si*?" Nacchio grinned down at him, his pistol resting on his thigh. His weapon was useless after his shot at Fisher. When Knighton didn't release the bridle, Nacchio raised his pistol as if to cuff him and jerked back on the reigns in an attempt to provoke the horse into pushing Knighton away. "Beware! This horse, she is impatient and likes to bite."

"Beware yourself," Knighton echoed. "You do not have time to reload, and I have a pistol aimed at your heart. I am unlikely to miss at this distance. Tell your men to ride back in the direction from whence they came."

Nacchio shrugged. "There is only you and that foolish young man. Why should we give up so easily when it is you who are at the disadvantage?"

"Go back, or I will shoot," Knighton repeated in an even voice. He would not allow them to pass, not when Pru was at risk. He did not know what drove Nacchio, but Knighton's will to stop him was stronger, whatever the motive. It had to be. "Even if one of your men manages to shoot me, it will not prevent me from pulling this trigger. Go back. Leave us in peace, and we shall all live."

Nacchio's dark eyes bored down from above cheeks darkened with black stubble. His sardonic smile never left his face, but after a moment, he tucked his useless weapon into his wide leather belt.

He held up his right hand where his men could see the gesture. "Opportunities arrive and opportunities vanish like our beautiful mist. Perhaps your advice is good—for now." Nacchio shrugged. "Who is to say what other opportunities may arise?"

Knighton gripped the reins of Nacchio's horse more tightly. "Tell your men to depart first. When I can't hear their horses any longer, I'll release you to join them."

"Are you wise to insist on such a ridiculous scheme?" Nacchio threw his head back and laughed. "Already one of you—that silly one on the horse—is wounded. Or dead somewhere on the road. Who is to say? So perhaps our opportunity, she is not gone, after all."

"Tell them." Knighton tapped Nacchio's knee with the barrel of his pistol.

"Never fear, signore." The captain gestured to his men and shouted a series of orders in a rapid patois that he clearly believed Knighton wouldn't understand.

But he understood the gist of it. Nacchio told his men to return to their quarters and assured them that there would certainly be another opportunity tomorrow or the day after.

Knighton did not relax or allow his expression to alter, despite an overwhelming sense of relief.

"You understand?" Nacchio asked as they waited for his men to ride far enough away for Knighton to release him.

"I understand that we have both—wisely—decided to live," Knighton replied in a dry voice. "Or am I mistaken?"

"You make no mistake. And so, now you will release me. Waiting is ridiculous for my men are already far away."

"And you will not follow us." Knighton made his remark a statement, not a question.

"There is no need." When Knighton released the reins, Nacchio wheeled his horse around to face the direction his men had taken. Then he glanced over his shoulder and grinned. "Tomorrow will be here soon enough."

With that, the captain nudged his horse's flanks with his heels and cantered after the other four riders. Knighton watched him go, wondering if he should have put a bullet into him while he had the chance.

The last thing he wanted was to meet Nacchio again while he was trapped inside the old coach on the road to Terni. Mrs. Ruberry's screams would deafen them all.

"Shall we catch up with the ladies?" Captain Marshall joined him, staring into the moonlight-silvered fog.

The soft sounds of Nacchio's horse slowly faded into the night as they stood there, listening.

"Yes, but keep alert. I would not be surprised if they circled back to try again. There may be another road or lane they can use that loops back to this one." Knighton waited another minute before starting down the road. His back felt exposed, and he almost stopped to look over his shoulder after a few yards.

"With luck, the ladies have already reached the village," Captain Marshall commented cheerfully, falling in step beside him. "And we won't be too far behind if it is only a mile."

"Did you see if that shot hit the lieutenant? Was it bad?"

Marshall shook his head. "I did not see."

"Watch for him, then." Knighton studied the road.

Here and there, small, dark splashes marred the dirt surface. The moonlight drained all color away, and the road was so rough that he could not tell if the splotches were simply dampness from the mist or if they were blood.

Had Fisher been wounded or not?

With the rapidly thickening fog, he could easily be lying a few yards from the edge of the road, and they would never see him. Unless he had been lucky enough to make it back to the village without assistance.

Either way, Knighton feared their difficulties were not over yet. It promised to be a long and unpleasant night.

Particularly for Fisher.

Amy Corwin

Chapter Five

The inn Charron drove them to was hardly the bustling, cheerful place Pru had hoped to find. If anything, it looked like an old, abandoned villa. The building sprawled untidily around a center courtyard and the main three-story structure had a sagging roofline with an assortment of chimneys leaning in odd directions.

One meager light flickered through the open door of the stables, and no other lamps welcomed them. All of the visible windows of the inn were dark.

Pru wasn't superstitious, but looking at the inn—if inn it was—seemed like a promise of further difficulties. When Hethering jumped down from the wagon, she held out one hand and had to restrain herself from begging him to get back into the vehicle and insisting Charron drive to a different hostelry.

Any inn would be better than this eerie place.

However, he strode through an arch and disappeared into the gloomy dankness, whistling a jaunty tune as he went. Luc jumped down and held up a thin hand to assist the ladies, while Charron yelled for the stable boy.

Miss Demaretti had just set foot on the ground when Hethering returned, still whistling *The Joys of the Country* and carrying a much needed and very welcomed lamp.

"Ah, signore, welcome! I am Buonfiglio De Viventis. Welcome to my inn, De La Fortuna." A short, plump man stepped in front of Hethering, rubbing his hands in a nervous way as his eyes flicked over them. Some locks of his dark hair stood up in little tufts while others were flattened against his round head, and as if aware of Pru's gaze, he patted his hair with one hand, trying to flatten it uniformly. "Apologies—my apologies—but it is late—we had not expected..." His words trailed off. He frowned and cast an uncomfortable glance at Hethering, who watched him with detached interest. "We are not prepared—we have few rooms." He sounded agonized, and his face wrinkled as if he struggled to keep back tears over such an abysmal lack of readiness. "If I may ask, how many are you?"

"Three ladies and five men," Hethering answered succinctly. "I am sure Charron and the boy will wish to stay in the stables with their horses."

"Eight?" Buonfiglio rubbed his hands together even harder. "*Mio Dio*, what will I do?"

"Give us rooms, I presume," Hethering answered cheerfully. He held the lamp up and stood sideways to wave at the entrance to the inn. "Ladies? Perhaps you would care to step inside? There must be a sitting room or dining room we can use while you prepare our rooms."

Pru nodded, and as she passed him, she plucked the lamp out of Hethering's hand to light their way into the gloomy hallway. Hethering eyed her with surprise, but didn't object, and the innkeeper, Buonfiglio, hurried after them, followed more slowly by Hethering.

"Right, please," Buonfiglio said in a breathless voice. "We have a good dining room you may also use as a sitting room—on your right, *per favore.*"

Leading the way with the lamp held aloft, Pru found the doorway a few yards further on and entered. In the flickering light, the room hardly appeared to deserve the appellation of "good dining room." A much-abused table stood in the center of the room, and a variety of wooden chairs were strewn about in no particular grouping. A sole, cushioned wing chair, that looked like it might once have been comfortable before mice stole most of the stuffing, stood near the black maw of a stone fireplace.

"Is there wood to light the fire?" Pru asked, moving toward the fireplace.

"Now? You wish a fire now?" Buonfiglio sounded shocked at the very notion.

"Yes. It is cold outside, and we would all appreciate the warmth." She bent and examined the fire irons, pleasantly surprised to find a few sticks already arranged in preparation for a fire. A wooden basket near the hearth contained one lonely pinecone, and she placed that under a few of the thinnest twigs. It would have been nice to have a bundle of thicker logs for fuel, but at least they wouldn't have to sit in the dank gloominess of the sitting room while the proprietor got their rooms ready. "Never mind. I will light the fire while you prepare our rooms."

"You will need more fuel than that," Hethering commented. "Where is the wood pile, Buonfiglio?"

"I will bring wood. But the rooms... The other man, Signor Savage, he has already taken the small room. What will we do?"

"I have no idea," Hethering replied, standing at Pru's shoulder and watching her light the pinecone with the flame from the lamp. "However, I am sure in an inn of this obvious size, you will find something suitable."

Although he made no comment about her attempt to light the fire, she felt crowded by his nearness, and his cool supervision irritated her. She pressed her lips together and concentrated on gently moving the twigs to catch fire from the rapidly burning pinecone.

After wringing his hands and frowning at them, Buonfiglio hurried out. He came back a minute later with a few thicker bits of wood, dropped them near the fireplace, and hurriedly left before anyone could ask him for anything else.

"Charming," Hethering murmured.

Mrs. Ruberry and Miss Demaretti huddled together behind Pru and held their hands out to the meager fire.

As if Hethering's inconsequential remark was the final, intolerable indignity, Mrs. Ruberry faced him. "You may find this inn charming, but I assure you the rest of us do not! Expecting us to spend even an hour here is beyond comprehension."

One of Hethering's dark brows rose. "It may be beyond your comprehension, my dear lady, but I assure you—whether you understand it or not—we will be staying here. Unless, of course, you prefer to join Mr. Charron in the stables."

Pru stood and dusted off her soot-smeared hands, trying not to laugh at the startled expression on Mrs. Ruberry's face.

Surprise soon turned to anger, however, as Mrs. Ruberry's brows snapped down and the lines framing her mouth deepened with a frown. "Jest if you like, Mr. Hethering. You may wish you had heeded my advice when you wake up in the morning with your throat slit and your wallet gone."

Hethering smiled in a superior way and slowly strode over to one of the wooden chairs and took a seat before he deigned to answer, "It is difficult to imagine waking to anything, except possibly a heavenly choir, with my throat cut. However, granting you that, I believe the only robbery we shall experience is the rate which our host will charge us for what I am sure will be grossly inadequate quarters."

"I will not stay in this dreadful place," Mrs. Ruberry reiterated in a strident voice.

"Oh, do be quiet," Miss Demaretti said in a haughty voice. "I am tired and wish to go to whatever chamber allotted to us. You must insist that the innkeeper provide us with a room," she glanced at Pru and raised her chin, "a *private* room. At once."

"I beg your pardon," Mrs. Ruberry said, her face flushing with aggravation in the firelight. Her mouth tightened with disapproval. "But you can hardly wish to stay *here*. You are too young to understand—"

"I understand perfectly," Miss Demaretti interrupted. "This is not the sort of place I would select as an appropriate lodging. However, complaining about it will not change the fact that we are here and unlikely to go further tonight. So for once, I beg you to be quiet and do as requested."

While Pru wouldn't phrase the request in precisely the way Miss Demaretti had, she couldn't help but be grateful to the young girl when Mrs. Ruberry's wide mouth snapped shut. After a tense moment, she dragged one of the spindly wooden chairs closer to the fire and released a puff of exasperation as she sat down. Miss Demaretti soon followed suit, although she elected to sit in the padded wing chair.

Pru was about to pull another wooden chair closer to the fire and sit when Buonfiglio returned. "*Mi scusi*, but there is not one bed left. As I said, Signor Savage took the last bed before you came. I am sorry."

It took a great deal of self-control for Pru not to march up to Mr. Savage's room and wrest him bodily out of bed. He might at least have considered Miss Demaretti instead of leaving the girl to spend the night shivering in front of an inadequate fire. Pru eyed the staircase through the dining room door and even took a step toward it before she thought better of it. There had to be other beds. Matters would be sorted out when the rest of the men, including her husband, returned.

She nodded tiredly and rubbed the back of her neck as Mrs. Ruberry proceeded to give the innkeeper a dressing down that he was unlikely to forget any time soon.

"Someone is coming," Mr. Hethering called, standing in the inn's doorway.

After trying to see around him, Pru went to the large window next to the door and peered out into the blackness. Mist oiled the glass panes with a heavy film of moisture and obscured the road, but if she strained, she could hear the clippity-clop of a horse approaching. The cadence was slow and stumbling, as if the animal were exhausted.

"Can you see anyone?" Pru asked Mr. Hethering as she rubbed one of the windowpanes with her handkerchief. All she succeeded in doing was to smear the smoke and grease on the cold glass and obscure her view even more.

"A horseman—my God!" Mr. Hethering rushed outside, letting the door slam behind him.

Pru followed him as quickly as she could, her heart pounding in her chest for fear of who might be approaching.

A shaggy, gray horse—not much larger than a Welsh Cob—walked into view, with a rider bent over and swaying with the horse's nervous steps. The skittish animal moved sideways when it saw Pru and Mr. Hethering standing outside the inn.

With a soft oath, Hethering dashed forward. As he neared the animal, it lifted its head and snorted, dancing of out of his reach. Its great, dark eyes rolled, showing the whites as it lifted its head and snorted, shying away from the lantern Pru grabbed on the way outside.

The rider slumped over the horse's neck and the reins dangled, trailing down the animal's sides. His black hat and cloak obscured his identity, but she saw with a guilty sense of relief that he was not her husband.

The horseman might not be Knighton, but he was still injured or ill. Pru's breath caught in her throat as she ran forward a few steps. "Who is it?"

"Fisher." Hethering grabbed the reins and drew the horse toward the arch leading through the courtyard to the stables. "Hold the lantern up—I think there is blood—"

"Blood!" Pru, who had started to follow him with the light held aloft, stopped. She flicked a quick glance at the road. "Where are the others? Where is my husband?"

There was no sign of anyone else, although the fog obscured everything further than a few yards distant.

Ignoring her question, Hethering rang the heavy bell near the stables for assistance and reached up to help Fisher dismount. The rider almost fell into his arms, and Hethering staggered under his ungainly weight. One of the stable lads responded to the bell and joined them, his hair propped up by bits of straw. He yawned, rubbed his eyes, and stumbled up to the horse, only managing to stay upright by flinging an arm over the horse's neck.

Hethering shoved the horse's reins into the young man's hand and shifted Fisher's weight.

A frown wrinkled his brow as he pushed Fisher's cloak back over his shoulder. "He has been shot!" Hethering exclaimed before drawing the unconscious man's arm over his shoulder. "You must assist me, Mrs. Gaunt. The door, if you please."

"Is he conscious?" She threw open the side door, her gaze fixed on the archway leading to the road. Where was her husband? What had happened?

Was he lying on the mountain road, dead or dying even as they stood here? The lantern in her hand shook and the light skittered over the two men and the walls, highlighting the scene with dramatic and frightening shadows.

"Barely aware, I should say," Hethering said through gritted teeth. "He is covered in blood."

"What about the other men? They may be hurt, too. Shot..." She glanced at the groom, still holding the horse's reins and eyeing them curiously. "I should take the horse and go back—we can not simply leave them on the road without assistance."

"I will go when we have settled Lieutenant Fisher. Where is that infernal innkeeper?" He propped Fisher against one of the walls in the hallway and glanced around with a scowl darkening his face.

"Wait here." Pru hurried into the smoky public room, only to find it deserted. There was no time to find a handy bell. She ran behind the bar, picked up a large, pewter pitcher and spoon, and beat the jug until the vibrations numbed her hand.

"What—what—what?" Signor De Viventis hurried into the room, his shirttails flapping and a startled look on his round face. His hair was once again standing up in small tufts like cattails dotting a marsh. "Mrs. Gaunt— what is amiss? What has happened?" He tried unsuccessfully to smooth his tousled hair with his hands.

"I am sorry to disturb your rest, but Lieutenant Fisher has returned and is injured. He must have a bed and a doctor."

"A doctor!" Buonfiglio's bloodshot eyes opened wider as he stared at her, his mouth open.

"Yes, a physician. There must be someone in the village, and you must send for him."

"A physician?" He continued to stare at her uncomprehendingly. "There is no physician in Benerosa!"

"Don't be foolish. There must be someone. Fetch him immediately."

"But signora, there is no one. We are a small village—we have no physician here."

"There must be someone you turn to in an emergency," Pru replied impatiently. As they dallied, Knighton might be bleeding to death on the road less than a mile away. She could not stand here and argue with this idiot.

"*La ostetrica.* There is only the midwife, Ghita Poverelli, signora. I swear to you there is no one else."

"Then send for her," Pru replied brutally. "And find a room. Lieutenant Fisher must have a bed without delay."

"What is it, Buonfiglio?" a middle-aged woman asked, coming into the room through the door the innkeeper had used and pulling a heavy, woolen shawl more tightly over her broad shoulders.

Beneath the gray wrap, she wore a voluminous white nightgown and a startlingly red kerchief tied around her graying black hair. Although she spoke with the innkeeper in a rapid Italian patois, Pru was fluent enough in the language to feel further incensed when she studied her with dark, gimlet eyes and asked, "Who is this woman?"

"A guest—there has been a carriage accident, my sweet," Buonfiglio answered quickly.

"A guest!" She flung her square, work-worn hands into the air and shook her head. "And where will she stay when the *Contessa* must have the entire third floor?" She hit her husband's heavy shoulder as he stared at her, his mouth working, and hands gesturing frantically for silence. She laughed in his face and shoved his shoulder again. "The haunted room? Is that where you will place your fine signora?"

A haunted room?

While Buonfiglio and his wife were obviously superstitious enough to consider a rentable room uninhabitable due to some sort of spirit presence, Pru was not. In her youth, she had spent many nights exploring purportedly haunted places in support of her father's desire to scientifically prove and document the existence of ghosts. Sadly for her father, Pru had proved to be more adept at dispelling the tales rather than substantiating them. To her dismay, her father had passed away still hoping to find his first, true spirit, and she still believed he could have found leprechaun gold long before he ever beheld a ghost.

A dusty, disused room did not frighten her in the least.

Nor did stories of wailing spirits, or whatever had frightened the innkeeper and his wife, fill her with dread. Such things invariably proved to be natural phenomena.

"Send for the midwife and have that spare room prepared. We have an injured man. He must have a bed— a *clean* bed. Do you understand?" Pru held Signora De Viventis' gaze until the woman looked away.

"Celestina will prepare the room, signora, while Buonfiglio goes for Ghita," Signora De Viventis said in a subdued voice. She flicked a glance at her husband.

The stubborn jut of his round chin indicated he did not favor his wife's plan. Worried grooves lined his forehead as he glanced at Pru and Hethering. "My wife, Fiorella, is perhaps optimistic. It is late, too late to go now."

"And so?" His wife locked glances with him. "It grows later still while you argue. Ghita is used to late hours—babies always prefer to arrive after midnight. She will come. Now, go."

"Where is this haunted room?" Pru asked, catching Fiorella's heavy woolen shawl before she slipped back through the door leading to her private quarters. "Is there a key?"

Fiorella stared at her as if in disbelief. "A key? Why would there be a key? No one uses that room—no one dares to. There is no need for a key. Use it if you dare."

"Where is it?"

"The room is at the end of the hall on the second floor," Signora De Viventis said.

"What about Celestina?"

"What about her?" Fiorella's dark, insolent eyes studied Pru's face.

"Will she change the sheets and prepare the room if it is reputed to be haunted?" Pru asked, feeling rushed and breathless with anxiety. She couldn't dawdle here any longer—she had to find her husband.

But what about Fisher? Could Mrs. Ruberry supervise the care of the lieutenant while Pru was gone?

"That one? Celestina will do as she is told." She shrugged. "The room will be ready in a short time, and then you may do as you wish."

Worrying about leaving Fisher, Pru had to drag her attention back to Signora De Viventis. She stared at her for a moment before she remembered they were discussing the maid and the room for Fisher.

"Very well, that should do. Mrs. Ruberry will take care of any details while I'm gone," Pru answered hastily.

"Gone? And where would a lady go at this time of night?"

"My husband has not arrived. I must find him. He may be injured."

"You cannot go alone." Fiorella's black brows wrinkled beneath her red kerchief and she moved to block the door. "Buonfiglio will go with you. You will wait for Buonfiglio. He comes soon with the midwife."

"No. I am sorry, but I can not wait any longer." Pru held up a hand when the woman's face darkened with anger. "I will take one of the other men with me, never fear."

"Other men!" The woman flung her hands into the air, heaved a long sigh, and rolled her dark eyes. "Our dog would do as well as those men. No, no. You must wait for Buonfiglio."

"We will see," Pru answered neutrally. She had no intention of waiting or arguing.

"*Si*. We see." Fiorella's round chin jutted out at a stubborn angle remarkably similar to her husband's, while the gimlet light returned to her dark eyes. "If you wish the horse, you will wait."

The proprietress seemed determined to thwart her. Pru bit her lip, shaking with frustration and anxiety. "If you will excuse me, I must see to the wounded man and let the others know of our arrangement."

"Arrangement. *Si*." She held out a plump, calloused hand. "And so we must have payment. Now, if you please."

"How much is that room?" Pru slipped a hand through the opening in her skirt to finger the coin purse she had secured in her pocket.

Knighton had been too proud to take money from his newly wealthy wife and consequently, Pru hadn't felt the need to carry a great deal of currency. As a result, she was nonplussed when asked to pay for Fisher's room. Asking the injured man for money, or worse, taking his purse out of his pocket, was unthinkable under the circumstances.

"For you, forty francs."

"Forty francs?" The sum was outrageous, far too dear for a room in such a dreadful inn. "That must be a mistake."

"No mistake. It is forty francs for that room." She crossed her arms and eyed Pru with the hint of a smile. "And fifteen more if you wish supper."

"That is outrageous as you well know! We are *spesati*—we have already paid for our journey to Terni." Pru straightened and held the woman's bold gaze. She refused to give in to such extortion when she and Knighton had given up the comfort of their own carriage to travel with others who had engaged a *vetturino* to drive them in his vehicle for a fixed price, specifically intended to avoid

63

being fleeced by greedy innkeepers along the way. "And we travel with *vetturino*, our coachman must have spoken to you about our arrangements when he arrived here."

Fiorella studied her in insolent silence. When Pru did not look away, her gaze flickered, and she dropped her gaze to the floor as she shrugged.

"You say the room is haunted," Pru said, trying a different argument. "Very well. I will give you twenty francs for the night for Lieutenant Fisher. He may wish to make other arrangements in the morning." Depending upon his wound, the lieutenant might not be in any condition to travel, but he could decide on his own arrangements. Assuming he was conscious to do so. Pru smiled grimly. "I suspect we will all make other arrangements tomorrow morning."

"Twenty francs?" Fiorella pressed a hand to her ample breast in a theatrical gesture. "You ruin us!"

"The room would not have been rented except for us," Pru pointed out. "You are fortunate to get twenty for it." She pulled her wallet out of her pocket and counted out two ten-franc coins from her small supply.

"And supper?" Fiorella took the proffered coins with alacrity and tied them into a corner of her shawl.

"I am unsure at the moment. Will you excuse me? I have tarried long enough." Pru escaped and ran down the short hallway to the small dining room where she had left the others.

When she entered, Lieutenant Fisher was sprawled over the rectangular table in the center of the room. Mr. Hethering held Fisher's lapel in one hand and was peering under the bloodstained jacket.

He glanced up as Pru neared the table, anxiously examining Fisher's pale countenance. "Was there some difficulty about the doctor?" he asked.

"There is no physician," Pru replied shortly. "The landlord has gone for the local midwife, though. He should return soon." She pressed the back of her hand on the wounded man's forehead. The skin felt damp and cold. She glanced worriedly at Hethering, fearing the worst. "How is he?"

"He has lost a great deal of blood." He shrugged. "It will be fortunate if they don't bleed the rest out of him in an attempt to balance his so-called humors."

"Has he regained consciousness at all? Has he said anything about the others?"

He shook his head. "No to both questions."

"Then I can wait no longer. I must go." Pru picked up the cloak she had draped over one of the ladder-backed chairs and threw it over her shoulders. "Do you have a pistol? I would appreciate the use of it."

"Pistol? Mine are locked away and will remain so." He straightened and gave her a look remarkably similar to the obstinate one Fiorella had given her when she announced her intention to rescue her husband. "You cannot mean to go out alone, Mrs. Gaunt."

"I do mean to do so." She held out her hand. "And I would appreciate it if you could lend me your firearm."

"I beg your pardon, but I will not do it. No. You must wait here." He glanced down at Fisher and frowned. "I will go when the doctor—"

"Midwife," she corrected.

He nodded. "Midwife, yes. When she arrives, I shall go in search of the others."

"They may be dead by then!" Pru flung at him, twisting her hands together. "Please, I beg of you, give me one of your pistols. I can not wait here, knowing that my husband may be lying injured, or worse, less than a mile away."

Mrs. Ruberry stood and approached them. "Pardon me, but perhaps I could be of assistance? If you wish to accompany Mrs. Gaunt, I can look after the gentleman, here, until the midwife arrives." She smiled in her self-satisfied way and added, "I am accounted to be an excellent nurse. Many a gentleman has shown true appreciation for my skill in such matters."

"I have no doubt about the appreciation," Hethering murmured.

Mrs. Ruberry ignored him and continued, "You may rely upon me, Mrs. Gaunt."

"Thank you." Pru reached out and clasped the woman's wrist for a moment, giving it a grateful squeeze, forgetting all about her previous annoyance with the older woman. "If you could watch over him, I would be in your debt. I have paid for a room for the lieutenant, and the maid is preparing it. Once the midwife arrives, you should be able to move him there."

"Room?" Mr. Hethering's brows rose in surprise. "I was given to understand they had no more rooms."

"Apparently, that was a misunderstanding. There is at least one more room, and I have paid for Lieutenant Fisher to use it. The maid is preparing it now." She stepped toward the door. "If you are going to accompany me, then do so. Otherwise, I intend to go alone."

Mr. Hethering exchanged a glance with Mrs. Ruberry. When she nodded with a confident smile, he strode toward the door and flung it open with a flourish. He executed a bow and stood aside for Pru to walk through the doorway ahead of him.

The mist closed damply around them as they walked quickly down the road. Pru was too preoccupied to speak and after a few abortive comments, Mr. Hethering grew silent as well. The tiny village around them slumbered, not a single candle burned to light the dark windows and even the dogs and cats remained hidden in the shadows, either asleep or watching them through the shifting patches of fog without making a sound. They had just passed the last, small cottage next to the village church when Pru heard the crunch of footsteps coming toward them. Her nape tingled.

Bandits? Would they dare to enter the village?

Despite Mr. Hethering's presence, she felt frighteningly vulnerable and alone.

66

This was not the time for cowardice, she reminded herself sternly. She stepped forward, ready to confront whoever was coming.

Mr. Hethering gripped her arm and held her back. "I beg your pardon, Mrs. Gaunt, but we don't know who is coming." He gave her a slight push toward a half-wall made of rocks that surrounded the church's side yard. Then he moved back to the center of the road and pulled his firearm out of his capacious coat pocket. "Please go on the other side of that wall."

For one second she considered ignoring his request. She hated to leave him alone when the presence of another person might reduce the danger to him, but in the end, she didn't argue.

The ever-present mist obscured the road, and whoever was approaching would not see either of them until the last minute. She stepped onto the scraggly grass and weeds at the base of the wall and leaned against the cold stones.

Odd sounds, magnified by the fog, echoed around them. Her nerves tightened until she wanted to scream just to break the tension. Slowly, the footsteps got closer and closer, but the unhelpful mist refused to reveal who approached.

Finally, a dark shape grew amidst the gray coils, walking confidently down the center of the road and heading straight for Mr. Hethering.

Chapter Six

The silhouette of a man blocking the road rose out of the mist at the outskirts of Benerosa. Knighton stiffened and held out an arm to bring Captain Marshall to a halt.

"Who stands there?" he called in Italian.

"None of your bloody business," came the cheerful response in English.

"Hethering?" Knighton laughed in relief and removed his hand from the grip of the pistol in his pocket. "What the devil are you doing here?"

To his surprise, another figure catapulted toward him. He flung out his arms as it hit him in the chest.

"Where have you been? Are you hurt?" Pru asked breathlessly, her pale face peering up at him. Her hands patted his arms and waistcoat, as if searching for evidence of holes or blood. "I have been nearly prostrate with fear. Oh, do say you are unharmed."

"I am unharmed, or was until you assaulted me." He chuckled before catching her in his arms and giving her a hard hug. When she smiled up at him, he kissed her forehead, equal parts relief and joy rushing through him.

Thank God, she had arrived at the village unharmed. The warmth of her slender form eased his anxiety. He breathed in the clean, lavender scent of her hair and pressed his face into her soft neck.

He had not realized how worried he had been. Anything could have happened. The wagon might have overturned, or worse, been attacked along the road. He should have gone with her to ensure her safety, instead of placing her in the care of others. He'd been an utter fool to let her out of his sight in such a dangerous place.

Thankfully, nothing had happened, and here she was, safe in his arms.

She hit his chest gently but insistently with a fist. "Well? Where have you been?"

"We had a bit of trouble on the road." He pulled her closer again and closed his eyes as he rested his chin on the top of her head. "Has Lieutenant Fisher returned?"

"He is at the inn," Hethering said, stepping forward. "He has been shot. I don't know how serious it is."

Pru lifted her head to look up at him, her beautiful eyes dark with concern. "We sent the innkeeper for a midwife—there is no physician in this village. It is too small."

"Then we must hurry." Knighton looped an arm around his wife's shoulders, keeping her near. "Lead the way, Hethering."

Mr. Hethering wasted no time. He turned on his heel and walked quickly back through the damp, swirling mist to the inn. The building loomed up, dark and sprawling, in the poor light. The only sign of welcome was the flickering, golden light in the huge window to the right of the door. A heavy wooden sign above the door, somewhat inexpertly painted and peeling, read *De La Fortuna*.

Despite the optimism of its name, the inn did not appear to promise much in the way of good fortune. In fact, quite the opposite.

When they entered the dining room, they discovered an elderly woman dressed in unrelieved black leaning over the table where Lieutenant Fisher lay. She glanced up at their approach, revealing a face that was such a mass of wrinkles that her brown eyes looked like small currants set in a crumpled lump of dough.

"Are you Signora Poverelli, the midwife?" Pru asked, surprising Knighton with the fluency of her Italian. She had been shy about speaking it during their travels, and given her lovely and undeniably expert accent, he couldn't understand her previous reluctance.

"*Si*, I am Ghita." The woman nodded and straightened to examine the newcomers.

"How does he fair?" Knighton asked in Italian, reluctantly removing his arm from his wife's shoulders.

Pru cast a glance around the room and then walked back into the hallway as a man, presumably the innkeeper, called her name. The two began a rapid, whispered conversation as Knighton turned back to hear Ghita's assessment of Lieutenant Fisher's condition.

The woman laughed and waved her gnarled hand over Fisher's bare chest. She had already removed his waistcoat and shirt, but the pale flesh was so streaked with blood that he appeared to be wearing a red vest.

"He will do well." She laughed again, gurgling to herself. "Unless he dies."

"Have you removed the bullet?" he asked more sharply than he intended, irritated by her callous attitude.

"No need, signore. It passes here," she poked a finger at the hole on Fisher's left side, "broke a rib or two, and out it passes again from his back."

Knighton leaned closer, thrusting back the strong urge to order her to depart and manage the care of wounded man, himself. She had done nothing that he could see except strip Fisher's unconscious body and watch the blood drip down his side.

Did she expect him to heal himself?

Then Knighton noticed a bit of white stuck out of the wound.

The broken rib she'd mentioned? When hen reached out, the midwife slapped his hand.

"No touch, signore!"

"What is that? Bone?" He did not withdraw his hand. His fingers hovered over the ugly wound, and he glanced at her, raising his brows.

"Si. Bone." She frowned at the fragment, but did not touch it. Her hands were occupied with a battered and chipped ceramic bowl and an earthenware jug. She uncorked the jug with a few of the yellow teeth she still retained in her mouth, and the harsh, acidic odor of vinegar wafted into the air.

The midwife poured the vinegar into the bowl and then dug around in a worn out, raveling brown cloth bag before withdrawing a wad of wool. She plunged the wool into the vinegar, squeezed out the excess liquid, and wiped the streaks of crimson off Fisher's chest. When she came near his wound, she glanced up at Knighton.

"Hold him, signore. If he wakes..." She shrugged, holding the wool just above the wound.

Knighton placed his hands on Fisher's shoulders, praying that God would show him mercy and allow him to remain unconscious. "Proceed."

She swabbed him until the wool was dark crimson. With a sigh, she rinsed the wool, but didn't squeeze out as much excess liquid this time. "Hold him. More tightly this time."

Her command, however, proved unnecessary. Fisher moved slightly when she removed the jagged fragment of bone and sponged the bullet hole torn through his side. Fisher's muscles twitched, but mercifully, he did not regain consciousness.

"Turn him to his side," she commanded, watching intently as Knighton eased the injured man onto his unhurt side. When the exit wound was exposed, she hurriedly washed that, too. As she worked, she flicked a quick glance at Pru, who had come back into the room. "Ask for a pot of honey, signora, if you would. To dress the wound, *si?* Old Buonfiglio will have one, but of course you will pay."

Pru cast an enquiring glance at Knighton. He nodded and watched her go before he carefully rolled Fisher onto his back. While the midwife was occupied digging through her bag again, he gently touched the bruised rib cage, trying to assess the damage to the bones and the woman's course of treatment.

Vinegar and honey. How little medicine had changed over the centuries. Even Pliny had recommended washing wounds in wine or vinegar and applying honey to help them heal.

Well, it had to be better than nothing. And the midwife's method might be primitive, but she appeared to know her business. Her hands moved with assurance and a deftness that belied her swollen, red joints and ancient face.

"Will this do?" Pru returned with a small pot of honey and handed that, along with a small wooden spoon, to the midwife.

"*Si.*" Ghita pulled a roll of linen out of her burlap bag and placed it on the table. Next to that, she placed two more wads of wool. "Pour the honey so." She ignored the wooden spoon and instead dribbled the thick, dark gold liquid over the two puffs of wool. "Now, hold him so he sits." She waited while Knighton propped him up before she quickly placed the wool over the wounds and proceeded to wrap the long strip of linen around his chest. "There. Now he lives. Or dies. God will decide."

"Thank you, signora," Pru said as the midwife rinsed her sticky fingers in the bowl of vinegar and wiped them off on her dingy black dress.

"*Si.*" She shrugged and picked up her bag before holding out a gnarled hand. "Fifty francs, signora. If you please."

"*Fifty?*" Pru's pale face grew even whiter. She glanced at Knighton. "It cannot possibly be that much."

"*Si.* Fifty." The price was exorbitant, as the knowing sparkle in Ghita's dark eyes acknowledged. Her smile widened with glee at their discomfiture.

As it was well after midnight, Knighton was in no mood to argue. He counted out a few gold coins and dropped them onto her lined palm. "I will escort you home, of course."

"*Si.*" Despite her ready agreement, she looked startled by the suggestion. Apparently, she was used to navigating the streets alone after delivering babies at all hours of the night.

"I will go—you stay with your wife." Hethering stood and adjusted his hat. "This inn is damnably stuffy, and I would just as soon go for a walk as try to sleep sitting upright in one of these abysmal chairs. It would be more comfortable leaning against a fence post, if you want the truth."

"But surely," Knighton looked at his wife, "there must be bed chambers. We cannot be expected to spend the night sitting in the dining room."

"Bad luck, but that is precisely it." Hethering's voice contained the smoldering hardness one usually hears when a man is trying to substitute humor for anger. "Oh, they do have one room, a *haunted* room, destined for Lieutenant Fisher. That is apparently the extent of it." He stuck out his elbow to Ghita and gave her a little bow as she let out a high, girlish giggle. "After you, signora."

Knighton watched the two leave before he turned back to Pru. "Is that true? There are no other rooms?"

"Apparently." Pru sighed tiredly and rubbed her temple.

He smiled, remembering Pru's past attempts to contact the spirit world. Perhaps she would have another chance to prove their existence after all.

"And it is haunted?" he asked.

"Theoretically haunted." Her red-rimmed eyes watered as she tried to stifle a yawn behind her hand. "I have doubts, of course. Though I have yet to hear the tale, and I am assuming, without any facts whatsoever, that the truth consists of a loose floorboard and possibly an errant draft."

The amusement in her eyes made him smile. "Well with any luck, we shall not be here long enough to prove or disprove your theory."

"I spoke to Buonfiglio, the proprietor, just a few minutes ago. There was one other room. Mr. Savage has it. Apparently, it is very small and used to be a servant's room at one point. It is too cramped to accommodate more than one. He took occupancy while the others came to fetch us with the wagon. In any event, I arranged for the lieutenant to have a bed."

"This is outside of enough." He ran a hand through his hair. Although it was dark when he approached the hostelry, the building had seemed very large. They could not have rented every single room. Who could possibly be interested in visiting an insignificant little village like Benerosa? "I refuse to believe this entire inn is full. From what I saw from the outside, it should have dozens of rooms."

"Well, it seems that there is a contessa in residence who has rented the entire third floor."

"A contessa? Where is the proprietor?"

"I don't know." Pru appeared startled.

He gently moved her aside and strolled into the public room. A metal ewer and spoon sat on the bar, and he picked them up. When he saw Pru standing in the doorway, he winked. "Under the circumstances, he will simply have to agree to allocate some of the rooms on the third floor to our party." He pounded the ewer with the spoon and was gratified when the portly man he had briefly glimpsed talking to Pru ran out of the door next to the bar, followed by an equally plump woman.

"Signore—signore! What is it now?" the man asked, moping his sweating forehead with the voluminous linen sleeve of his nightshirt.

"Rooms, if you please."

"Rooms! Did Signora Gaunt not explain? We have no rooms. None."

"You have some, I believe, on the third floor," Knighton replied calmly.

"The third floor!" The innkeeper and his wife exchanged glances. "The contessa must have the third floor. There is no room there for others."

"Must have or wishes to have? Precisely how many rooms are on that floor, and how many are in the contessa's party?"

The innkeeper shrugged, holding his hands out, empty palms upward. "There are six rooms, but free? It is not for me to say."

"Then you will speak to the contessa and inform her that any unoccupied rooms on the third floor are urgently required."

"He will not!" The innkeeper's wife stepped forward with lightning in her eyes and thunder in her voice.

"Fiorella..." The innkeeper tried to push her back through the open door, but she planted her feet and stood her ground.

"No. We will not." She crossed her arms. "You speak to her. If you dare."

Pru placed a hand on his arm. "Perhaps it will not be so bad—"

"No. You will have a proper bed." Knighton pressed his palm over her cool fingers. "I will speak to her if no one else will."

"Oh, Knighton, no." Pru's grip on his arm tightened. "You cannot intrude on an unknown woman at this hour. It would be indecent. Perhaps..." She removed her hand from his arm and straightened. "Perhaps it would be best if I were to speak to her."

"As you wish. I cannot prevent you." The innkeeper's wife flicked her hand at them. "If the contessa agrees, it is forty francs a room. To pay what the contessa would, you see, it is forty francs."

Knighton's teeth ground together at the monstrous sum. First Ghita and now this. Despite the feeling of being cheated, he was in no mood to argue. "Agreed."

"No, Knighton, please don't be so foolish for my sake." Pru's lovely mouth drooped as she studied him with shadowed eyes. "That is far too much. It is outrageous."

"If it will provide you with a comfortable bed, I am satisfied," he replied.

The proprietress nudged her husband, and he held out one fat hand, though he couldn't seem to meet Knighton's gaze.

He shook his head. "You will receive payment after we, that is, after Mrs. Gaunt," he amended, "has obtained permission to use the rooms on the third floor from the contessa."

"*Si*," the proprietor agreed, despite the resumption of a thunderous frown on his wife's hard face.

Pru cast Knighton one rather tired glance before she headed for the stairs. He shifted uncomfortably. Placing the burden on his wife made him feel like a heartless ass, but he had to admit that if anyone was capable of convincing a contessa to let them have any unoccupied rooms, it would be his lovely, and very persuasive, wife.

Chapter Seven

Mid-way up the stairs, a sensation of light-headedness hit Pru. She paused and gripped the handrail until the strange feeling passed. When she glanced over her shoulder, she was not surprised to see Knighton staring up at her, one booted foot on the lowest step.

"What is it?" he asked sharply, climbing a few more steps.

"Nothing." She glanced up into the darkness of the landing, her stomach growling hollowly. What had she last eaten? Breakfast. And then she'd been ill.

Well, she would not give in to such a weakness, and particularly not here. Sick or not, she refused to remain in this dreadful inn one more day than they absolutely had to. But first, she had to try to obtain sufficient rooms for them all.

When she took a deep breath and placed her foot on the next stair, Knighton leapt up the staircase and halted her with a hand on her arm. "Allow me to speak to her. You are unwell." His eyes searched her face. "I should have realized—you have had nothing to eat—you should return to the dining room and order a late supper. Senor De Viventis is waiting downstairs to be paid. He can easily fix you something while he waits."

"No." She laughed to take the sting out of her refusal and touched his cheek gently. "I had better be the one to speak to the contessa if we want any hope of sleeping in an actual bed tonight." When he frowned as if ready to refuse, she continued, "And perhaps you could speak to our illustrious innkeeper about a small supper for me. I will not be long."

After meeting her firm gaze, he nodded and descended the stairs while she headed in the opposite direction. On the landing, she paused again, unsure which closed door concealed the contessa and feeling slightly ridiculous at the prospect of knocking at each door in turn until someone answered. A cold draft, smelling of dust and the musty odor of damp straw, brushed past her face. She sneezed abruptly several times and swallowed, forcing her attention away from her unsettled stomach.

She had raised her hand to knock at the first door on her left when a woman holding a lamp opened the door at the end of the corridor.

The woman was dressed in a plain black dress with a modest cap on her head, and her dark hair was twisted into a tight knot at the nape of her neck. The rough, wooden floorboards creaked terribly, and when Pru had stepped into the hallway, the woman obviously heard her soft footsteps.

She held up her lantern and faced Pru. "Who are you? What are you doing there?" She strode forward and stopped a yard away, blocking the hallway. "You must return downstairs at once. This floor is occupied."

"I beg your pardon, but I am looking for the contessa."

"The contessa? Who are you to want the contessa?"

"Mrs. Gaunt. My name will mean nothing to her, however I must speak with her."

"You must do no such thing." Because the woman held the lamp up to her right, it illuminated that side of her face while casting the left side into shadows. That, and the shadows created by her brow and nose, gave her a curiously forbidding and angry appearance, despite her smooth, unlined skin.

Pru ignored the woman's statement and continued. "Is she awake?"

A loud tapping noise, like someone beating a stick against the wooden floor, came from the room the woman had recently left.

She glanced over her shoulder and then back at Pru. "I must go. And you must leave as well."

"She is clearly awake. I will not return downstairs until I speak to her." Pru held her ground. It was late, and she was too tired to go back to her husband without at least attempting to complete her task.

"I will not argue with you." She turned halfway around and tilted her head, obviously listening. The sharp rapping echoed down the dreary corridor again. With each insistent tap, a thin trickle of dust sifted down from the ceiling and fell through the halo of golden light cast by her lamp.

"I shall speak to her," Pru insisted firmly.

"Very well. So be it." She walked back down the hallway and halted at the door at the very end. She gave one long, calculating glance at Pru before she knocked softly at the door.

"Come!" The peremptory command was as clear as if the speaker stood next to them instead of on the other side of the closed door.

The woman put a hand on the doorknob, took a deep breath, and opened the door. "Contessa—"

"I heard voices, Domenica," the regal lady standing in the center of the room said.

She was dressed in a heavy, black silk *robe à la française* with a tight bodice, back pleats hanging loosely from the neckline, and a great deal of lace framing her neck and wrists. One of her gnarled hands rested on the knob at the end of an ebony cane. Her white hair was tightly braided and then twisted around her head to form a coronet beneath a crowning cap of white lace. Diamonds glittered at her ears in the golden lamplight, and her dark eyes were just as hard and bright as the jewels when she caught sight of Pru standing in the doorway. "Who are you?"

"I beg your pardon, contessa." Pru sketched a hasty curtsey. "I regret that we have not been properly introduced, and that I must make your acquaintance under such undesirable circumstances, but I must speak to you."

The contessa stiffened and, if anything, her rigidly upright posture grew even more unyielding. "I see no need to speak to anyone in this dreadful hovel. Leave at once."

"Contessa, please hear me out—"

"Are you deaf or simply an imbecile?" As the contessa frowned, the skin sagging over her jawline tightened, revealing a glimpse of the handsome, and perhaps beautiful, woman she once might have been. "Domenica, see this person out."

"I will not leave until you have heard what I have to say," Pru said calmly, though her heart throbbed so frantically in her chest that she was sure the two ladies in front of her had to hear the low thuds.

"Indeed." A light flashed through the contessa's dark eyes. For a moment, Pru thought she smiled in amusement. "Then I must ask you to do so as rapidly as possible."

"There has been a carriage accident on the road. One man was shot."

At this, the two woman exchanged glances. Pru could not read their expressions, but they seemed to echo each other as closely as a reflection in a mirror.

"Is he dead?" the contessa asked finally.

"No, we hope not. He is resting in the room below this one—"

"The haunted room!" The contessa appeared to pale, although her skin was already so white that it was difficult to be sure. "Buonfiglio must have been desperate indeed to rent that room."

Pru nodded, resisting the temptation to question the contessa about the mystery surrounding the chamber below. "As there are six more of us stranded here, we are in dire need of additional rooms. If you would allow us to occupy the empty chambers on this floor, we would be very grateful."

"Impossible. That rascal, Buonfiglio, should have informed you of this."

As the contessa spoke, her maid placed her lamp on a small table nearby and smiled maliciously at Pru, her countenance expressing her pleasure at being proved correct. She seemed to enjoy her employer's aristocratic snobbery and general unhelpfulness.

"It is just for the night," Pru said.

"I do not like to be disturbed. I always occupy the entire floor when I am here, and I am not inclined to change. Now, I wish to retire." She waved one hand at Pru, fingers bent and swollen with arthritis, and motioned toward the door.

"I assure you, no one will make any noise. We are exhausted and have no wish to disturb or discommode you." Pru blinked and forced herself to concentrate. Despite her efforts, she could not help weaving slightly as another wave of dizziness darkened the room temporarily.

"You are unwell?" the contessa's sharp eyes caught the small, uncontrollable signs of her weakness. Another slight smile curved her thin lips as her dark eyes brightened.

"I am simply tired. If you would allow us the use of any spare rooms, I would sincerely appreciate it."

"Who are these travelers you speak of?"

"My husband, Mr. Knighton Gaunt, and myself. Two other men, Mr. Hethering and Captain Marshall, and Miss Catherine Demaretti and her chaperone, Mrs. Ruberry." It was everything she could do not to smile. She sensed that the contessa was relenting, or at least curious, and Pru didn't want to do anything that might make her change her mind, including a display of premature joy.

"Demaretti?" The contessa again exchanged glances with her maid.

"Yes. I understand she is traveling to her cousins in Rome."

"I am acquainted with the family. They are rather...tempestuous. I hope your Miss Demaretti does not exhibit such traits."

Pru shook her head, although she felt the warmth of a blush redden her cheeks. "She is well-behaved and will not disturb you." At least, she hoped that would be true.

"You are unsure of this." The contessa held up her hand to stop Pru's protest. "One can only hope your party will not occupy the inn long enough for her presence to

81

make itself known." She took a deep breath. "I have decided. You may have three of the rooms on this floor—those furthest from this one. You may wish to move that wounded man, as well. The room he occupies is not healthy. And there must be no noise. I will not tolerate any noise. That is all. You may go."

"Thank you, contessa." Pru turned, rapidly leaving before the elderly lady could change her mind.

She was hurrying down the corridor to the stairs when she heard the slap of leather soles on the floor behind her. Her heart sunk. She hadn't even reached the stairs before the contessa changed her mind. With a heavy sigh, Pru turned to see the maid, Domenica, carrying her lamp again and striding toward her with her free hand holding her long, dark skirts out of the way.

"Signora Gaunt, la contessa asked me to speak with you."

"Yes?" Pru glanced at a nearby closed door with regret. They had almost had the chance to have a decent night's sleep.

"That man—the wounded one..." her voice trailed off with uncertainty.

"Lieutenant Fisher?"

"*Si.* You must move him to one of the rooms on this floor. That room—the one where he sleeps—is *cattiva*, um, bad. Evil. You understand?"

"Yes, but surely, for one night it will not harm him. It would be difficult to move him now. He is resting. It might be worse for him to climb or be carried up the stairs."

"It is far worse if he dies in that room," Domenica replied sharply. She gestured at the closed door next to her with the lamp, causing the flame to flicker wildly. "You can have this room and three others if you will but move him. The three next to this one are unoccupied."

"While I appreciate the contessa's concern, I confess that I don't understand her insistence concerning

Lieutenant Fisher. What precisely is wrong with that room?"

"It is haunted—evil!" she repeated, a fleck of spittle forming at the corner of her mouth with the intensity of her words.

"In what way?" Pru asked patiently. "You say it is haunted. Every haunted place I have investigated has a story. What is this room's tale?"

"You have investigated such places?"

"Yes, though that hardly matters now. What I would like to know is the story of this inn. Why is it haunted?"

"It is an old tale." She held the lamp up a fraction higher and glanced over her shoulder. Her head tilted, as if listening for a moment before she stared at Pru as if gauging her ability to hear the tale without becoming hysterical. Then her dark eyes flashed as she looked from one side of the deserted corridor to the other, peering into the shadows and moving the lamp around.

What did she fear? There was no one there except the two of them. Surely, there was nothing more fearsome occupying the inn than a few badly made beds, wood rot, and a rat or two.

"Perhaps you do not know?" Pru prodded her in a bored voice. She glanced at the stairs as if preparing to go.

"Know? Everyone here knows but you foolish English. It is the girl—and you brought another of the same name with you." She crossed herself and once again stared into the wavering shadows. "Many year ago, oh, a hundred at least, a young girl, only sixteen, ran away on her wedding night. Signorina Demaretti. She was to marry her father's friend, but she was young and did not wish to marry an old man. She wanted a young, handsome man. So she fled with her lover to this place. But her father could not let her shame herself, or his family, so and pursued the lovers." She paused to cast a quick look over her shoulder at the contessa's closed door. "Did you hear anything?"

"No," Pru answered impatiently. "I suppose the father caught the lovers here and killed the young man."

"He killed *both* of them in their bed in that very room. Beheaded them both with one magnificent stroke of his sword."

"I see. And now the young lovers haunt the inn—"

"No. They say only *she* haunts the room as penance for her evil. You see she begged for mercy while her father drew his sword and then cursed him. The blade struck her lover first before it killed her, too. They say her lips were still moving with the words of her curse as her head rolled across the floor. She swore she would never rest while any men of the Demaretti line remained alive." She studied Pru's face. "If you investigate such things, you must have heard this tale. It is quite famous."

"Indeed, I have heard many remarkably similar tales." The story was so predictable that Pru had to clench her jaw to keep from yawning. So many hauntings seemed to be caused by a disobedient young woman fleeing from an unwanted marriage. The girl either killed herself or was murdered by her father, brother, or the elderly, and frequently hideously ugly, suitor. "In any event, Lieutenant Fisher is unrelated to the Demaretti family, and Miss Demaretti is obviously not a young man of that line so I doubt anyone will be bothered in what is left of the night."

"I have tried to help you—warn you—you cannot say otherwise. Now I must go. La contessa requires my presence." She turned and fled to the door at the end of the corridor, leaving Pru alone with the echo of her words rattling around in her mind.

Surely, there was nothing in the room that could harm Lieutenant Fisher. Unfortunately, the contessa's warning, followed by Domenica's tragic story, made her uneasy. She did not wish to discover that she had been wrong about ghosts at the lieutenant's expense. But wouldn't it be equally unwise to move the wounded man?

She rubbed her eyes tiredly and descended the stairs.

Tonight the fates would have to decide. She was simply too exhausted.

Chapter Eight

By the time his wife returned to the sitting room, Knighton had already instructed the remaining travelers to gather what they needed for the night and be prepared to retire. Pru smiled in response to his enquiring gaze, and her eyes twinkled despite the deep shadows under them.

So she had been successful, just as he'd hoped. His wife was remarkably convincing, and even a contessa would have found it difficult to resist her if there were any empty rooms remaining.

"There are four rooms." As she handed her lamp to Knighton, a small frown compressed her mouth. "They suggested we move Lieutenant Fisher to one. Do you think we should?"

"He is in a room now. Why would we move him?"

Pru flushed. "I suppose it is nonsense, but they insist that the room he is in is haunted." When he took an impatient breath, she added hastily, "The room had not been used for a while. The air may be bad."

"Then he can open a window." He knew that his wife still cherished the somewhat forlorn hope that one day she might actually discover the true haunting her father had so diligently searched for. However, he doubted that the momentous discovery would happen at this pathetic inn. To temper his answer, he touched her arm gently with one hand and gestured with the candle to the room where the others waited. "I spoke to Buonfiglio and persuaded him to supply a small supper for you and the others. There is a bit of some sort of rabbit stew he called *pappardelle all lepre*, bread, and some quite good cheese. Hethering is having some boiled tongue, and there is enough for you, too, if you wish."

She did not look quite as pleased by the menu as he'd hoped, but she did try to smile. The expression did not reach her eyes. "I don't suppose there are any pickles? For some reason, I have a desire for something tart, something with a touch of vinegar."

"Of course." He guided her to the small, combination sitting and dining room, praying she would lose her wan appearance after she'd eaten. "There is a bowl of various pickled vegetables on the table. Can you try, however, to eat some of the ragout, or stew, or whatever it is? It is warm, and you need something more than a handful of pickles."

"Yes, dear," her voice trembled with laughter as she meekly agreed.

"Minx," he whispered, his lips brushing her ear before she walked gracefully to the scarred but mercifully well-scrubbed table and took a seat.

To his relief, she managed to eat an entire bowl of the *pappardelle all leper,* the dish deliciously redolent with bacon and cloves. Apparently still hungry, she followed this with several pickles and a piece of bread with cheese. Her cheeks gained a touch of color as she ate and laughed with the other travelers as they joined her. Within a few minutes, they had consumed everything the innkeeper managed to find in his larder.

Pru appeared decidedly more cheerful when she finally placed her empty bowl on the table and glanced at him. "This may be a wretched inn, but I cannot complain about the food. I feel much refreshed."

"Good." He nodded in relief. Perhaps whatever had made her ill earlier had lost its grip on her, and she would enjoy the rest of the journey to Terni and from there, to Rome.

"Did we understand that there are rooms for us?" Mrs. Ruberry asked hopefully, wiping her fleshy lips on her handkerchief.

"Yes." Pru said. "If you and Miss Demaretti share one room, and the captain and Mr. Hethering share another, we should be well accommodated on the third floor. My only warning is that we have been given the rooms on sufferance by a contessa who insists on absolute silence. So if we can be as quiet as possible, we should all pass a good night."

"Or what is left of it," Mr. Hethering interjected. "I, for one, have no intention of marching up and down the corridor or banging on doors, even if I were so inclined. Lead on, Mrs. Gaunt."

Captain Marshall stood with alacrity and bowed to Miss Demaretti, sweeping his hat out in a broad gesture toward the stairs. "May I assist you, Miss Demaretti? And Mrs. Ruberry, of course." He took the girl's bandbox out of her hand and looped its ribbons over his arm.

"Go on, then." Mrs. Ruberry waved impatiently at the stairs before picking up her worn leather portmanteau. "Take the lamp and light the way. I have no desire to stumble up the stairs in the dark. I should not like to break a limb in this dreadful place."

"Of course, of course." Captain Marshall retrieved the lamp from the table and his own leather bag before preceding the rest of them up the staircase.

Pru and Knighton took the room closest to the contessa's end of the corridor. The ladies took the next room, and then two remaining men took the third room, nearest to the stairs.

Knighton closed and bolted their door, determined to get a good night's sleep. The rest of the night proved to be thankfully quiet, at least for him. He was dimly aware that Pru had gotten up at one point, but he had rolled over and gone back to sleep without speaking. When he finally woke up again, she was sleeping beside him. Her lovely, intelligent face was flushed with slumber and though she had braided her dark hair before bed, a few strands had worked loose and curled around her forehead. He brushed the soft strands aside, watching her sleep. She was so beautiful with her black lashes fanned out against the plump rosiness of her cheeks that his heart ached with love.

She could have married a rich man, a titled noble, and yet she had chosen him. Why? In his darkest moments, he still wondered if she ever regretted her decision, or if she wished that she had gone to London, instead, to flirt and enjoy herself as a member of the *Ton*.

His breath caught in his throat when she moved and let out a long sigh. Her lips opened briefly as if speaking in a dream, and a slight smile dimpled the corner of her mouth. Her patrician features held both strength and character, promising that she would be just as beautiful at eighty as she was now.

His wife. She was nothing short of a miracle, a blessing he had somehow received.

He studied her for another minute, breathing in the warm fragrance of her neck and hair before he eased out of bed. After last night, Pru needed what little rest she could obtain. He dressed as quietly as he could and left, closing the door gently behind him to avoid waking her.

On his way downstairs, he stopped by Lieutenant Fisher's room. He knocked on the door and was somewhat surprised when someone other than Fisher bid him to enter.

"Mr. Hethering," Knighton said, startled. "What are you doing here?"

"Thought someone should see if the gallant lieutenant survived the spirits haunting the inn." Hethering smiled, flashing his teeth. He ran a hand over his black hair, smoothing back the white streak as if calling attention to its uniqueness and settled back in the creaking wooden chair he occupied.

Knighton found his amused glibness a trifle irritating, but he was at least an interesting traveling companion.

"How is he?" Knighton studied Fisher's face. The watery sunshine streaming through the dust-streaked window revealed an unhealthy gray pallor.

Was Fisher's wound festering, despite the midwife's care?

"Alive." Hethering shrugged, accompanied by another creaking protest from his chair. "Other than that, I have no opinion."

89

Knighton strode to the bed and pressed the back of his hand against Fisher's forehead. No fever. A small mercy. "Has he regained consciousness?"

"Not that I am aware. He was asleep when I entered and remains so."

"Undoubtedly for the best." He glanced at Hethering. "I don't suppose you have explored the breakfast possibilities of this wretched inn, have you?"

Hethering got to his feet and smoothed the lapels of his dark blue coat. "When I went down a few minutes ago, Miss Demaretti and Mr. Savage were speaking with our proprietor." He grimaced. "I believe they were rather fruitlessly requesting hot chocolate. And buns."

"Shall we see what they managed to obtain?" Knighton opened the door and gestured for Hethering to precede him, casting one last glance at Fisher. If Charron had repaired his carriage, they could not leave Fisher here alone.

Which meant some of them would have to stay behind with him.

Remembering Pru's illness the previous day, he considered suggesting they remain. He could send word for the coachman he'd sent ahead to Rome to arrange for lodgings to come to Benerosa. Riding in their own carriage might be best for Pru, after all.

As he followed Hethering down the stairs, one of the man's comments struck him anew. "Did you say Miss Demaretti was in the dining room alone with Mr. Savage?"

"Yes. She seemed quite distressed, as well. It appears a pot of chocolate is essential to her wellbeing in the morning."

"She was without Mrs. Ruberry?"

They reached the bottom of the staircase, and Hethering gave him a curious glance. "I did not notice if that august lady was present. I confess I was not looking for her. Why?"

"Mrs. Ruberry seemed quite assiduous in her duties as chaperone. It struck me as unusual that she would

90

permit Miss Demaretti to come downstairs without her, or leave her alone with a strange man." Particularly knowing that other gentlemen like Mr. Hethering were likely to be kicking about in the inn, searching for diversions to pass the time.

If Knighton had a daughter, he would not want her to be in the presence of such a loose screw without at least a dozen duennas in attendance.

Hethering laughed and stepped aside for Knighton to enter the dining room ahead of him. "Fear not. Methinks Mrs. Ruberry will be in attendance soon enough. She will not leave her little lamb to wander too far without her when there are so many wolves about."

Upon entering the small room, Knighton discovered Miss Demaretti and Mr. Savage seated at opposite ends of the rectangular table. Miss Demaretti was sipping a cup of *caffè e latte* that was so light it appeared to be simply milk that had stood next to a pot of coffee for five minutes or so. Mr. Savage held a roll gingerly between his fingertips and was turning it this way and that with an air of suspicion and distaste. With a long-suffering sigh, he broke it in half, spread some butter on one piece, and took a small bite.

"Good morning, fellow travelers," Hethering said boisterously as he pulled out one wobbly chair and took a seat at Miss Demaretti's elbow. He grinned at her and even spared a good-natured nod to Mr. Savage, who stared at him without expression and returned to examining his breakfast.

The girl gave him a flirtatious smile as she delicately selected a roll with two fingers and removed it from under the napkin folded over an overflowing basket. She placed it on a plate and gently put it down it in front of him with another glance from under her thick lashes.

"Good morning, sir. Would you like some *caffè e latte*?" she asked, stumbling a bit over the foreign phrase.

Amy Corwin

"Indeed, yes. And how are you this," Hethering glanced at the window, noted the sunshine streaming through, and continued, "fine morning?"

"Quite well, thank you." The young lady blushed and took a sip of coffee to cover her dimpled smile. "How are you, Mr. Hethering?"

"Tremendous! And you, Mr. Savage?" Hethering asked. "How do you fare?"

"As well as can be expected, considering the unfortunate circumstances." Savage barely accorded him a glance as he concentrated on buttering the remaining half of his roll with remarkable precision.

"Is your chaperone, Mrs. Ruberry, well?" Knighton asked, taking the chair next to Savage.

"I have not the faintest notion." Miss Demaretti flicked him a glanced and shrugged as she poured herself more of the coffee and milk mixture. "I have not seen her this morning."

"Where is she?" Knighton asked a bit more sharply than he intended.

"How should I know? She was gone by the time I awoke." Miss Demaretti's wide forehead wrinkled with a frown. "And if you must know, I found it excessively inconsiderate of her to leave like that, without a word. I have no maid with me, you see, so it was quite awkward to complete my toilet this morning."

While Miss Demaretti's parents could have selected a better chaperone, Mrs. Ruberry hadn't struck Knighton as the type of flighty woman who would rise at an outrageously early hour and go for a stroll to enjoy the morning mist. If anything, he would have predicted that she would remain in bed, snoring heartily, for as long as possible.

His earlier unease intensified. He had no real reason for his concern, but he could not ignore the uncomfortable feeling. "Did she leave a note, or mention where she was going?"

Once more, Miss Demaretti shrugged and poured a cup of *caffè e latte* for Mr. Hethering, giving him another dimpled smile as he took the cup from her. Single men obviously interested her more than married ones like Knighton. She even topped off Mr. Savage's cup for him before putting the pot back on the table.

When it was clear that she wasn't concerned enough to answer, Knighton rephrased his question. "When did you last see her?"

"Last night, I suppose." She glared at him and said coldly, "I fail to understand why you should expect me to make note of her schedule. She is *my* chaperone. I am not *hers*."

"I am merely concerned that she appears to be missing." Knighton poured himself a cup of *caffè e latte,* stared at it with distaste for a minute, and then took one of the rolls.

Maybe the beverage wouldn't be so objectionable in the company of a dry bun.

"Maybe she went out to explore the village," Savage commented before taking another piece of bread.

"The village? This squalid little place?" Hethering laughed. "From what I saw of it last night, it would take her all of five minutes to explore every dark corner of it. Assuming, of course, that she stopped to draw that picturesquely abandoned cottage at the edge of the churchyard."

"Then where is she?" Knighton hadn't meant to express his thought out loud, but having done so, he wasn't entirely surprised by Miss Demaretti's callous answer.

"Perhaps she ran off with that dreadful ruffian who stopped us on the road," she replied nastily. "Or met some fascinating young shepherd on the hillside. She is, after all, quite old enough to manage her own affairs."

"I am concerned that she may have met with an accident," Knighton said, having the satisfaction of seeing her blush. He hadn't considered the frankly terrifying prospect that Mrs. Ruberry may have gone for a walk and

93

been waylaid by the bandit who accosted them the previous evening.

If she had, it might prove awkward to obtain her release as. Try as he might, he couldn't imagine the Demaretti family being concerned enough to pay for the release of a woman who was little more than a servant. Particularly if Miss Demaretti was any indication of their general character. And since rich women rarely decided to hire out as chaperones, it was unlikely that Mrs. Ruberry would be able to pay any kind of a ransom herself.

"Well, I have not seen her, and that is all I can tell you," Miss Demaretti concluded.

Knighton was contemplating his *caffè e latte* and simultaneously wondering if he was worrying over Mrs. Ruberry to no purpose and if there were any other beverages available when he heard voices. Some of the shadow lifted from his heart. One of the voices was Pru's.

Just as he stood, Pru walked through the door, followed closely by Captain Marshall and a pale, wobbling Lieutenant Fisher.

"Fisher!" he exclaimed, stepping forward for fear the wounded man would collapse at his feet.

Pru smiled at Knighton with a triumphant gleam in her dark eyes. "You see, Lieutenant Fisher. I told you that no one expected you to come downstairs for breakfast. I could easily have brought you a tray."

"And I would be more than happy to assist you upstairs again if you wish," Captain Marshall added. Then he glanced at Hethering. "I noticed you borrowed my pocket guide this morning, Hethering. If you would return it, perhaps the lieutenant and I can look through the schedules. There must be other coaches passing this way, eh Fisher? At any rate, it is foolish to get out of bed until our carriage is pronounced ready." He gripped the sick man's elbow, but Fisher shook him off.

"I am quite capable of navigating a few stairs, though I appreciate your concern." He wheezed, and a drop of sweat rolled down the side of his face. Smiling manfully, he pressed a hand to his side and waved Pru to the table before slowly following.

Knighton gave his wife his chair, absurdly proud to do so. He noted the other men watching her and couldn't help believing that their gazes turned envious when Pru smiled up at him and caught his hand briefly. She gave his fingers a warm squeeze before picking up the pot to pour two cups for Lieutenant Fisher and herself. Captain Marshall waited on the other side of the table for everyone to be seated before he pulled out his own chair.

"Where is Mrs. Ruberry?" Pru glanced around the room. "Is she feeling unwell?"

Captain Marshall exchanged a glance with Miss Demaretti.

Knighton watched the two curiously. Had the pair managed to send Mrs. Ruberry on a wild goose chase to allow them time alone?

"That seems to be the question. No one has seen her since last night." Knighton held the basket of rolls out to his wife and then Fisher.

The lieutenant's skin was gray, and deep circles emphasized the lines of pain around his eyes. He struggled awkwardly with shaking hands to break his roll apart and take a bite. Although he managed a few more mouthfuls, he finally had to place the roll on his plate as he wheezed and jerked in an attempt to stay upright. He appeared to be regretting his decision to leave his bed, but he was obviously too proud to admit defeat.

Knighton caught his wife's gaze and shook his head. Her compressed mouth revealed her disapproval of Fisher's rash action. Knighton could only assume that Fisher feared being abandoned at the inn if Charron should get his carriage repaired today and wanted to prove that he was well enough to travel.

Knighton couldn't blame him. He wouldn't want to be left kicking his heels in this dismal village either. Although he'd only seen it in the dark, it didn't appear to have much to recommend it, and the innkeeper hadn't done anything to make it more agreeable. In fact, the dry, splintered state of the floorboards, the ever-present dust, and the general air of neglect made it clear that he hoped any guests would only stay the night and be gone as soon as possible come daylight.

He was just pondering the likelihood of obtaining another pot of *caffè e latte* when the front door clattered open.

Charron staggered into the room, red-faced, sweating, and wheezing as he tried to catch his breath. When Knighton stood, Charron stared at him and gestured to him to wait while he mopped his brow with a grimy handkerchief.

"Accident—" Charron gasped. He waved his handkerchief vaguely in the direction of the road where they'd left his carriage. "The lady—" he caught sight of Miss Demaretti and his eyes widened. "You! But we saw you—I thought... I thought it was the young lady—one of our ladies..." He bent over to grip his knees and catch his breath. "Come quickly."

Chapter Nine

Only one lady was missing, unless it was the contessa renting rooms on the third floor.

"Is it Mrs. Ruberry?" Knighton asked, his chest tight.

An oily bead of sweat rolled down Charron's bulbous nose. He shrugged and mopped his brow again and blew his nose. "It is difficult to say." He cast a puzzled glance again at Miss Demaretti.

The young lady was looking at Captain Marshall, a strange expression on her face.

Knighton examined Charron's perspiring face. He appeared almost ill with worry.

How bad could it be? Surely she wasn't dead.

"Mr. Hethering." Knighton gestured to the seated man. Hethering was nearly as tall as he was and appeared to be fit. A good man, perhaps, in such an emergency.

Savage watched them unhelpfully, leaning back in his chair, with his small hands clasped over his trim belly. He didn't appear to have any intention of exerting himself.

Seated at the table, Fisher frowned and flicked an uncomfortable glance at Miss Demaretti, clearly irritated by his inability to offer any assistance and embarrassed to admit it in front of the young, and very attractive, young lady.

"Certainly. At your service." Hethering rose hastily, almost knocking over his chair. He glanced at Captain Marshall.

Marshall had shoved an entire roll in his mouth and took a long swallow of his *caffè e latte* to help him swallow as he stood up. "I will join you."

"Wagon—we must have the wagon," Charron moaned, wringing his hands.

Hethering strode to the door. "I will speak to the stable boy. The one we had yesterday should do."

"Perhaps I should go with you." Pru placed a hand on Knighton's arm. "If it is a lady, I might be of some assistance."

When Knighton glanced at Charron, the stout coachman shrugged, shook his head, and mopped his brow.

Knighton was loathe to involve Pru in what might be a terrible accident. Worse, she might be exposed to further danger if the ruffians of last night should return. Unfortunately, she was also correct in that if the woman was hurt, having another lady present might prove useful.

"Very well," he agreed slowly.

"Let me get my cloak and our medical case." Pru ran out, and he heard her light, quick step on the stairs before he could respond.

Hethering strode through the front door just as Pru returned, her cheeks flushed from running. She had already draped her dark blue cloak over her shoulders and carried the small, leather satchel containing the medical supplies they'd packed for traveling.

Knighton put his hand against the small of her back and escorted her through the front door with the other men trailing after him. The long-bed wagon from last night stood on the road, with the stable lad holding the reins of the team of raw-boned draft horses they'd used last night. The horses snorted in the cool morning air and stamped their feet, clearly restive.

As Knighton helped his wife up onto the single bench seat, Hethering and Marshall climbed into the back and settled into the piles of straw lining the bed. When Charron began to climb up next to Pru, Knighton pushed him aside, took the seat, and gestured to the stable boy to hand him the reins.

"I drive." Charron stared up at Knighton, his hands on his hips. "I know where she is, *si*?"

Knighton flicked the reins. "Get in the back, or we will go without you."

"Go then." Charron flicked a hand at them. "And good luck to you."

"Thank you." He lifted the reins and clicked his tongue, ignoring the coachman's ill humor.

The horses' ears twitched, and they thudded forward a step before Charron yelled, "Stop!

The wagon shuddered and before it even rolled to a halt, Charron caught hold of the back. The other two men helped the portly man up, and he had barely lurched onto the wagon when Knighton clicked his tongue again. They set off with a rattle and a jolt.

There was only one main road running through Benerosa, and the horses seemed determined to maintain a sedate pace, regardless of any encouragement to go faster, so Knighton did not have to pay a great deal of attention to his driving.

"What happened, Charron?" he asked.

"Who knows? I did not see." Charron's coarse voice floated over his shoulder.

"Then how do you know there was an accident? Where did it occur?" Knighton persisted.

"I go to look at my coach in the daylight. You understand. And I saw her."

"At the carriage?"

"*Sí*. That is, on the side of the mountain. You will see."

What on earth had Mrs. Ruberry, if it was Mrs. Ruberry, been doing returning to the coach alone?

If she had been alone.

Perhaps she thought she had forgotten something. Her plump fingers, bedecked with a half-dozen gaudy rings, arose in his mind. If she had lost a ring, she might have returned to locate it for fear that it would be stolen.

In truth, there could be a hundred reasons why she might have found it urgent to return to the coach.

They reached the disabled carriage quickly, and even before Knighton brought the horses to a halt, Captain Marshall and Mr. Hethering jumped down onto the road. Charron waited until the wagon came to a complete halt before he laboriously, and with much huffing and aggravated mumbling, climbed down.

Knighton assisted Pru to alight and was about to join the other men at the edge of the precipice on the far side of the road when Mr. Hethering turned toward him.

Hethering held up a hand. "Perhaps your wife ought to wait by the carriage."

"Should I remain here?" Pru gave Knighton a troubled glance. "It must be terrible."

"I will call for you if there is any assistance you can give." He gave her hand a squeeze as she nodded and returned to stand next to the wagon.

He strode to the edge of the road and stared down the rock-strewn hillside. The morning mist, eluding the rapidly brightening sun, curled over the ground like smoke, hiding some of the trees and boulders and making the shadowy slope look remote and dreamlike. At first, all he saw were stone fragments, boulders, and shrubs clinging to the sharp incline. Then he noticed some smudges in the dirt. Darker streaks on the ground pointed downward, like an arrow marking a tumble of color. Red, white, and black jumbled together in a small heap halfway down the hillside.

No wonder Charron had been surprised to see Miss Demaretti—her red cloak with its white ermine trim was unmistakable.

What was Mrs. Ruberry—if it was Mrs. Ruberry— doing with the girl's cloak?

"Did anyone bring a rope?" Knighton asked.

"There was one in the wagon." Hethering went back to the vehicle and grabbed a coil from the bed, shaking off bits of straw as he returned to the edge. He glanced around, frowning. "There is no place to serve as an anchor. The wagon won't do. It is likely to roll down the side of the mountain and drag you with it."

Knighton studied the side of the road. The nearby trees were stunted and twisted. Certainly, they were not strong enough to hold his weight, and although there were rocks, none of them had enough mass to provide a firm anchor. However, with only three wheels, the heavy, old fashioned coach wasn't going anywhere. He slipped the rope around both axles and knotted it.

Before he could return, Captain Marshall had looped the other end of the rope around his waist and stepped over the edge, his boots sliding a few feet before he steadied himself with one hand.

When he caught Knighton's frown, he smiled. "I could hardly let you go with your wife watching, could I?"

Hethering shook his head, a rueful expression on his face as he tentatively stepped down the slope a yard and picked up the taut rope to stabilize it for the captain. He halted and watched Marshall briefly before sliding another yard over the rubble.

So many heroes.

Perhaps it was the thought of Miss Demaretti awaiting them at the inn, or the possible glory of being the one to rescue her chaperone, that made the two men so eager to risk their lives. Knighton eyed them with a sour taste in his mouth. This was not the time nor the place for bravado and bragging. If anything, it appeared to be a tragedy that would only bring sadness in its wake.

As he studied the two men scrambling down to the crumpled heap, he realized it was highly unlikely that their rescue efforts would meet with success. That pile of clothing wedged against a large boulder a twenty yards below the edge of the road never moved. There would be no smiles and no happy ending to their adventure, at least for the lady involved.

Involuntarily, he remembered the glances exchanged by Miss Demaretti and her gallant captain that morning, the glances of conspirators. Had the pair already known what had happened to Mrs. Ruberry? An ugly and suspicious thought.

However, once it intruded upon his mind, he couldn't ignore it. He glanced back at Pru, thankful once again for her company. She understood people and their motivations, and she was more charitable in her

Amy Corwin

assessments than he was. She always seemed to see through to the heart of the matter.

Sometimes, it was humbling, and at first, he had resented her flashes of intuition. Her talent made inquiries seem too easy, almost effortless in the face of his own methodical plodding through facts. Even though they had only been married a few months, he now relied on her compassion and judgment to temper his reasoning.

Nonetheless, despite her influence, logic and the bare facts remained his *métier*, a necessary balance to his wife's sensibilities. Pure sensibility could lead them astray as easily as misinterpreted facts.

Had Pru also noticed Miss Demaretti and the captain's reaction? He wished that he had the time and privacy to discuss the matter with her. He glanced over at her, but she was stretching her neck and standing on tiptoes, trying to watch the rescue activity on the slope. The captain was toiling up the hillside with the body, presumably Mrs. Ruberry, slung over his shoulder.

Knighton helped Hethering draw up the rope, yard by yard, to keep it taut until the captain stumbled over the edge of the road. Unbalanced, he fell to his knees in the dirt. The woman's body toppled limply out of his grasp and landed with a dull thud that made Knighton wince.

Before he could warn her away, Pru ran to the woman and eased her onto her back, exposing Mrs. Ruberry's slack face. Her empty blue eyes, hazy with death, stared at the clear sky above, and her mouth hung open, exposing a surprisingly good set of strong, white teeth. An ugly gash broke the skin and exposed the bone over her right eye.

No bruising around the cut, though. Post-mortem? Had she been thrown down the hillside after she died? He studied the ground directly in line with her original position.

"She's dead," Pru said, pressing her palm over the eyes to close them, but her gesture proved useless. Mrs. Ruberry's eyes remained open.

"Are you sure?" Captain Marshall breathed heavily as he slipped the rope off over his head and got to his feet.

"Yes. Quite sure." Pru glanced at Knighton and stood, brushing the dirt off her skirts.

They stood in a semi-circle around the body, staring down at it as if hoping they were all mistaken, and that Mrs. Ruberry would sit up, laugh, and claim in her raucous voice that the entire thing had been a splendid joke.

"She must have walked too close to the edge of the road and fallen," Hethering commented, winding the rope and throwing it into the back of the wagon. "If she returned here last night, it would have been easy to make such a misstep in the dark."

Unlikely. Knighton studied him. Did Hethering actually believe such a nonsensical idea? It was inconceivable that she would have returned to the coach alone and at night. Particularly after they had been accosted by bandits twice already and Fisher had been shot.

"Perhaps," Knighton remarked, keeping his doubts to himself.

"We should return to the village. Miss Demaretti is alone—I should have considered her situation earlier." Pru studied the road nervously and clasped her arms protectively over her waist.

"You had no way of knowing if Mrs. Ruberry returned here on her own or suffered such a tragic accident," the captain said, casting equally worried glances in the direction of the inn. "However, Mrs. Gaunt is correct. There is no reason to linger. We should return to Benerosa as quickly as possible. Miss Demaretti will be worried." He picked up the body and gently placed it in the wagon and climbed in after it.

Knighton assisted his wife to settle onto the seat and gave her the reins. Then he worked with Hethering and Charron to turn the long wagon around without sending it over the edge. As soon as that was accomplished, he climbed into the seat next to Pru and accepted the reins.

No one spoke as they rattled and clattered back to the inn, but Knighton knew the others must be as preoccupied as he was with questions about Mrs. Ruberry's death. Pru sat quietly beside him, her brows drawn down into a worried frown.

Something told him that Mrs. Ruberry's death had not been the tragic accident someone had intended it to appear. And even more curious, the woman had been wearing Miss Demaretti's cloak.

Did that mean the girl was involved?

Or had she been the intended target?

Chapter Ten

"How could she? My cloak is quite ruined!" Miss Demaretti dabbed her eyes with an extravagant, lace-edged handkerchief.

If he'd remained a hundred yards away, Knighton might have believed she wept for her chaperone's dreadful and untimely death. As it was, after listening to a litany of Mrs. Ruberry's failings, he realized the girl's tears were not related to grief.

He turned away, disgusted, and caught Captain Marshall's gaze.

"She is upset—shock—you know. She does not mean anything by it." Marshall looped an arm over the girl's shoulder and dragged her back, protesting, into the inn.

Pru stared after the pair, chewing her lip. "I suppose I ought to see to her. I cannot leave a young girl like that unchaperoned."

"I don't see why not," Knighton said gruffly. "Cold-hearted little chit."

"She is only sixteen." Pru smiled ruefully. "Girls at that age can be very hard-headed."

"Cruel. And spoiled."

Pru laughed and then pressed her fingers over her lips in embarrassment. "Perhaps. However, that simply means she needs a firm hand. And she truly may be in shock over the tragedy. I should check on her."

"The captain has her well in hand." He caught her wrist. "Please. I need your assistance. I don't believe Mrs. Ruberry simply tripped and fell."

"But the hem of her cloak was torn." Pru gingerly reached into the back of the wagon and pulled at the mantle's hem, revealing a rent in the left front side. "She must have caught her foot in the hole and lost her balance." She smoothed out the red wool, her hand lingering for a moment on the soft ermine trim.

He could see a brief flash of desire in her face as she apparently remembered how elegant the cloak had looked on Miss Demaretti the previous day.

Knighton caught Pru's hand, but didn't comment. He'd been unable to convince her to purchase a new wardrobe after she had inherited her cousin's estate, and he still felt frustrated by her seeming inability to spend money on herself. But whenever he brought the matter up, she just laughed and shook her head at the extravagance of buying new clothes when she had a trunk full of perfectly good garments.

Certainly, she'd purchased a few new things for their honeymoon, however. And all of the items were understated though undeniably elegant.

Nothing was as splendid as Miss Demaretti's red, ermine-trimmed cloak.

Well, he could change that. As soon as they arrived in Rome, he would purchase a new cloak—blue, her favorite color—trimmed in ermine. It was little enough to do, and she deserved that, and better. Despite her obvious illness the last few days, she had never once complained. She always considered others first.

Her strength of character and kindness never failed to surprise and awe him.

Miss Demaretti could learn a great deal from his wife.

"You look pale, my love," he said. "Are you sure you are well? I am selfish to ask you to remain here."

"Not at all." She pressed a hand over her waist and gave him a smile. "I am well enough, I believe. What do you require?"

"I am afraid you will need to prepare Mrs. Ruberry for burial." He gripped her shoulder and squeezed it reassuringly when she stared at him with wide, horrified eyes. "Request the assistance of a maid. You should not have to do it alone. For now, though, I feel we must examine her, and it would not be appropriate for me to do so."

She studied his face and then nodded, although a reluctant frown turned down the corners of her mouth.

The wagon stood in a corner of the inn's courtyard and fortunately, they would not be easily observed, or disturbed, as there were no windows overlooking the corner. He assisted her to climb onto the bed of the wagon and felt her momentary recoil as she leaned over the dead woman. The body lay on its side, one arm pointing straight up, the other crooked and broken beneath her. Her neck was also broken and twisted awkwardly, her ear almost resting on her shoulder. Her legs were drawn up and bent in a way she would undoubtedly find horribly uncomfortable, were she still alive.

"If you remove the cloak, I can lay her out more properly," he suggested, gently pulling on one cold ankle.

The limb resisted his efforts to straighten it. Rigor mortis had already fixed her body in its tumbled state. He eyed it and his wife bending over the still form and wished he had not involved her.

Pru struggled to unwrap the heavy cloak and turn the corpse on its back, growing paler as she worked. When the cloak pulled free, she thrust the heavy fabric into Knighton's hands and abruptly turned aside to grip the side of the wagon. Her breath rushed in and out in loud gasps.

"Are you sick?" he asked.

She held up a hand, begging for a chance to regain her self-control. After a minute, she scrambled down to the ground and pressed her fingers against her mouth. "I'm sorry—I cannot—the smell..." Her throat worked convulsively.

"Go lie down. I should never have asked you to help me."

"No." She shook her head. "I will be fine in a moment." She walked a few steps away and took a deep breath. "It was just the smell. And I saw—" The muscles in her jaw tightened. She closed her eyes and her forehead glistened with small beads of perspiration. "You were

correct to suspect something. She was shot. Her chest...
Oh, Knighton, it was awful."

So that was the answer to the mystery.

Someone had shot her and then dumped her down
the steep slope, most likely hoping that either she would
not be found, or that the post-mortem injuries would hide
the fatal wound.

One look at his wife's distraught face made him
speak more firmly. "Go to bed. And don't worry about that
chit. I shall make arrangements for another female to see
to that revolting young woman. You are not responsible for
her well-being."

A light, forced laugh escaped through Pru's fingers,
still pressed against her pallid lips. "She is not that bad."

"No, you are correct. She is far worse."

"The poor maid is going to have enough work." Her
eyes flicked toward the wagon's sad burden. "I should do
something."

"There must be other women in the village. Don't
let it worry you. Get some rest. I shan't be long." He kissed
her on the cheek and waited until she went inside before
turning back to the corpse.

He climbed onto the bed of the wagon and
examined the woman's wounds. The broken bones and
gashes had obviously occurred after death, for the
surrounding skin lacked the bruising it would have
developed if she had been alive when they occurred. The
injury that had precipitated her death was the bullet that
left a hole immediately under her left breast. Rolling her
over exposed a very ugly exit wound. Her entire back was
stiff with dried blood.

There was obviously no point in digging for the lead
ball. It had left the body when she'd been shot. However,
it might be worth his while to see if he could find the bullet.
Locating the place where she had been shot might tell him
something about the circumstances surrounding her
murder. It might even reveal evidence leading to the
identification of the murderer.

He frowned, thinking about last night as he climbed out of the wagon.

Although he had slept fitfully, he could not remember hearing a gunshot. The murder could not have occurred in, or near, the inn, or they would have heard the shot. He picked up the cloak from the side of the wagon where he'd draped it. The silk lining was spattered with blood and pierced with two holes on the left side going through the front and the back. The tumble down the rocky hillside had caused additional tears and embedded large smudges of gritty dirt.

The garment might be useful as evidence to whatever authorities investigated.

He glanced at the body, considering what else might be learned from the pitiful figure. Would it be too much to hope that there might be a bit of the wad left in the wound? While unlikely, he climbed up and made a more thorough examination.

Mrs. Ruberry had been wearing the same dark green traveling dress with black piping that she'd worn the previous day in the coach. So she had not changed into her night clothes before going out. A closer examination of the cloak also revealed burned areas that reeked of gunpowder.

Whoever had killed her had fired at fairly close range. Close enough for the burning gunpowder to singe her clothing.

Distasteful though it was, he probed the wound and searched for any foreign objects. To his surprise, he found a bit of a gold chain and locket driven into her chest by the force of the shot. The rest of the chain had dug into the folds of skin at the back of her neck. She had clearly worn the jewelry under her clothes, hiding it from view.

Resisting the urge to study the necklace more closely, he pulled out a handkerchief and placed the bits of gold into it before turning his attention once again to his unpleasant task. Small pieces of bone, and even some stones and bits of dirt, made the search more difficult. He had nearly given up before he found it. The wad was wedged deeply into the wound, almost at the exit point in her back.

Knighton removed it and added it to the small collection in his handkerchief. He would examine all of it later, in private.

He started to drape the ruined cloak over the body when he realized that the maid might dispose of it when she prepared the body for burial. He folded it awkwardly and bundled it under his arm. With luck, the local constable, or authorities, would arrive soon, and he could hand all of these depressing items over to him.

Just as he jumped down to the ground, the inn's side door opened. A woman came out and stopped abruptly when she saw him.

The girl—woman, he realized as she finally came closer—was rail thin. Her fine brown hair straggled out from under a dingy white cap and her sharp nose hung over a pointed chin, giving her a rodent-like appearance. Her twitchy manner didn't help the impression, for she acted like a mouse caught in the middle of the floor and surrounded by a dozen cats. Her brown eyes flicked to Knighton several times before she dropped her gaze and began twisting her tattered apron between reddened, chapped hands.

Belatedly, she dropped a curtsey. "Signore?"

"Are you the maid here?"

"*Si*, signore." She curtsied again. Her mumbled Italian was a little difficult to understand as she seemed to have an exaggerated patois even more distinct than the innkeeper's rapid speech. "The signora said to come."

"Not a very pleasant job, I am afraid. What is your name?"

"Celestina, signore."

"This lady has met with an unfortunate accident and will need to be prepared for burial." When she frowned and opened her mouth, he held up a hand. "I will pay for your services and the funeral. As I am unfamiliar with your priest, I would appreciate it if you could either make the arrangements or send him to me so that I might see to matters. The young English lady should be able to provide you with appropriate garments from the lady's trunk. Is that clear?"

"You wish me to speak with our priest?" Her wide eyes indicated her disbelief at this request.

"Yes. I don't know him. Do you understand?"

"He will not be pleased, signore."

"No doubt. However, it must be done."

She continued to stare at him, twisting her apron, a frown crimping the skin between her eyes. "It cannot be done. She has no last rite. Our priest—he was not called for the last rite. It cannot be done."

"Well, it will have to be done. She must be given a proper burial. You may send your priest to me if he objects."

"*Si.*" She shrugged at last and turned back toward the door. "I get clothes. And sheet." She glanced at him over her narrow shoulder. "You pay for sheet?"

"Yes. I will pay. I will pay for everything. Just get it done."

"*Si*, signore. As you wish."

As he watched her leave, Buonfiglio came outside, his round face wrinkled with fear. His plump hands kept flattening the hair on the side of his head in a nervous gesture.

He cast a glance at the wagon and blanched. "Is it the missing lady?"

"Yes, it is Mrs. Ruberry."

The innkeeper crossed himself quickly and murmured what sounded like a short prayer. "Not good, this is not good."

"Indeed, it is not. You will need to send for the authorities. A death certificate must be sent to her family in England, if she has any remaining."

"Impossible! It is impossible. I will be ruined. To have a guest murdered in her very bed." He wrung his hands dramatically. "I am ruined."

"She was not murdered in her bed. And despite your commendable concern, I should imagine that if a ghost on the second floor does not drive away business, then this certainly will not."

"Ghost! *Mio Dio,* now we shall have another. Oh, what will we do?"

"I doubt you even have one phantom. If you do, it is not particularly active. Lieutenant Fisher spent the night in that haunted room of yours without any ill effect that I could see."

"Not all the night, signore. Not at all."

Knighton studied the innkeeper. "What do you mean, not all the night?"

"Did you not know? Me, I saw him in the dining room."

"When?"

"Late, very late. I do not know the time, but the others had retired already."

"Did he speak to you? What did he want?"

Buonfiglio shrugged. "He did not see me. I do not know what he wanted, but he went into the dining room, and I heard the sound of the door. Crazy English, *Mio Dio,* must I stay awake all night to unlock and lock the door? Meaning no offense, of course. But only by the goodness of my heart do I do this."

"How long was he gone?"

"An hour? Maybe more." He shrugged again, clearly unconcerned about the implications of Fisher leaving the inn in the middle of the night. "Who can say?"

So Fisher had been awake and outside during the time when Mrs. Ruberry could have been murdered, considering the state of the body. However, though the wounded man could undoubtedly wield a firearm, he could not have carried her corpse in his condition.

Unless he had lured her to the mountainside, shot her, and then simply let her tumble over the edge. That would certainly explain the facts as they knew them.

The theory made it even more urgent that he find the site where she died. It would be the only way to know if it was possible that Fisher had been involved. And if he had not, then perhaps he had seen something. Or someone else.

Buonfiglio's curious stare caught Knighton's attention. "You will contact the authorities, then? And tell them to bring a physician for the death certificate." If nothing else, Knighton could take the certificate with him. When they returned to England in the spring, he could let any remaining members of Mrs. Ruberry's family know about her unfortunate death.

"*Si.* If they will come." Buonfiglio didn't sound overly confident that the authorities would arrive any time soon.

"Make sure they do, or I will hold you responsible." Knighton ignored the innkeeper's final shrug. He strode into the inn with the tattered, red cloak under his arm, determined to obtain some answers.

The authorities might not be interested in Mrs. Ruberry's death, but Knighton was. He had no intention on traveling to Rome in the company of a murderer.

Chapter Eleven

Pru gazed at Miss Demaretti with exasperation.

"I am nearly seventeen—I do not need a chaperone, and no one will thank you for interfering." The girl's brown eyes flashed with anger. "My cousins live in Rome, and we are nearly there. There is no sense in hiring another old woman. I am perfectly capable of sitting in a carriage without one."

"How do you think your cousins will react when you arrive alone?" Pru asked gently, struggling to make the girl see reason. "It is simply not *done* for a young lady to travel by herself, no matter how short the distance."

"They will say nothing." Miss Demaretti thrust her chin out in a gesture that unfortunately reminded Pru of a mule taking the bit between its teeth and jerking its head to go in the wrong direction. "And if they do, I shall return home. I never wanted to come to this dreadful place anyway. I *hate* Rome."

"How do you know when you have never been there?" Pru covered her mouth to hide her smile.

Despite her amusement, Pru was sensitive enough to catch the slight tone of unhappiness in the girl's last statement. Her parents had obviously sent her off for whatever reason without consulting her. Perhaps they had grown exasperated with her peevishness and tantrums.

"Why would I enjoy it? They will no doubt keep me locked up to suit their old-fashioned notions of propriety."

"I hardly think they will lock you in your room." *Unless you go on in this manner and deserve it.* She touched the girl's hand. "I understand your concerns, Miss Demaretti, and would not like it, myself, if I had to be saddled with a stranger less than fifty miles from my destination. However, this is a foreign land. You must consider your own safety and comfort. You mentioned earlier that you missed Mrs. Ruberry's services as a maid this morning—wouldn't you prefer to have someone to assist you?" Inwardly cringing at the performance she was about to make, Pru straightened and assumed a critical and haughty expression. "I understand the ladies in Rome are very fashionable, and I would not want to be seen in such a haphazard state, myself. Of course, I have always preferred a certain elegance in my appearance, and I understand it is not something everyone can achieve. Your appearance was unavoidable this morning, I am sure. Nonetheless..." She let her words drift off, implying that Miss Demaretti's hasty and casual toilet left much to be desired.

The girl's quick blush and rapid blinking betrayed her inexperience and a touching lack of confidence. She understood the criticism only too well and took it painfully to heart. Her slim hands smoothed the golden-brown wool of her traveling dress over her lap before she caught herself and clasped her hands in her lap.

"A—a maid would be useful," she stammered, eyeing Pru's ice blue wool traveling dress with a touch of envy in her eyes.

"Indeed." Pru gazed around the room in apparent boredom while her mind raced. Where on earth could she find a woman suitable to act as a chaperone for this girl in such a small village? Would the contessa know? She seemed familiar with Benerosa. "The contessa might advise us." She gave Miss Demaretti a casual glance. "If you are truly interested."

"Oh, yes." Miss Demaretti stood, her eyes flashing with excitement. "I have not met her, but I'm sure she can suggest someone. Shall we call on her now?"

Pru hurriedly put a hand over her mouth and covered her smile with a yawn. While she had hoped Miss Demaretti would respond to her gentle prodding, she had not expected such quick and enthusiastic response. If she hadn't had the girl's best interests at heart, Pru might even have felt ashamed of herself for playing on Miss Demaretti's sensibilities.

"Certainly." Pru rose and shook out her skirts.

"And please, call me Catherine," Miss Demaretti placed a hand on Pru's arm and glanced up at her shyly.

"I would be honored." Pru considered the matter, but there was their age difference to consider, and Catherine might not continue to accept her authority if she were to give her the use of her first name too quickly. "Are you ready?"

"Yes." Catherine hesitated with one dainty foot hovering above the first stair. "Is she a terrible dragon?"

"No, she is not too dreadful if one shows her the proper respect."

"Oh, I shall. Honestly. It was only when that awful Mrs. Ruberry hovered over me that I, well, I scarcely knew what I said. I am not usually so saucy or cruel." While Catherine sounded sincere, Pru wasn't convinced that Mrs. Ruberry was entirely to blame for the girl's heartlessness.

As she started up the stairs behind Catherine, one hand on the rickety handrail, Pru found herself once again questioning the contessa's presence in Benerosa. Why would a contessa stay in such an inconsequential, and frankly depressing, place? There were no picturesque ruins, or even falls such as those Pru hoped to visit near Terni. The cascade at the Velino River, just a few miles from Terni, reportedly fell 1,068 feet on the flank of a ravine and formed three successive, spectacular falls. That prospect was the prime reason for them to join the small group of travelers and take the more indirect route to Rome, rather than following the coast.

The village of Benerosa lacked any such points of interest and seemed to be in a desolate area infested with brigands. To make matters even more inexplicable, Pru had gotten the impression that the grande dame was a frequent resident at *De La Fortuna*, although the contessa had not explicitly stated it. Perhaps she had gotten such a notion because Buonfiglio seemed so resigned to giving up the entire third floor to the contessa.

They reached the contessa's door, and Catherine stood aside to let Pru take the initiative. Straightening, she knocked firmly.

The maid, Domenica, opened the door almost immediately. When she saw Pru, she stood aside to permit the two women to enter. To their surprise, they found the contessa seated at a lovely little oval table. A silver tea service was spread out over the table with a delicate teacup and plate near the contessa's hand.

When she saw Pru, she gestured at the teapot. "Would you care to join me, Mrs. Gaunt?"

"It would be a pleasure," Pru said, stepping aside to draw the girl forward. "And I hope we are not disturbing you. I brought Miss Catherine Demaretti with me to introduce her and seek your advice on an important matter that concerns her deeply."

Walking past Pru to assume her position behind her employer, Domenica gasped at the mention of Miss Demaretti's name and cast an agitated glance at the contessa. "But she is—" she broke off abruptly, flushing.

Except for a slight tightness around her mouth, the *grande dame* managed to control her reaction better than her servant. She studied Catherine, her sharp gaze traveling from the girl's lacy cap down to her shoes.

Pru waited, watching Domenica's more expressive face. What could possibly have caused such consternation? Had she thought it was Miss Demaretti who had died, instead of Mrs. Ruberry?

When the contessa nodded, Pru asked formally, "Contessa di Mordano, may I present Miss Demaretti?"

The contessa lifted one hand and gestured for her to move forward.

Pru turned slightly and continued, "Miss Demaretti, the Contessa di Mordano."

Catherine curtseyed and had the sense to remain silent.

"Be seated," the contessa commanded. "Miss Demaretti travels to Rome to visit her cousins, *si*?"

The young lady cast an agonized glance at Pru, clearly too overawed to speak.

"Yes, contessa," Pru answered. "And that is the difficulty, I am afraid. Miss Demaretti's chaperone has met with an accident here in Benerosa. She cannot go on without one."

"Of course. That is obvious." The contessa waved and nodded impatiently.

"I was hoping that perhaps we might trespass upon your kindness and ask for your advice regarding any ladies in the neighborhood who might be suitable."

The contessa gave a dry laugh like the rattling of twigs and shook her head. "Benerosa is small. There are no ladies here. However, I know a woman, a distant cousin, who may do well enough. She is widowed." She waved her hand dismissively. "Her husband was a fool—improvident. You understand. It is difficult for her."

Was that why the contessa came to Benerosa? To visit an indigent relative? Whatever the reason, Pru was relieved to hear that there might be someone suitable nearby. She had no desire to chaperone the flighty, stubborn girl all the way to Rome, even if she could have convinced Knighton of the necessity for it.

"Thank you," Pru said. "I am grateful to you for the suggestion."

"I will write an introduction you may take to her today." The contessa poured two additional cups of tea. "Sit. Please. It is pleasant to have company, is it not?"

"Yes." Pru took a seat and waved Miss Demaretti to the wooden chair next to her.

"How is it you remain in Benerosa?" The contessa held out a delicate porcelain plate of biscotti. "I had understood you broke your journey only for one night."

"The accident—I am afraid we must make arrangements for a burial."

"Ah, I see. A fatal accident." She shrugged. "Sadly, these things happen. If that idiot priest gives you difficulties, I will speak to him." The contessa smiled in a way that made Pru pity the poor man. She then gestured to her maid, who promptly brought a portable writing desk and stood holding it awkwardly while the contessa took out a heavy sheet of paper and carefully dipped a quill in a small, silver pot of ink. "My cousin will do as I ask. You will find her satisfactory. She had a daughter—once."

"I am sorry," Pru murmured.

"The foolish child ran away." The contessa's dark eyes sparkled with malicious amusement. "She is unlikely to allow it to happen again. *Si?*" She folded the letter in thirds and handed it to Pru without sealing it. When she caught Pru's confused expression, she laughed, again. The sound was more like the rustle of sere, brown leaves than merriment. "I will not waste the wax for a seal. I have no need to hide the contents, and she well knows my writing. Her name is Justina Ursini. Buonfiglio will show you the way to her house. Now you must go." She leaned back in her chair, a padded and exceedingly ornate piece of furniture that some might call a throne, and closed her eyes briefly.

Astonished at the sudden dismal, Pru studied the contessa, alarmed to see how tired and old the *grande dame* appeared in the murky light. She kept the drapes closed, but the strong autumn sunshine peeped through in long streaks around the heavy curtains, and the light showed every wrinkle and fold in the contessa's papery skin. Dark circles under her sunken eyes emphasized her fragile air, and Pru, remembering the purple shadows under her own father's eyes before he suffered his fatal heart attack, wondered if the elderly lady had a weak heart.

In any event, their brief visit had been enough to weary her. Pru stood quickly and touched Catherine's arm. The girl had just taken a sip of the tepid tea and sputtered awkwardly, trying to hide her reaction behind her handkerchief. When she recovered, Catherine stood up quickly, her cup and saucer rattling in her hands before she placed them with a jerk on the low table.

"Thank you again for your advice and allowing us to visit you," Pru said.

"Thank you, Contessa. It was lovely meeting you." Catherine sunk into a low, graceful courtesy.

Domenica held open the door, waiting impatiently for Miss Demaretti to rise and leave. They had barely crossed the threshold when it was shut behind them with a snap.

"Do you think Mrs. Ursini is anything like her cousin?" Miss Demaretti asked in a nervous voice as they hurried along the hallway.

"I honestly don't know. However, I should not worry excessively over it. We shall visit her this afternoon, and you can see if she suits you." Pru gave the girl's arm a light squeeze. "Never fear. I shall not foist her upon you if she is a dragon." Although perhaps a dragon was precisely what the girl needed if she became this well-behaved after just a few minutes with a very elderly one.

"Should we go now?" Catherine's hands fluttered to her neck. "Oh, my cloak..."

"Perhaps you can wear Mrs. Ruberry's?"

The girl frowned, clearly unhappy with the idea. Pru could almost read her thoughts. The girl's cloak had been trimmed in ermine, and her chaperone's had been not only drab, but well-worn.

"If you wish, I can speak to my husband and see if we may remove the ermine from your old cloak. You will not want to attach it to Mrs. Ruberry's, however, you might obtain a new cloak in Rome and have a seamstress reattach the trim."

"Oh, yes. That is an excellent idea. You must ask him immediately." How quickly she reverted to her previous, callous attitude.

"When we return."

"Of course," Catherine replied in a slightly meeker voice. "And Mrs. Gaunt, I do appreciate your efforts on my behalf." She touched Pru's hand. "You have been so kind to me despite..." She trailed off, blushing. "Well, despite everything."

120

"Of course." Pru smiled at her. "Now, collect your cloak. I shall see if I can find our illustrious proprietor to guide us to Mrs. Ursini."

"And the captain? May he not attend us, as well?"

Much as Pru thought that Catherine had already encouraged the young captain quite enough, she had to admit that she would feel safer with another man attending them, particularly an armed one. They had already had one difficult encounter with ruffians, and although it was now daytime, she didn't relish the thought of another unpleasant adventure.

"Very well. If he is not busy and wishes to walk with us, he may do so." Pru sighed ruefully at how old and stuffy she sounded. It was demoralizing to think that sixteen-year-old Catherine probably viewed her in the light of an elderly aunt, despite the fact that she had not yet turned thirty.

"Thank you, Mrs. Gaunt. If you wish, I'll fetch our cloaks and ask Captain Marshall to accompany us. I'm sure he will be quite pleased."

"No doubt." Fleetingly, Pru thought of Catherine's red cloak with the ermine trim. She had never been one for bold colors and flashy clothing, but just once...

No. She was too old to change now, and it was foolish to even think about it. Leave such things to others more suited to flamboyant styles. Nonetheless, she couldn't help feeling just the slightest bit of longing over the young lady's elegant fur-trimmed cloak.

Fiorella appeared, dusting rag in hand, before Pru could even take a seat to wait for Catherine, and she took the opportunity to obtain directions to Mrs. Ursini's house. It seemed the widow rented a room above the local cheesemaker's establishment, and it was just down the street a few blocks. As Pru thanked her, Catherine came clattering down the inn's stairs with the captain in tow. Chattering blithely to the young man, who wore a slightly bemused expression, she handed Pru her cloak. The captain tipped his hat to Pru when he caught her gaze upon him and then seated his stylish haberdashery more firmly on his wavy blond hair.

Studying him, Pru could understand Catherine's fascination. Captain Marshall was a very handsome man. His large blue eyes were framed by exceptionally long lashes, and his perfect nose ran straight and true to a soft, gentle mouth. But his nearly perfect features could not make up for his rather weak chin. That feature seemed to indicate he'd be no match for the willful girl if he successfully gained such an alliance. He didn't appear to exhibit much strength when it came to the fairer sex. Mrs. Ruberry had effectively cowed him in the carriage, and Catherine seemed to find it just as easy to give him orders now.

"I understand you ladies require an escort," the captain said, holding the door for them.

Pru settled her cloak around her shoulders, although the sun was out and the day was as fair as one could wish. While the temperature was cool, it was by no means cold and had never yet fallen below freezing, despite being mid-October. But she was reluctant to go outside without something around her shoulders.

"Yes," Pru murmured as Catherine tucked her hand confidently through the captain's elbow.

When he offered his other arm to Pru, she took it, hoping that Mrs. Ursini would be at least as firm as Mrs. Ruberry had been, particularly with the charming captain.

"Mrs. Gaunt says I must have a chaperone," Catherine confided as they set out.

The captain glanced at her. "A chaperone? What on earth for? Did you not tell her—" Pru felt his arm stiffen. She wished she could see his expression and Catherine's, but the two were staring at each other, and she was not a party to their silent conversation.

"Of course I discussed it with her," Catherine said at last. "We agreed it would be for the best. At least until we arrive in Rome."

"I am sure Miss Demaretti's cousins would expect her to be properly chaperoned, even after she arrives," Pru said.

"Of course," the captain agreed, although his lower lip jutted out in a disappointed way.

For one fleeting instant, Pru wondered if the good captain had been relieved when he discovered Mrs. Ruberry was dead. Without her, he was free to court Catherine and do as he pleased.

Had he grown so annoyed with the chaperone that he'd helped matters along? It could account for a good many factors that had been worrying Pru. The captain may have sent a note to Catherine to meet him, and that note might have been intercepted by Mrs. Ruberry. She might have decided to teach him a lesson by donning the girl's cloak and proceeding to the assignation in disguise.

Caught off-guard, the captain may have lost his temper and murdered her. The action would have removed an annoying obstacle from his plans to marry the young, and obviously wealthy, girl. Assuming he meant to marry her.

It all made a horrifying sense. Pru stumbled and clutched the captain's arm more firmly. No, in truth, she could not believe it of him.

However, the captain's arm felt stiff and unyielding under her hand, and weak chins did not mean a complete lack of temper. And after ridding himself of one chaperone, he could hardly relish confronting a second one.

She was so consumed with the thought that she hardly noticed where they were until the captain paused.

As it happened, Fiorella proved correct in her assessment that they could hardly miss the building where Mrs. Ursini lived. The cheesemaker's shop was the largest edifice on the street and was surprisingly well-built and elegant, with large windows displaying an assortment of cheeses and other goods that were appetizingly arranged to tempt the peckish. The warm breeze was filled with the milky scent of fresh cheese, although every once in a while, Pru caught a whiff of the less pleasant odor of sour milk. Her stomach twisted in reaction to the odors, and she pressed her handkerchief against her lips, hoping to avoid being sick.

Why did so many scents bother her?

It was terribly annoying. She didn't *feel* ill and had no discernable fever, and yet her stomach remained easily upset when some strange odor wafted near. The sudden weakness didn't make sense. She'd never been sensitive before, even when they crossed the English Channel, so why now when they were on solid ground?

In summary, she was fast losing patience with herself.

She was still frowning as they entered a side door that led upstairs to what she presumed to be the apartment rented by Mrs. Ursini. Captain Marshall knocked smartly on the door, and it was opened before he even lowered his arm.

"Do I have the honor of addressing Mrs. Ursini?" Captain Marshall asked in schoolboy Italian.

The short, plump, dark-haired lady glanced at the captain and then examined Pru and Catherine with sharp, brown eyes. "*Si*. And you are?"

Pru gently edged Captain Marshall aside and held out the contessa's note. "The Contessa di Mordano suggested we speak with you."

"*Si?*" A dimple flashed in one plump cheek and her dark eyes twinkled. "You are friends of the contessa?"

"Acquaintances," Pru clarified. "Are you Mrs. Ursini?"

"*Si*. Come in, come in." Mrs. Ursini stood aside, waved them inside, and then chivvied them into a small sitting room that overlooked the narrow street at the front of the building.

The room was simply furnished with several mismatched chairs, a low table, and a settee under the double-window. A wooden tray graced the low table and sported several plates.

Trying to make conversation, Pru off-handedly commented, "You must be pleased to see the contessa—"

"The contessa?" Mrs. Ursini stared at her. "Why would she come here?"

"Perhaps I misunderstood. She mentioned you are related. I thought she must come to Benerosa to visit you."

"No, you misunderstood. She does not come to visit *me*." Mrs. Ursini laughed. "I am cousin to her first husband. Most assuredly, she does not come to see me."

"First husband?" Pru repeated.

"*Si*. She has three husbands." When Mrs. Ursini caught sight of Pru's startled expression, she laughed and shook her head. "Not all at once, you understand. The third was the conte—before he died, of course."

"Then why does the contessa come here? Who does she visit?" The questions slipped out before Pru could stop them.

"This is not for me to say. You must ask the contessa."

"Of course." Pru felt dazed. If the contessa was not here to visit Mrs. Ursini, then why had she come to Benerosa? She examined the woman's merry face and felt more confused than ever.

"Sit, sit," Mrs. Ursini motioned to the chairs. "There is very good prosciutto and cheese, help yourselves, please. It is most excellent. The landlord does not mind if I borrow a few bits of his lovely cheese now and again as it is so delicious. And, of course, the prosciutto." She beamed at them as they selected chairs and sat down. "Coffee, *si?*"

"That would be lovely," Pru replied, feeling a trifle overwhelmed as Mrs. Ursini left the room abruptly. In the depths of the house, they could hear the woman speaking in rapid Italian to someone before she bustled back into the room and took the remaining chair.

She clasped her short-fingered, plump hands in her lap and fixed her birdlike gaze on Pru. "You are good friends of the contessa?"

"As I said, we are acquaintances." Pru waved at the folded note Mrs. Ursini had in her lap under her hands. "I believe the note will explain—"

"*Si, si.* I am sure it explains, but you will tell me, *si?*" She beamed at Pru.

Smiling back, Pru cast a quick glance at Catherine to gauge her reaction. While Pru had developed an immediate liking for the small, plump, sparrow-like woman, she was not the one who had to tolerate her company on the journey to Rome.

Except, of course, in the carriage.

Catherine stared at Mrs. Ursini with a slightly overwhelmed expression on her face. Captain Marshall appeared equally startled and sat with his hands on his knees and his mouth slightly open as he eyed her.

"I apologize," Pru said at last. "I neglected to introduce ourselves. I am Mrs. Knighton Gaunt. This is Miss Catherine Demaretti and Captain Marshal."

Mrs. Ursini smiled and nodded at them. Before Pru could speak, a young maid came in. The delicious scent of coffee filled the room as she shakily set the tray down on the edge of the table. After one quick, agonizing glance at Mrs. Ursini, the maid fled, shutting the door behind her.

Mrs. Ursini poured the coffee and urged them to sample the thin slices of meat and cheese on small pieces of toasted bread.

"As I was saying," Pru continued, balancing a cup of coffee on her lap, "the contessa recommended we speak to you. Miss Demaretti needs a chaperone to accompany her to Rome—"

"Rome!" Mrs. Ursini clapped her hands twice and then clasped them together over her breast as her large, brown eyes flashed with excitement. "*Si!* I would go to Rome. This I will do. Rome is so beautiful, *si.*"

Pru glanced at Catherine, unsure if the girl would appreciate Mrs. Ursini's seemingly boundless enthusiasm.

"My previous chaperone died," Catherine said in a stern voice, obviously intended to quench the woman's eagerness.

"*Si*." Mrs. Ursini shrugged and rolled a bit of prosciutto around a wedge of white cheese. "These things happen. It is so sad." She popped the entire thing in her mouth and twinkled at Catherine, her dimples creasing her cheeks. "But you are young. You must not grieve. In Rome we will see the *fête* of the birth of Christ at *Santa Maria Maggiore*—it comes December 24th—and you will forget your sadness, *si*? We have much to enjoy. You will like Rome and forget your troubles. There is much to see."

Catherine cast a helpless glance at Pru.

"I am pleased that you are interested." Pru took one more sip and placed her cup on the table. "We merely wanted to introduce ourselves and determine if you might be available. We must discuss it, of course, and make our decision. Thank you for your hospitality, Mrs. Ursini. I have enjoyed meeting you very much." She stood.

Catherine and Captain Marshall quickly followed suit, exchanging glances.

"*Si*." Mrs. Ursini stood, looking from one face to another, clearly anxious. "You leave? So soon?"

"You must understand that Miss Demaretti needs time to consider. It is an important decision."

"*Si, si*. I will come to *De La Fortuna* this evening. Young ladies must not be left alone overnight, *si*? Then we will know if we will suit."

"Yes. That is an excellent notion," Pru agreed.

At least she would not be responsible for Catherine's actions, assuming the girl could be persuaded to hire the irrepressible Mrs. Ursini. She hoped Catherine would see the sense in it. She was lucky that Mrs. Ursini was not a sour, ill-disposed specimen like the contessa or— not to think ill of the dead—a coarse, overbearing harridan like Mrs. Ruberry.

She sighed to herself as they started back to the inn. In truth, if Pru had children of her own, Mrs. Ursini was precisely the type of smiling, warm-hearted woman she wouldn't mind seeing in her own nursery.

If she had children...

Pru pushed the wistful thought firmly from her mind. She was almost thirty. She'd learned long ago that wishing for something wouldn't make it true, and it only hurt worse when one dwelled upon it.

For now, it would be enough if Catherine would agree to a new chaperone so Pru would not have to worry about her and could enjoy the rest of their trip.

They almost reached the inn when Captain Marshall slowed. Given the tilt of his head and the muted sounds of whispering coming from Catherine, Pru guessed that the girl was resisting their return. Pru couldn't entirely blame her.

The sun was out and the sky was a lovely, pale blue with nary a cloud to cast a cold shadow. While the village was small and sprawled untidily against a hilly backdrop, exploring it was definitely more appealing than returning to the musty, dark inn. Even the air was as cool and crisp as a succulent apple.

"Would you care to go for a walk?" Pru asked, anticipating Catherine's reluctance to sit inside on such a glorious day.

Catherine stepped smartly around the captain and faced Pru. Her round cheeks were flushed and her eyes flashed with temper. "I will not do it—I simply will not!"

"Do what?" Pru stared at her in confusion. "We don't have to walk if you are too tired."

"I will *not* have that—that *woman*! Old Ruberry was bad enough, but this one is scarcely more than a *peasant*." Catherine's hands tightened into fists at her sides as she leaned forward to glare at Pru. "An interfering old biddy. You are not my mother—you have no authority over me. You cannot force me to take on that creature!"

"Catherine!" Pru exclaimed, shocked at her reaction.

Frowning, Captain Marshall grabbed Catherine's arm and shook it, but she pulled away, her face tight with anger. "I will not, I tell you!"

"Cath—Miss Demaretti," Captain Marshall said. He flicked a wary glance at Pru and caught Catherine's arm again. "You are upset—hysterical—the death of Mrs. Ruberry, you see." He looked at Pru uncomfortably and shifted from one foot to the other before glancing down the street. "Perhaps a walk would do you good, as Mrs. Gaunt suggested."

Catherine rounded on him. "You said you loved me, that we would—"

He shook her arm again and then grabbed her hand to pull it through the crook of his elbow. "No nonsense now, Miss Demaretti. What you need is a good, long walk to clear your head."

"I suppose I could go with you." Pru caught sight of her husband just outside the inn as Catherine's sharp words whirled through her mind. *She thought she and Captain Marshall would do what? Marry? Run away together?* Had Catherine simply been on her best behavior, trying to divert suspicion away from her plans when she agreed to interview Mrs. Ursini?

Pru's previous, uncomfortable speculation rustled like a mouse tunneling through dead leaves. She desperately wanted to talk to Knighton. His cool logic would soon put her dreadful thoughts to flight. He might even have resolved the mystery by now.

As if aware of her, Knighton glanced their way. A warm smile lightened his saturnine face as he waved at her. Her heart leapt in response.

"No need," Captain Marshall said. "Mr. Gaunt is waving to you. Perhaps he wishes to speak with you, Mrs. Gaunt. I shall escort Miss Demaretti. She will be quite safe, I assure you."

"She must have a chaperone," Pru answered sharply.

Catherine scowled at Pru. "I am not a child! I do not need anyone."

"Never fear." Captain Marshall smiled and patted Catherine's hand. "We shall remain in plain sight at all times. I would do nothing to tarnish her reputation."

Pru studied the captain, who was clearly straining to present an honorable and reassuring appearance. "Perhaps a walk would be the best thing. I trust you, Captain Marshall, to conduct yourself appropriately. And if you would be so good as to discuss the advantages of having a chaperone like Mrs. Ursini, I would be grateful."

"Most assuredly." The captain dragged Catherine away and started toward the village before Pru could reconsider her hasty agreement.

She watched them as they walked quickly in the opposite direction, but not too quickly for her to miss Catherine's petulant words, "But you promised..."

What exactly *had* he promised to her and under what conditions?

Chapter Twelve

"There you are," Knighton said as his wife joined him. "Where did you go?" He stopped himself just in time from admitting that he had been worried when he went into the inn and found her gone.

"I escorted Miss Demaretti to a woman, Mrs. Ursini, recommended by the contessa to take Mrs. Ruberry's place."

Knighton laughed. "Poor woman. I hope she had enough sense to refuse."

"No decision was reached, but I sincerely hope she does not decline. If Mrs. Ursini does not chaperone that child, then I will have to do so." Frowning slightly, Pru's thoughtful gaze followed Captain Marshall and Miss Demaretti as they strolled down the street away from them.

"God forbid." He studied his wife's face, relieved to see that she was not as pale today as she had been the previous evening. "Are you well?"

"Yes." She smiled up at him, her gray eyes brilliant in the autumn sunshine. "I believe it was simply a touch of travel sickness. I feel much better, although at times, certain smells... Well, I am quite well today at least." Her expression changed, however, as she glanced again toward the village. "I have had the strangest notion." She gave a brief, uncertain laugh. "You will think me ridiculous, but when I was walking with Miss Demaretti and Captain Marshall, I had the curious idea that the two of them knew something about Mrs. Ruberry's death. I thought Catherine—well—in truth, she does not seem overly grief-stricken by the loss of her companion."

Knighton chuckled. Catherine Demaretti was not the sort of girl to let anything concern her unless it had an unfortunate result for herself. Losing her interfering chaperone could only be seen as amazingly good fortune from her perspective, for it granted her the freedom to do exactly as she pleased.

He sobered quickly, however, when he caught sight of the concern in Pru's eyes. "Did she say something to you?"

"Not directly, no," Pru admitted. "It is simply that—you will think I have gone mad."

"Never." He pressed a reassuring kiss on her brow and hugged her, warmed by a bolt of sheer joy that shot through him.

"Stop that—what will the others think?" Pru blushed prettily and glanced around.

"That I am very lucky."

"Don't be ridiculous. In fact, I was hoping you would have the good sense to tell me that I am a silly goose for even entertaining the strange thoughts I have had."

"What strange thoughts?" He examined her face, suddenly serious.

"Well, I wondered if Captain Marshall sent a note to Miss Demaretti to meet him last night. Mrs. Ruberry might have intercepted the missive, and she may have taken Catherine's cloak and arrived at the rendezvous intending to teach the captain a lesson." Pru gripped Knighton's arm and gazed up at him, her eyes dark with anxiety. "He might have killed her in anger when he realized it was Mrs. Ruberry instead of Catherine."

Much as he wanted to reassure his wife, her words raised and strengthened his own doubts. A sense of danger tightened his shoulders and neck as he turned slightly to watch the two young people, who were nearly out of sight at a bend in the road. Should he stop them? Was Miss Demaretti hanging on the arm of a murderer? Or were they conspirators?

They could very well keep on walking, and Marshall could not only escape with the girl, but with murder.

But escape to where? They had no carriage and were miles from Rome. No. They were young, but not that foolish. He hoped.

"I wish I could alleviate your worries, my dear. However it does explain the cloak."

"Yes, it does," she agreed in a small, miserable voice. "I wish the notion had never occurred to me."

"Unfortunately, it did." He pulled her hand through the crook of his arm and started back to the inn. "But be of good cheer. The two young lovers are not the only ones engaging in suspicious activities." He opened the door and stood aside for Pru to enter.

"You think someone else was involved?"

"Our injured man appears not to be quite the complete invalid we thought he was."

"Lieutenant Fisher?" Pru untied her cloak and in a graceful movement, swirled it off her shoulders and folded it over her arm. "What possible reason could he have for murdering Mrs. Ruberry?"

"You mean beside the fact that she seemed bent on making our journey as miserable as possible?" he asked dryly.

Pru laughed. "Well, he was one of the fortunate men who could escape from her if he wished and sit on the carriage roof. So he can hardly complain. He did not have to endure what the rest of us suffered."

"True." Suddenly remembering the locket he'd found around the dead woman's neck, he drew it out of his pocket. "Mrs. Ruberry was wearing this. I hope there are no children or husband to grieve for her."

"No. She told me several days ago that she was a widow. And she never mentioned children." Pru gently took the locket from him and inserted her thumbnail to pry it open. She gasped as she studied the small miniature inside and then handed it to him. "It—it is the lieutenant, is it not? A younger version, but still him."

He studied the tiny portrait. The artist had been skilled and, despite the small size of the painting, had captured the lieutenant's large nose with its bump between the close-set eyes to perfection. He, or she, had even managed to use the same unusual blue-green color for the eyes as Lieutenant Fisher exhibited, and the thinning blond hair in the portrait held the identical glint of orange-red.

"It does appear remarkably like Lieutenant Fisher," he agreed slowly.

"Why would she have his portrait in a locket? Were they lovers?" Pru caught his arm. "You don't think they arranged to meet on this trip, do you?"

"I don't know. I do know, however, that he did not stay in bed all night. He was seen walking around the inn after the rest of us retired for the night." A prickle of foreboding itched between his shoulder blades. He shifted his shoulders as he examined the miniature one last time before clicking it shut and slipping it into his pocket.

"Oh, Knighton. You don't think he murdered her?"

"I believe he knew her and was roaming around last night. Beyond that, we should not speculate without more information."

They were still discussing Fisher when they heard a series of thuds outside the inn and a brief, muffled shriek. Knighton strode to the door and yanked it open, only to have Pru brush past him.

"Captain Marshall!" Pru exclaimed. "And Mr. Hethering!" Apparently, the captain and Miss Demaretti had returned from their brief walk and had run into Hethering.

At the sound of Pru's voice, Captain Marshall staggered and lowered his fists. Hethering, seizing the opportunity, landed a solid punch on the captain's jaw and sent him sprawling into the dust.

Miss Demaretti shrieked and went down on her knees in the dirt beside the unconscious man, pulling his dusty head into her lap. "How *could* you?" She glanced up at Hethering, who had straightened and pushed back the distinctive lock of white hair from his forehead.

Wearing a lop-sided grin and eyes twinkling with satisfaction, Hethering shrugged. "To the best man and so on and so forth." His smile widened when the girl caught his gaze. He winked at her and straightened his cravat.

Instead of anger or shock, Knighton was surprised to see a look of speculation briefly narrow Miss Demaretti's eyes. Apparently, the gallant captain had a rival in the form of the older, and much more sophisticated, Mr. Hethering.

"What happened?" Knighton asked as Pru pulled a bottle of smelling salts out of one of her pockets and bent down to wave it under the unconscious man's nose.

"Nothing serious," Hethering answered airily. "Captain Marshall simply forgot himself for a moment."

Marshall coughed and sputtered and roughly knocked away the bottle of salts as he sat up. Miss Demaretti stood and shook out her skirts. Her gaze flickered from Marshall to Hethering, and Knighton wondered which of the men was coming off in a more favorable light. While some women might consider Marshall romantically wounded, Knighton thought Miss Demaretti just predatory enough to prefer the winner over the injured. She did not seem to be the type to enjoy sitting beside a sickbed and caring for another person.

Hearing Hethering's voice, Marshall staggered to his feet, a scowl darkening his dusty and bruised face. "I forgot nothing, you arrogant—" He cut himself off when he caught sight of Pru and Miss Demaretti watching him. "Miss Demaretti has no need of your services, sir, and I will thank you to remember that."

"Oh, I have no doubt you would thank me to remember it," Hethering answered in a bland and ever so slightly bored voice. "However, I believe we will leave the decision to Miss Demaretti, shall we?" He bowed to the young lady and with elaborate courtesy, offered his elbow to her.

After a quick glance at Marshall, Miss Demaretti took Hethering's arm and allowed him to escort her into the inn under Marshall's furious gaze. When Marshall moved as if to follow them, Knighton stopped him with a hand on his chest.

"She will be fine," Knighton said. He nodded to Pru and was relieved when she smiled and followed the other two inside.

"That cad!"

"My wife will ensure Miss Demaretti's safety. Now exactly what happened?"

"That scoundrel interrupted us just as we were returning and tried to convince Catherine that I had something to do with her chaperone's death! Said she was not safe with me—as if she would be safer with that womanizing scoundrel."

"Would she be safer? Or did you have something to do with Mrs. Ruberry's murder?"

The captain flung an angry jab at Knighton, but he dodged it easily and caught the young man's arm before he could try again. "Get ahold of yourself, man. It is a simple enough question. I expect a simple answer."

Marshall swiped the back of his hand over his swollen mouth and cast a bitter, furious glance at the door to the inn before eyeing Knighton with loathing. "I had nothing to do with it, sir. If it is any of your business."

"Why should I believe you?"

"It is the truth! Why would I kill that woman?"

"To clear your path to Miss Demaretti, I would suppose."

"I had no need to kill her. If I wanted to, we could have run away at any point on this ridiculous journey. And if that is your thought, you might just as well consider that bounder, George Hethering. If anyone needed a path cleared, he is the one."

"I will certainly keep that in mind, Captain." Despite the young man's swift temper, Knighton realized that he was unlikely to confess anything at the moment. He was far too concerned about what Miss Demaretti might be doing in the inn. "If you think you can keep your temper under control, we can join the ladies."

"I can." Marshall brushed the dust and straw off of his coat, his face still flushed with anger and a livid bruise forming on his chin. "If that scoundrel inside can control his."

"Then we will go inside anyway, although I am inclined to believe neither one of you will be able to keep that promise for long."

Had Pru realized she now had two men who might be contenders for the role of murderer, based upon her previous speculation? It seemed that young Miss Demaretti was a regular Helen of Troy, strewing conflict and war like rose petals wherever her dainty feet trod. Which one would she select, if either, and what would happen when she did decide?

Hethering was most likely only interested in the girl's dowry, while the earnest young captain seemed to actually adore her. Sadly for him, Hethering was older, much more sophisticated, and understood how to exploit any opportunity granted him. On the whole, Hethering's experience gave him a definite edge. However, Miss Demaretti's future aside, both men were likely suspects and bore watching.

When he followed the captain into the dismal parlor that the benighted carriage's passengers had appropriated for their use, he nearly ran into Marshall's back as he stopped just inside the entryway. A tap on the shoulder got the captain moving again. Knighton glanced around, saw his wife, Miss Demaretti, and Hethering seated at the table in the center of the room and moved toward them.

Miss Demaretti was pouring a cup of the inevitable, and quite execrable, coffee for Hethering as she dimpled and exclaimed over the button that had come loose from his jacket during the bout of fisticuffs outside. Hethering's small, self-satisfied smile and languid look gave him the appearance of a well-fed cat basking in the sun. Pru watched both with an exasperated expression on her face.

"Have you seen Lieutenant Fisher?" Knighton bent over his wife's shoulder and asked softly.

"Fisher?" Hethering glanced up at him. "I should think he is abed in his room, haunted though it may be. Why?"

Pru caught his eyes and shook her head, obviously indicating her ignorance of the wounded man's current location. "Would you like me to check on him?"

"No—I wish to speak to him and can ascertain well enough if he needs anything." He nodded at Hethering.

"I will go with you." Pru stood quickly. "Someone should check his bandages, and if he wishes a bowl of broth, I can get it for him."

He suppressed a smile and held out his arm. She clearly wanted to be present when he questioned the man about his likeness in the locket worn by Mrs. Ruberry. Well, he could use her perceptiveness and almost uncanny ability to read the emotions others might wish to keep hidden.

To his relief, Fisher was in his room, which appeared to be a perfectly normal—if small and slightly dusty—accommodation. Fisher was ensconced in a narrow bed with several well-washed blankets of indeterminate color pulled up to his chest.

When he saw Pru and Knighton in the doorway, he threw back the covers and struggled to sit up.

"Oh, do be careful—you will reopen your wound." Pru rushed forward and supported him with her arm around his shoulders. "Knighton, please. Can you push the pillows forward so he can sit up?"

He awkwardly arranged matters to allow Fisher to lean back. When Pru released him, he settled against the pillows with closed eyes. The skin around his lips was white from his effort, and although Knighton could see that the man was clearly in pain, he couldn't help but wonder how much was real and how much was playacting. Fisher had certainly been well enough to amble around the inn last night.

Try as he might, however, Knighton could not fit Fisher into the role of murder. His wound would have made it difficult for him to throw Mrs. Ruberry down the hillside. Of course, he could have forced her to that spot on the road and shot her there, allowing her body to tumble away on its own.

Yet another reason to find the site where she had been shot. If that was even possible at this late date.

"How are you feeling?" Pru sat on a three-legged stool next to the bed, leaving Knighton to perch either on the edge of the bed or to stand.

He elected to stand.

Fisher shrugged and then winced, obviously regretting the gesture. "Why are you here? Is the carriage repaired?"

"I am unsure." Pru glanced at Knighton.

He shook his head. The state of the carriage was the least of his concerns. "We are here about Mrs. Ruberry."

"What about her?" Fisher kept his face impassive although his eyes were hard with dislike. Perhaps he had had his own share of private arguments with the opinionated woman.

Knighton pulled the locked out of his pocket, flicked it open, and handed it to the man. "I found this necklace around her throat. Would you care to explain?"

A sharp, dry laugh escaped Fisher. "How could I possibly explain the trumpery jewelry that woman might choose to wear?" He tossed the necklace back to Knighton.

"That is your portrait, is it not?" he asked.

"It could be anyone."

Pru delicately plucked the locket out of Knighton's hand and studied the miniature, obviously comparing the likeness to Fisher. Her gaze flicked from him to the portrait and back again. "Do you have a twin brother, then? For if this is not you, it must be your twin. Perhaps there is a name on the back." She ran her thumbnail around the edge of the miniature to ease it out of the gold frame.

Frowning, Fisher watched her for a moment, his fingers playing with the hem of the covers before he said in a voice suppressed by rage, "Very well, yes. It is indeed my portrait—make of that what you will."

"How did Mrs. Ruberry come to be wearing your likeness in her locket?" Pru asked, her voice light and almost disinterested. Knighton was pleased at her initiative and edged back a step to let the conversation progress more naturally.

Fisher seemed to relax a bit and lose a small measure of his hostility when she spoke to him. He laughed again, though not with amusement. Bitterness tightened his mouth. "Ruberry—I should like to know how she came upon that name when she should rightly have been Mrs. Fisher."

"She was your wife?" Pru's eyes widened in surprise.

"Yes. Once. Was still my wife, in fact, though I begged her for a divorce." He glared at Pru, but Knighton could see that the man was looking through her, as if Mrs. Ruberry—that is, Mrs. Fisher—stood behind her. "It certainly didn't stop her from bigamy, did it? Mrs. Ruberry, indeed."

"She was a bigamist?" she asked.

"Must have been, mustn't she? How else could she call herself Ruberry? But when *I* wanted a divorce for my own chance at happiness, it was all, 'oh, no, I couldn't possibly' from her."

"I'm sorry," Pru murmured, her soft mouth drooping in sympathy.

If Violet Ruberry refused to give Fisher a divorce, perhaps he had decided that he'd force an end to their legal ties in a more permanent fashion.

"Where did you go, last night, when you got out of bed?" Knighton asked when Pru cast a questioning gaze in his direction.

"I don't know. I—something woke me up. I couldn't sleep—my side was annoying me—so I got up. Standing relieves it a bit. So, I walked around."

"Did anyone see you?"

140

"Well, obviously someone saw me or you wouldn't have known that I left my room." Fisher's lips twisted, but he refrained from indulging in profanity with Pru sitting nearby.

"Did you go outside?"

"Ah, so you don't know everything." He smiled, though his eyes remained hard. "Yes. I went outside."

"Where did you go?"

"No-where in particular. I simply walked. That is all." He closed his eyes and leaned back, a small V of pain creasing the skin between his brows.

Pru glanced up at Knighton and raised her eyebrows, obviously thinking they should leave the man to rest.

Knighton studied Fisher's pale face, unsatisfied. Fisher had the best motive for murder of all of them. He obviously hated his wife and wanted a divorce, presumably to remarry.

What better reason could there be?

"Why did you go on this trip?" Knighton asked abruptly.

"Isn't it obvious? When I discovered she was accompanying that chit to Rome, I followed along, hoping to convince her to agree to a divorce. There would be plenty of time to talk to her along the way. It seemed like as good a plan as any."

"Did you have any reason to believe she would finally agree?"

"None at all, except perhaps for common decency." He rubbed his forehead. "And she had set herself up as a chaperone. I thought—I mean—she was attempting to appear like a proper lady."

"So you thought you could use that to convince her to accept the divorce," Knighton stated.

"Yes. And you need not think it was blackmail. It was the decent thing for her to do, assuming she wished for once in her life to behave with a modicum of propriety."

"Did you speak to her at all?" Pru asked.

He shook his head. "She clung to that girl the entire time. Refused to see me alone."

"And yet... She wore your portrait in her locket. Against her heart," Pru pointed out softly.

"Well, what of it?" Fisher asked savagely.

"Perhaps she still loved you. In her way," Pru replied.

Fisher stared at her. He was already so pale that it was difficult to be sure, but it appeared to Knighton as if his skin grew even whiter at the suggestion. "She left *me* less than a year after we wed. *I* did not abandon *her*." He covered his eyes briefly with his cupped right hand and breathed heavily as he rubbed his face. "Those are not the actions of a woman in love."

"It is difficult to say. Some run away from the things they want the most for fear of being hurt. And after all is said and done, she kept your portrait." Pru patted his arm, though he did not appear to notice her soothing gesture.

After a moment to allow Fisher to get control of his emotions, Knighton continued, "What was she wearing?"

"Wearing? That old cloak of hers, I assume. And that green dress. Is that not what she was wearing?"

Knighton shrugged. Fisher identified the dress correctly, but not the cloak.

"Well, if that doesn't satisfy you, why don't you ask her cousin? Perhaps she confided in him. I don't know anything else, and if you don't mind, I would like to get some rest. If possible in this wretched bed."

Pru stood and looked first at Knighton and then, pointedly, at the door.

"Cousin? Who is her cousin?" Knighton asked, ignoring his wife's signal to depart.

Fisher smiled again and this time, his eyes crinkled with amusement. "So you are not omniscient after all."

"I doubt any of us are. Who is her cousin?" he repeated.

"Why, our quiet little Mr. Savage."

"Savage!" Knighton exclaimed in surprise. The last person he would have suspected of being related to the flamboyant woman was the quiet little Mr. Savage. "How do you know he is related to her?"

"I met him years ago when I was searching for Violet. After she ran away. But he knew no more than I."

"Why was he on this trip?"

Fisher ran his hand tiredly over his face again. "He didn't confide in me. I honestly don't know. Ask him."

As Knighton studied him, Pru pulled on his sleeve and stood on tiptoes to whisper into his ear, "He is exhausted, Knighton. Please, we should go for now. You can come back later, if you wish."

He pressed his wife's slim fingers against his arm briefly. While he was far from satisfied with Fisher's answers, he still had doubts that Fisher's health would have allowed him to murder anyone, regardless of the strength of his motives.

And he had given them an interesting lead to follow. Mr. Savage would definitely be worth questioning.

"I will send up some broth, Lieutenant Fisher," Pru said. "And I hope you can get some rest."

"Good day," Knighton added, his palm resting against his wife's back as they turned toward the door. "I will inform you when the carriage is repaired."

Fisher leaned back, eyes closed, and didn't bother to speak. He lifted one hand in farewell before settling the covers over his chest. He looked ill and weak and somehow, telling the sad story of his marriage to Violet seemed to have deflated him, or stolen a bit more life out of him. Even his golden hair seemed more gray than gold, and Knighton couldn't help a brief stab of sympathy.

Violet had led Fisher a merry dance, and in the end, he'd only been abandoned one more time. If Fisher cared at all, it had to cut him deeply.

Chapter Thirteen

"I would never have thought Mr. Savage was related to Mrs. Ruberry," Pru remarked as they descended the stairs.

"I was just as surprised as you were," Knighton said.

She caught the attention of the thin, overworked maid, Celestina, and ordered a bowl of soup be sent up to Lieutenant Fisher posthaste. When the maid, wide-eyed and lips white with terror, objected because the wounded man inhabited the haunted room, Pru almost lost her temper.

"It is daytime now, Celestina. You can have no possible reason to avoid that room. And you cleaned it yesterday, did you not?"

"Yes, signora, but—"

"Then do as I asked. You could already have done so if you had not wasted time arguing."

Celestina swept a quick curtsey and ran off toward the kitchen. Pru watched her go, wondering if the girl would keep running, or if she would actually do as requested.

"Where do you think he is?" Knighton eyed the door to the lounge.

"Who? Oh, Mr. Savage. I haven't the least notion." She smiled ruefully. "He is so quiet that I never remember if he is even in the room. Are you going to question him now?"

"Yes. I see no reason to delay. I'm sure Charron is working on getting that carriage of his repaired. I'd like to resolve this and leave as soon as possible."

"But we can't leave before the funeral, can we?" The thought of getting back into that jolting, ill-sprung conveyance made her stomach curl. Then she realized that she would no longer be required to keep the windows closed, now that Mrs. Ruberry was gone.

So even she had a motive for disposing of the good lady. She could finally open the windows and get a breath of cool, crisp air. And avoid Violet Ruberry's appalling perfume.

"No. I'm hoping Buonfiglio managed to arrange that." Knighton ran a hand through his thick, black hair. "And we must wait for the authorities. If we can present them with the murderer, we can travel on to Rome with a clear conscience."

"If they even evince any concern," Pru replied dryly. "Which does not appear likely."

Knighton laughed. "There is that. Since Napoleon was routed and the French gave up their control of the Papal State and its environs, such matters have been a trifle lackadaisical. Or so I hear."

"The French did appreciate the law and order. Nonetheless, I wish we could just..." Her words trailed off as she realized how cowardly she would sound if she said she wished they could simply abandon their little group and make their own way to Rome.

Knighton gave her a brief hug and kissed her forehead. "The last few weeks have not been especially pleasant for you, have they?"

"Oh, no. I have enjoyed our trip so much." She stared up at him, determined to convince him even if she did feel untruthful. The last few days had been the most difficult, and she had been terribly homesick for England, not to mention the sickness which had crept up upon her lately.

"Don't lie, my love." He tilted her chin up with his fingers and studied her face searchingly. "Do you wish to return home?"

Oh, yes! But—if they went now, they would never see Rome. How could they end their honeymoon so close to that grand city? It would be like quitting a race a yard away from the finish line.

She shook her head. "No. We must at least visit Rome."

"And the falls?"

"Yes," she replied wistfully. "And besides, we sent our carriage with my maid and your valet ahead of us to rent and prepare rooms in Rome while we visit the falls. We must go on if for no other reason than to collect them."

"Oh, bother. Let them find their own way home."

"Knighton! You cannot mean that." She laughed as he swung her around and gave her a lingering kiss.

"I do mean it," he said as he released her. "We shall go on only as long as you wish. Remember, say the word, and we will return home."

"I will, but what about Mr. Savage?"

"Yes. We do need to question the little weasel, don't we?"

Unable to help herself, Pru giggled and nodded. Savage did have a way of quietly arranging things for his own comfort, despite any discomfort it might cause others. "Yes. If we can find him." A sudden thought sobered her. "What do you think of Mrs. Ruberry wearing Catherine's cloak? I cannot decide if it was important or not. I mean, if Mr. Savage or Lieutenant Fisher shot Mrs. Ruberry, then I cannot see that it signifies. But if not, well, I'm afraid it may mean that Captain Marshall may have killed her. Or even Mr. Hethering."

"That is the question, is it not? Either the cloak meant nothing, or it presents us with two other possibilities. Hethering or Marshall may have thought they were meeting with Miss Demaretti. When they discovered their mistake, they may have killed Mrs. Ruberry in anger, as you postulated. Unfortunately, there is also the possibility that whoever killed Mrs. Ruberry thought they were shooting Miss Demaretti. It was night, and she was wearing the girl's very distinctive cloak."

"Oh, Knighton, you cannot possibly believe that someone would have tried to murder that child! What conceivable reason could they have had? She is only sixteen!"

"It may be unlikely, but we must consider it all the same."

146

She didn't want to believe anyone would be cruel enough to murder such a young girl, but her husband was correct. It was a possibility. Until they had more information, they could not dismiss it, much as she might want to.

Pru sighed and entered the parlor, hoping that Mr. Savage would still be sitting next to the fire where he had ensconced himself after breakfast. Unfortunately, as soon as she stepped inside, the sense of tension filling the room halted her. Knighton gently moved her aside as he entered behind her.

A dark-haired, slim man dressed in the green uniform with the white and yellow cockade of the cavalry stood ramrod straight in front of the fire. He faced Mr. Savage, who remained seated. At the sound of their footsteps, the stranger turned to face the doorway.

"Ah, more English, perhaps?" His quick glance flashed over Pru and then Knighton and returned to study Pru. A slow smile curved his generous mouth, and his brown eyes, framed by ridiculously long lashes, twinkled. He looked pleased to see her and a bit too admiring.

Her cheeks warmed, and she glanced at the floor.

"I am Knighton Gaunt." Knighton stepped forward, hand outstretched. "And this is my wife, Mrs. Gaunt."

"Maggiore Tiberio Lupino, signore." He shook Knighton's hand and nodded to Pru. "Signora." He smiled, flashing brilliantly white teeth beneath his luxurious mustache. "Signore is fortunate."

"Yes, well, I suppose you are here about Mrs. Ruberry." Knighton gestured for Pru to take a seat on one of the wooden chairs nearby.

She complied, watching the handsome major with quite unreasonable dismay. He did not appear to be the seasoned official she had expected.

"Signora Ruberry? Ah, *si*, the dead woman. Very bad." He clasped his hands behind his back as he faced her husband. "I have been discussing this matter with your friend, Signor Savage."

"Indeed?" The dry tone in Knighton's voice made Pru stiffen. Her husband obviously had expected the authorities to contact him, first, as he had collected what little evidence there was in the case.

Hopefully, Maggiore Lupino would not take umbrage at that and refuse to work with them. She could already feel a kind of shifting between the two, as if they were engaged in a subtle tug of war.

Maggiore Lupino smiled again, although there was a glint in his dark eyes that suggested he was not as amused as his expression seemed to indicate. "*Si*. Perhaps you would care to add something?"

"As I don't know what Mr. Savage has told you, I am not sure what to add."

The major waved to a couple of chairs in the corner of the room. "*Per favore*, signore. We talk."

Knighton strode over to the chairs and took the one angled with its back to the uncurtained window. Still smiling, Maggiore Lupino sat in the remaining chair. After a quick glance at Mr. Savage's remarkably disinterested face, Pru got up and moved her chair closer to the two men and pulled a slim volume of poems out of her pocket.

If anyone had objected to her nearness, she would justify her movement as necessary to get enough light to read. However, despite her swiftly concocted excuse, no one appeared to notice or even care. The two men eyed each other.

"So, Signor Gaunt, what is your view of these matters?"

"I should tell you that I am an inquiry agent in London," Knighton said before the major raised one hand to stop him.

"This is, of course, interesting, but hardly important. I am here now. You must tell me what you know, and then you may carry on to Rome."

Knighton studied him briefly, before giving one, sharp nod. "I would not dream of interfering. The first we knew of the tragedy was when our coachman, Signor

Charron, came to the inn and requested our assistance in rescuing a lady who appeared to have fallen down the hillside. We did not realize it was Mrs. Ruberry until we managed to bring her back up to the road. When we examined her, we realized she had been shot and then either thrown or allowed to fall over the edge of the road. We have not ascertained why she went out last night, or why she was wearing her charge's cloak—"

Again Maggiore Lupino held up a hand to stop him. "*Si*. I have heard of this cloak. Edged with ermine, is it not? She must be quite wealthy to own such a thing."

"Yes," Knighton agreed.

A moment of thoughtful silence stretched between the two men. Pru glanced up from her book to find that the contessa's maid, Domenica, had come in at some point and stood a few feet away. She had moved so quietly that no one had been aware of her presence or observation of the two men.

When she caught Pru's gaze, she leaned over and whispered, "The maggiore is investigating, *si*?"

Pru nodded, a flash of irritation tightening her brow. She wanted to hear what her husband and the major were discussing, not gossip with a maid. As if aware of her feelings, Domenica smiled and pressed her index finger against her lips.

"For me, I see the answer clear enough." The major braced his hands on his thighs and leaned forward slightly. "You have not mentioned the *banditi*, but Charron and Signor Savage described them well. I know these men. All is clear. The bandito, Pasquino Nacchio—*Capitano* Nacchio, as he calls himself—has made trouble for me before. This cloak with the ermine—she was a foolish woman to wear such a thing—she made him believe she was rich, *si*? She goes out for the air, he sees her, and so..." He shrugged. "These things happen."

"That could, of course, be the answer," Knighton said slowly. He glanced at Pru.

She caught his gaze and understood the uneasiness in his eyes. He did not agree with the major, but he was loathe to dispute the too-easy solution.

Even Domenica shifted with an impatient movement. She frowned, deepening the lines on her plain face.

"*Si*. It is the answer. And the poor lady will be buried tomorrow—I have spoken to the priest. Then you will be on your way, *si*?"

"You are convinced, then?" Knighton asked.

"*Si*." The major smiled again and stroked his luxurious mustache.

Instead of arguing as he clearly wanted to do, Knighton stood and held out his hand. "Will you be staying here?"

"*Si*. I stay for the funeral and the arrival of my men. We will see to the *banditi* this time, do not fear."

"Of course." The two men shook hands, and Knighton stepped around the major to join Pru. "Would you care for a walk, my dear?"

"Yes, after I speak to Domenica." Pru hastily shoved her book into her pocket through the slit in her skirt and stood. She smiled over her shoulder and said, "It was a pleasure meeting you, Maggiore Lupino."

"*Si*." The major bowed deeply. "Enjoy Benerosa, Signora."

"Were you looking for me, Domenica?" Pru asked.

The maid dragged her increasingly hostile gaze away from the major, who stood with his hands clasped behind his back and a benign smile on his handsome face. "*Si*. The contessa wishes to know if you find Signora Ursini."

"Yes, we did. Please thank her for us, I am grateful for her suggestion. I believe Signora Ursini will suit us very well."

"*Molto buona*. I tell the contessa. *Grazie*." Domenica gave a sharp nod and the barest hint of a courtesy before walking past Knighton to the stairs.

"Shall we go?" Knighton asked, once more offering his arm to Pru.

They had barely gotten outside before Pru tugged on Knighton's elbow to slow his pace. "Maggiore Lupino appears to be an intelligent man, does he not?"

"Yes. And undoubtedly lazy."

She shook her head, trying not to laugh. "Not lazy, my love. Efficient. Do you think Maggiore Lupino could be correct? That the bandits killed Mrs. Ruberry?"

"I think it is an easy answer, and one that pleases him."

"Easy, yes, but it could be true, could it not?" Pru frowned and almost missed her step as Knighton, seemingly at random, turned in the direction of the small church at the outskirts of the village. "It would be nice to be able to continue on to Terni."

"Of course it could be true. The problem is that we have only begun to look into these matters. I doubt whether Lupino is even aware that Mrs. Ruberry's husband and cousin were both traveling with her."

"But his theory does account for the cloak. Capitano Nacchio may very well have seen the ermine trim and thought she had jewels or other valuables. Or that she was Miss Demaretti. He might have killed her when he realized he had a penniless chaperone instead of a young, rich heiress to kidnap."

"Why would Mrs. Ruberry meet him? Or walk along a deserted road when she knew bandits were in the area, and in fact, used that very road?"

"That is the difficulty, is it not? After all our experiences on the road, I cannot imagine why she would go for a walk at night in a strange village. I would have been terrified to do so." Pru glanced around at the rutted, dirt road they were following and the extremely humble wooden buildings. "She would not have gone out alone," she stated firmly. "She must have had a note requesting a rendezvous."

"But where would she have gone? Where would a woman feel comfortable going in an unknown village at night?" Knighton frowned, glancing around.

The village, while not exactly squalid, was not exactly begging for exploration. There were no fascinating shops or Roman ruins that might entice a lady to forsake the admittedly few comforts of the inn to go wandering around in the dark. A small farm, a few houses with chickens roaming around their yards pecking at the dirt in a desultory fashion and businesses like the blacksmith and the cheesemaker.

So where would Mrs. Ruberry go at night?

Up ahead, a small, stone church marked the edge of the village. It looked forlorn and inexplicably cold, despite the grainy afternoon sunshine glittering over the gray stones.

"A church." Pru paused, suddenly sure. "She would have felt safe meeting someone at the church."

Knighton nodded. "And everyone in our group knew where it was. We all passed it on the way to the inn." He studied the edifice, his brow wrinkling in thought. "Surely she would not have entered it. The doors were most likely locked."

Several well-worn stone steps led up to the wide, double doors in front, and the front stoop offered little in the way of shelter. The location was too exposed, too out in the open. An assignation there might have caught the attention of the priest, or someone in the village who was unable to sleep.

As her gaze traveled over the tall building, she spotted a gate and side entrance to an enclosed churchyard. Beyond that was a small, covered porch. A gnarled, elderly tree shaded the tiny alcove, giving it an even more private aspect.

Of course to go there, one would have to be willing to walk along the narrow path past several ancient grave markers. At night. Not precisely a cheerful prospect.

"Look, Knighton." She pointed at the porch. "That would have been ideal, would it not? If she was not afraid of going through that portion of the graveyard." A small, iron gate with a simple latch allowed them to enter the church's side yard and the fringe of the small graveyard that stretched past the tree.

"Mrs. Ruberry did not strike me as a nervous woman," he said. "A few old gravestones would not frighten her."

"No, perhaps not." She looked back, trying to see the inn. A bend in the road, a small copse of fruit trees and several houses intervened. A shot from this location might very well be muffled enough to remain unnoticed. She studied the gravestones. "However, you never know what superstitions someone cherishes. And at night, even the most sensible person can be subject to fancies and fears."

She released Knighton's arm as he strode forward, his gaze running over the headstones near the path, the tree, and the alcove. Pru watched him for a moment before she picked up her skirts and walked quickly to the covered entryway. There were no leaves or debris on the well-worn steps, and when she tried the iron handle of the heavy door, it proved to be locked. The space was tiny and private, with barely enough room for two people to stand comfortably and talk.

Even though the huge tree had lost its leaves, the thick branches wove themselves above the roof of the porch and shadowed the interior, making it gloomy, chilly, and damp. The corners of the porch were dark with moisture, but clean. Someone cared enough to sweep away any debris and dirt. Unfortunately, that meant that there was nothing there to indicate whether Mrs. Ruberry had met anyone on the porch or not.

When she turned around and descended the three steps to the dirt path, Pru noticed Knighton hunched over, scraping at the trunk of the tree with his knife. A moment later, he straightened, refolded his pocket knife, and turned to her with a grim smile.

"I believe this is indeed the spot where Mrs. Ruberry met her killer." He held up a small lead ball between the thumb and forefinger of his right hand. A partially blackened scrap of red material lay in the palm of his left.

Pru touched the burned fabric and realized it was barely more than a few threads that the bullet had apparently caught as it passed through her. Pru swallowed. She could hardly bare to think of it. But it was over, and Mrs. Ruberry was beyond feeling any pain.

She took a calming breath and cleared her mind. "We knew she was shot. I am unsure that finding the location where it occurred will change anything."

"Perhaps." He rotated the ball between his fingers, barely seeming to hear her. Then he held the missile up to the light and stared more closely at it. "There is a flaw, a small depression, in the ball." He glanced at her, his dark eyes glimmering with excitement. "We may be able to match that to the mold used to form the bullet."

She shrugged. "I don't see how that will help. Surely whoever shot her would not carry the mold around in his pocket."

"Not in his pocket, my dear." Knighton grinned and pulled out his handkerchief to carefully wrap around both the lead ball and scrap of red fabric. "His pistol case would contain not only the tools necessary to clean and keep the weapon operational, but the mold as well. So he could produce correctly sized rounds. If I can find the case, I can determine if this bullet could have been produced by the accompanying mold." His eyes grew intense as he gazed at her. "Several of the men brought pistols with them—"

"As you did," she reminded him.

He nodded. "Of course. Most men traveling these days bring something with which to defend themselves. We simply need to find the man whose mold produced this ball."

"Why do I feel it will not be quite that easy?"

He pulled her hand through the crook of his arm and guided her through the narrow gate to the road. "I have no doubt that it will not be easy. Nothing in an inquiry of this sort ever is. But it is a start."

"Are you going to give your evidence to Maggiore Lupino?"

She felt his arm stiffen under her hand. "Not yet," he replied slowly as if considering his answer. "I think in this case, it would be better to present the evidence and our conclusions in their entirety to the efficient Maggiore Lupino."

"I agree. He will not like it unless you prove it was Capitano Nacchio." She smiled a little sadly. "Unfortunately, even then, I believe he will not appreciate your efforts. He will see it as interference. He does not seem like a man who will tolerate much interference."

"No doubt you are correct, my love. As always. But I have never allowed one man's aggravation to prevent me from discovering the truth."

"Let us hope, then, that the others cooperate and do not complain to the maggiore."

"Let them complain." Knighton shrugged. "It will not stop me."

Chapter Fourteen

Knighton was about to open the inn's door for his wife when Hethering came through, followed closely by Miss Demaretti. He was amused to see the girl once more in Hethering's company—the man had to be at least twice her age—but perhaps his glibness and maturity managed to seduce her away from her previous *amour*, the earnest young captain.

"Good afternoon, Mr. Gaunt." Hethering smiled and tipped his hat to Pru. "Mrs. Gaunt. Beautiful day for a walk."

"Yes," Pru replied in a bland voice, her gaze bouncing from Hethering to Miss Demaretti.

"We are off for a walk to see the sights. Care to join us?" Hethering asked.

"No. We just came back from the church." Knighton watched Hethering's face but his genial, composed expression did not change.

"Ah, yes. A magnificent example of early perpendicular, if I am not mistaken." His eyes twinkled with amusement.

"Early perpendicular?" Miss Demaretti repeated, her forehead wrinkling with confusion.

Knighton managed to suppress a smile. Beside him, Pru snorted as she tried to avoid laughing at Hethering's glib humor.

She quickly raised a gloved hand to cover her mouth before she said, "Yes, well, I am sure Mr. Hethering can explain such architectural details to you."

Hethering flashed a wolf's grin at Knighton and his wife and picked up Miss Demaretti's hand to tuck within the crook of his elbow. "Once you see the bell tower, I am sure you will understand the principle, Miss Demaretti. Of course, it may easily be late horizontal, given the roofline, but I am certain it is either one or the other. If you will excuse us, Mrs. Gaunt? Sir?"

He strode off in the direction of the church, Miss Demaretti interspersing small, running steps with her rapid walk to keep up with the quick pace he set.

Knighton watched them for a minute before Pru tugged on his arm. "I am not sure we should let them go alone."

"She will be perfectly safe. He knows we have seen him with her. She may not learn much about religious architecture, but she will most certainly return alive and well." He opened the door and stood aside as his wife entered the dim recesses of the inn.

Turning to follow her, the door was jerked out of his hand. He paused on the threshold to find a short, plump woman behind him. She was dressed entirely in black and eyed him with a critical frown on her plump lips.

"Signora Gaunt!" The woman bobbed and stretched on tiptoes to try to see past his shoulder.

Knighton stepped inside and held the door for the woman. "She is inside."

"*Si, si.* I saw her enter. You are Signor Gaunt?" Her wide smile wrinkled the skin around her brown eyes and flushed a pair of dimples out of hiding. She touched the base of her neck. "It is I, Signora Ursini."

Pru peered around him. "Oh, Knighton, yes. This is Mrs. Ursini. We are hoping she can accompany Miss Demaretti to her cousins in Rome," she clarified with a relieved smile. "I am so pleased to see you again, Signora Ursini."

"Then it is settled?" Mrs. Ursini asked hopefully. She briefly lifted a small, brocade bag she held in her left hand. Clearly, she had been a bit precipitous and assumed the answer would be yes.

"Oh, dear." Pru cast a quick, troubled glance at Knighton. "I am not sure Miss Demaretti has had time to consider the matter."

"Bah." Signora Ursini shrugged and brushed past Knighton and Pru to enter the inn. "She is too young to decide. As long as it suits signora, it is settled."

157

Pru exchanged a bemused look with Knighton and followed her. At the last minute, she had to step aside as Celestina brushed by with a bowl of some foul-smelling liquid and mumbling, "*Scusi, scusi.*" She disappeared into the back of the inn before anyone could remark.

White-faced, Pru gagged, clearly affected by the lingering odor. "Excuse me—" She pressed her hand over her mouth and pushed past Knighton to run outside. The door hadn't even closed when he heard her retching.

When Knighton moved to follow her, Signora Ursini held him back. "She returns soon. Better if you do not follow." Her broad smile lit her brown eyes again as she peered up at him. "When does the little one come?"

"Little one? I beg your pardon." Knighton stared at her, confused and trying to listen for any further noises from Pru. There was nothing but silence outside.

"*Bambino.* When does it arrive?"

"Baby?" *Baby*? No wonder Pru had developed an inexplicable case of travel sickness! Even their terrible Channel crossing hadn't caused her this much trouble. Shaking with a fierce surge of joy, he grabbed Signora Ursini's well-padded shoulders and impulsively kissed her round cheek. "If Miss Demaretti is so idiotic as to refuse your services, we shall be privileged to hire you. Buonfiglio will show you to Miss Demaretti's room. I must see to my wife."

Blushing furiously, Signora Ursini laughed and waved him off. "*Si, si.* I will find the room, never fear."

Outside, Pru was leaning against the wall, her eyes closed, and her fingers still pressed against her pale mouth.

"How are you feeling?" he asked. How the devil could he tell her she was with child? Surely she must have guessed by now. Awkwardness, and an amazing sense of joy, surged through him. He could hardly stand still. He wanted to throw his arms around her and shout his happiness to the world.

She had to know—had to at least suspect.

Pru waved her hand briefly and then hurriedly pressed it against her mouth again.

"Signora Ursini does not believe you are suffering from travel sickness," he said, his voice sounding oddly loud, even to him.

Her eyes flew open, and she studied his face, but didn't attempt to say anything.

"Had you any suspicions?" he asked.

"Suspicions? Suspicions of what?" she whispered in a hoarse voice.

Another jolt of sheer elation filled him, making it almost impossible to speak. "Is it possible—do you think—that you are with child?"

"With *child*?" If possible, she turned paler. Her gray eyes grew huge in her wan face. "Oh, Knighton, do you think it could be true?"

He couldn't control himself any longer. He pulled her against him, wrapped his arms around her, and gave her a long hug. His *wife*. And child. With a chuckle he said, "We are not *that* ancient, Pru. I think it is entirely possible."

"It would certainly explain a great deal." She gave a small, watery laugh. "I had wondered."

Still holding her shoulders, he pushed her away enough to look down into her beautiful face. "I may have acted a bit impulsively just a few minutes ago."

"You? Impulsive?" She laughed again, although a little V of worry crinkled the skin between her brows.

"I am afraid I informed Signora Ursini that if Miss Demaretti proved too silly to accept her services, we might hire her, instead."

Pru's hands tightened on his lapels. "Oh, Knighton, I'm so glad you did. I was thinking she was just the sort of comfortable woman I should most like to have helping me if I ever had a child." Standing on tiptoes, she pressed a shaky kiss against his cheek. "I'm so happy, I hardly know what to do. And it is so dreadful, isn't it? I mean, here we

159

are laughing and happy when poor Mrs. Ruberry is over in the church, waiting to be buried."

Although she was right, Knighton couldn't find it within himself to replace his elation with grief. He pressed a kiss against her forehead, and after a brief embrace, looped an around her slender shoulders to escort her into the inn.

"Go upstairs and rest," he suggested. "Is there anything you need? Any food you particularly desire?"

"Not at the moment." She giggled, her eyes glowing, and slipped out from under his arm. "I think I will take your advice, though, and take a brief nap. I just wish you would make sure Mr. Hethering does indeed return with Miss Demaretti. And let her know that Signora Ursini is here. It may be best if we present her as a *fait accompli,* at least until we get to Rome. To be truthful, I don't feel capable of chaperoning that child any longer, and I shudder to think what her cousins would say if she showed up without any chaperone at all."

"Consider it done. Now off with you. I will be up later to see how you are doing."

She nodded and wended her way up the stairs, an abstracted, thoughtful look on her face.

A child!

While he was tempted to stand there forever, thinking about holding his child, *their* child, in his arms, or watching Pru cradle the baby on her warm lap, he had other matters to resolve. Major Lupino had a workable theory that would certainly make the other members of their party happy, but it did not make Knighton happy. While Lupino might have hit on the truth through luck, the theory didn't feel right to him. And he could not, in good conscious, allow the real murderer to travel with their party to Terni and eventually, Rome.

He would not allow him anywhere near Pru. Not if he could help it.

Recalling his original purpose of interviewing Mr. Savage, Knighton entered the sitting room-*cum*-dining room allotted to them. The last time he had seen him, Savage had been comfortably ensconced in the one and only padded wing chair next to the fire.

As anticipated, he was still there, sipping a cup of tea with a placidly satisfied look on his face.

"Mr. Savage, may I join you?" Knighton pulled one of the ladder-backed chairs away from the table and placed it to Savage's right.

"If you wish," Savage answered in a bland voice before taking another sip of tea. He didn't even bother to look up. If anything, he seemed to relax further and crossed his small feet at the ankles in a neat and precise manner.

"Are you well?" Knighton studied him, trying to read something in his face that would enable him to draw Savage into a conversation.

"Quite well." Mr. Savage's rather non-descript face, well-groomed salt and pepper hair, and plain brown jacket and trousers seemed designed to be unnoticed and unremarkable. He looked like one would expect a law clerk to look—unassuming and as dry as one of the legal tomes lining the shelves behind him. The impression was so strong that Knighton bit his tongue to keep from asking him if he did, indeed, work in a law firm.

"Have you any thoughts about Mrs. Ruberry's tragedy?"

A faint glint of amusement briefly lit Savage's brown eyes. But he blinked and swiftly dropped his gaze to focus on the fire as he took another sip. "I am afraid I have no thoughts on the matter." His tone, riddled with soft sarcasm, implied that he rarely considered anything that did not have a direct impact upon his comfort.

At least that was Knighton's rather annoyed reaction to his response. Clearly, approaching the topic obliquely would be a wasted effort with Savage. "I was surprised to discover that you are Mrs. Ruberry's cousin."

He stilled, his cup half-way to his mouth, and glanced at Knighton. Savage's face was mask-like in its

161

lack of expression, but he blinked several times before he could control himself. "Indeed."

"Lieutenant Fisher mentioned it in passing. You must be saddened by her death. Were you close?"

"As I never spoke more than two words to the woman, I cannot claim to be prostrate with grief over her demise," he said in his precise, dry voice. His tone brought to mind the rattle of pages being turned in an old book.

"I see. Were you even aware that she was your cousin, then? I understood from Fisher that he had enlisted your aid in locating her a few years ago."

"He did. However, we failed to locate her." He declined to elucidate or confirm if he realized the woman in their carriage was his missing relative.

Frustration chafed Knighton. The process of questioning Savage was akin to getting a stubborn dog to drop a meaty bone and seemed just as unlikely to result in success.

"So were you aware that Mrs. Ruberry was your cousin?"

His brows rose, and he gave a slight smile before taking yet another annoying sip of tea. "Would it have occurred to you?"

"Then why did you pay for a seat in that particular carriage?"

"I wished to see the cascade of the Velino River, of course."

"You did not recognize her?" Knighton persisted.

"Did I not already say that I had never met the lady previously? The last I knew, her name was Mrs. Fisher."

"It is quite a coincidence, then, is it not? That you should be riding in the same carriage, unawares?"

"Indeed, yes." His brown eyes studied Knighton briefly before he returned his gaze to the ashes of the fire dying in the fireplace. "You seem very interested in these matters. May I ask why?"

"I am curious by nature," Knighton replied, a trifle flippantly.

"You informed Maggiore Lupino that you are an inquiry agent in London." His mouth twisted with distaste as he spoke.

"I am."

"That, I suppose, explains your interest. Did our gallant lieutenant hire you to find his wife?"

"No." The muscles in Knighton's jaw tightened as he found himself being questioned instead of the reverse. He wrestled control back with a more direct inquiry. "Do you have anything to gain by Mrs. Ruberry's death?"

"Gain? What could I possibly gain by the death of a woman so impoverished that she had to act as companion to that wretched child?"

"Then you do profit. I must send word to my agency to ascertain precisely how much."

Savage smiled blandly, a malicious gleam in his eyes. "The matter is hardly that mysterious. And as I have stated twice before, I never met the woman and was unaware of her relationship to me."

"How do you profit, then?"

"You could discover it easily enough. For the sake of your *curiosity*, however, I will tell you. I have nothing to hide, Mr. Gaunt. My uncle was gravely ill when I left his home in Shropshire."

"An odd time, then, for you to take a trip to Terni for your pleasure," Knighton murmured.

Savage frowned briefly. "I could do nothing for him if I stayed. No one could."

"Of course. But continue—I take it you are an heir?"

"He favored the female side of his family, felt they deserved some sort of independence." Distaste sharpened his features, drawing sharp lines between his brows and around his mouth. He clearly did not agree with his uncle's opinion. "He informed me that the bulk of his estate would go to Violet Fisher, née Savage, if she could be found. If she was dead, however, I would become his heir."

"Your uncle must have been well-off."

"Moderately so."

"Then you had quite an incentive to determine Violet Fisher's fate, did you not?"

"It might appear so. I have never been overly concerned with the possibility that I might be his heir. Does that satisfy your curiosity, Mr. Gaunt?"

"It does not worry you that your uncle may have passed away prior to Mrs. Ruberry's death?"

"Not particularly. In fact, I had always expected that to be the case. You may investigate my affairs if you wish, but you will find that I am quite comfortable and am not in any particular need of his money. And unlike the other men in our group, I did not feel the need to carry a weapon with me." His slight, superior smile indicated his disdain for Knighton and the others who had come prepared for difficulties on their journey.

"But it never hurts to have a few more funds, does it?" Knighton returned Savage's smile grimly as he stood. There seemed little reason to continue their unproductive discussion. "Thank you for answering my questions, Mr. Savage. I appreciate your patience."

Savage nodded before Knighton strode away, deeply unsatisfied.

Savage might not need his uncle's money, but that did not mean he didn't want it. Men were rarely happy with what they had when there was the chance that they might obtain more.

And there was something irritating about the self-contained, tidy little man. Unfortunately, the image of Savage shooting his cousin, who was a few inches taller and much heavier than he was, and then dragging her down the road to fling her off the side of the hill was frankly ludicrous. Knighton just couldn't imagine him bestirring himself sufficiently to do such a thing. Or risking the inevitable stains on his neat little suit.

Savage had also confessed that he had not brought a pistol with him, and Knighton felt sure that if he searched his luggage, he would not discover one. If he had had a weapon before, he had already disposed of it.

Savage struck Knighton as the sort of man who would leave nothing to chance.

The sun had already set when Knighton stepped outside. Shadows darkened the houses huddling together along the main road in the village, and he could see a few flickering lamps through the windows of those closest to the inn. The night hid the sagging roofs and ill-maintained street, softening everything into a mellow, almost cozy view.

The door behind him creaked, and Marshall joined him. "Have you seen Catherine—Miss Demaretti?"

"She was going to look at the church."

"Alone?" The question rose shrilly in angry disbelief as Marshall stared at him.

Dear God, this was the last thing they needed, another fight between Hethering and Marshall.

Knighton felt his muscles tighten, although he answered calmly enough, "Mr. Hethering escorted her."

"You knew, and you let her go? With him?"

"It was daylight." Knighton shrugged. "And I was just going to find her when you joined me. You may accompany me if you wish, but only if you give me your word that you will behave with due respect to both Miss Demaretti and Mr. Hethering."

Marshall stiffened. "I beg your pardon, sir. I fail to see why I should do anything of the kind."

"Then you may wait here."

"I—I shall behave with perfect propriety." Marshall appeared disconcerted and glanced in the direction of the church. When he finally looked at Knighton, he had difficulties meeting his eyes. "As I always endeavor to do."

"Very well. Come."

Knighton set off at a brisk pace. Despite his gentle reminder about Marshall's earlier contretemps with Hethering, he was worried about Miss Demaretti, too. They should have returned to the inn by now. The church was hardly interesting enough to keep the pair there after dark.

They had just reached the small gate leading into the side yard cemetery when they heard the creak of a large, wooden door opening. Two figures appeared on the front stoop. The hinges of the front door protested again as the taller figure turned back to pull the doors closed behind him.

"Catherine!" Marshall called.

A sharp cry met his call and the smaller person, Miss Demaretti, ran down the stairs and flung herself into Marshall's embrace. "Oh, I am *so* glad to see you, Frederick."

"What is it?" Marshall lifted his head to watch Hethering descend the steps at a sedate pace. "What has happened?"

Miss Demaretti glanced over her shoulder, giving Knighton the impression that Hethering had done something to frighten her. "Nothing. That is, I have only been visiting the church. It is just so dark now—I lost track of time—and the shadows inside frightened me. I did not know it was so late." She took a deep breath and seemed to recover her composure, although she kept a tight grip on Marshall's forearms. "*Banditi*," she flicked a perfunctory glance at the road, as if to excuse her previous nervousness with something more mundane, "you know. We should return to the inn."

"Of course." Marshall flung an arm around her slender shoulders and escorted her toward the hostelry.

With a bored look on his face, Hethering strode forward to follow the young pair.

Knighton stepped into his path. "What happened in there?"

"Happened?" Hethering chuckled and tried to walk around him.

"Yes, happened. The girl was frightened—what did you do?"

"I did nothing. You heard her. Who would have expected such a bold chit to be so sensitive to the shadows in a church? And once she let her nerves run away with

166

her, she remembered the ruffians we met on the road and panicked."

"Anyone could see that the bandits were an excuse and a poor one at that. Something happened. I can guess what."

"Guess away," Hethering replied blandly. "I confess I have no interest in childish games, and I do not want to miss whatever meager supper Buonfiglio and his delightful wife can concoct. I suspect our host keeps country hours, given his performance when we arrived last night."

Hethering seemed to be a man driven by his appetites. But it was not Hethering's empty belly, but his appetite for money, that concerned Knighton.

"You tried to force yourself upon her, did you not?" Black anger surged inside him. He had no use for such men, who thought their every whim should be satisfied without effort or consequence. "The truth, if you please. I can ask Miss Demaretti if necessary."

"Ask away. You will get no gratification from that quarter."

"If you believe she will say nothing for fear of embarrassment or humiliation, you are wrong."

The girl might not speak to Knighton, but she would most certainly talk to Pru. His wife had the patience and sympathy to convince the very walls to speak, if needed. And while it annoyed him that others often responded to emotional appeals rather than the logic that had always driven him, he could not deny its effectiveness.

"She will say nothing because there is nothing to say. Now, shall we join the others?" While his light, casual tone was eminently reasonable and believable, the tension in Hethering's rigid back and neck belied his words.

Unfortunately, there was nothing to gain by arguing in the street, and Miss Demaretti had appeared unharmed, despite whatever had happened.

"Yes." Knighton nodded. "You are probably correct about supper. I do not think Buonfiglio is a man who enjoys late nights, or serving late dinners."

"No, indeed." Hethering laughed and walked more quickly through the gathering gloom. "And perhaps after supper we can have a game of commerce, or whatever suits your fancy." When Knighton frowned, Hethering continued quickly, "Come, you must give me the chance to reverse my previous losses."

Gambling didn't interest Knighton. Particularly after discovering in a previous game that Hethering lacked the immediate resources to back his bets and could only promise to pay his debts when they reached Rome. But with a long evening in front of them, games of chance were as good a diversion as any. Cards and alcohol tended to loosen a man's tongue, as well, so it might prove to be more than simply a way to while away an evening.

Chapter Fifteen

The long hours of darkness after their sparse meal seemed unusually tedious to Pru. She had never been interested in cards, and she was not the least bit tired after sleeping for well over an hour that afternoon. Catherine furnished a good fifteen minutes of excitement screaming and stamping her foot about the presence of Mrs. Ursini, but even that diversion ended eventually, once more leaving them without much to entertain them.

Catherine's pale face was still wet with angry tears when she sniffed and flounced over to a chair and sat down with a loud huff. "I have no need of a chaperone."

"Be that as it may, Mrs. Ursini has been hired. She shall accompany you to Rome," Pru repeated, she hoped for the last time.

After taking a sip of red wine with a thoughtful, meditative look smoothing his face, Knighton nodded and flicked a glance at her. "Mrs. Ursini will ensure there is no more awkwardness with the other passengers. I am sure you will find that reassuring."

Pru watched Catherine blush and stare at her lap as she tapped her toes on the floor. Knighton had told her that he suspected Hethering of trying to convince the girl to marry him and in so doing had frightened her—perhaps by becoming overly coercive. However, it had not taken Catherine long to recover, or to decide that she preferred to avoid the annoyance of a chaperone, no matter how much she seemed to need one.

"I am not a child," Catherine said, her lower lip slightly more protuberant than usual. In fact, her stubborn expression made her look even younger than her sixteen years and more in need of a mature companion than ever.

"Of course not," Pru replied soothingly. "But that is the difficulty, is it not? Sometimes one must accept things that are unnecessary, or even ridiculous. As a young woman, you would not want to do anything that might bring shame to your family. Responsibility can be so wearying, can it not? It makes one want to scream for the frustration of it all."

Catherine eyed her, clearly unsure how to respond to her statement, which seemed to include the girl in the company of mature women who bore the need for propriety as best they could. She straightened and assumed a calm demeanor, imitating Pru as closely as possible.

"Yes. I suppose I must. It is only until we arrive in Rome, however."

"Naturally," Pru agreed.

The two women spoke for a while longer, going through acquaintances to determine if they knew anyone in common either in London, or possibly in Rome. Sadly, they could not hit upon any friends, or relatives, known to both. Catherine, not having come out yet, begged Pru for tales of London and the Season, but Pru could not supply any details. She had been traveling the length and breadth of England with her father, searching for the truth behind ghost stories and local legends, at the age when most young ladies were presented to Society. Therefore, she had no real knowledge of Almack's Wednesday night balls, or any other venues popular with debutantes.

By midnight, they had both exhausted every possible topic of conversation and were ready to say good night.

Pru stood and walked over to her husband, resting a hand on his broad shoulder briefly as he played his current hand. She smiled with pride as he calmly won the pot.

"Are you retiring?" He glanced up at her as the other players made discontented noises at the loss of the coins and vouchers clustered in the center of the table.

"Yes. Will you be up soon?"

He glanced at the other players before grinning and saying, "Very soon."

"Good night, gentlemen," she murmured before walking toward the door.

She was surprised to find Catherine at her side when she got to the staircase. The girl looped her arm through Pru's and gave her a small smile before climbing the stairs with her.

"You think I'm a frightful little beast, don't you?" She flicked a shy glance at Pru.

"Not at all." In fact, that artless statement pretty well summed up Pru's precise feelings.

"I just—well—no one *listens* to me."

Pru sighed. How many times had she felt precisely the same way? More times than she could count. "I understand, but you must be patient. We are all young, once, and we all experienced the same frustrations. I think, if I were you, that I would be happy to have someone like Mrs. Ursini with me while I was traveling through a foreign land. She is a very happy woman and seems exceedingly understanding. I'm sure you will find her sympathetic."

"Maybe so, but I wish for once others would try to understand that I would much prefer to be alone."

Pru's heart nearly broke at the girl's words. Catherine did not know what it was like to be alone, to have no one to talk to for guidance or support. Pru did. Before she had met Knighton, she had ached with the desire to have a friend she could trust, to share both the pains and pleasures of life. Loneliness could be terrifying when one lay awake at night, wondering how to make ends meet, or avoid the advances of married men, who seemed to think a woman without a protector was fair game.

"Being alone is not something to wish for, Catherine. You are fortunate. Enjoy it. You will be in Rome in a few short days, and then you may look back at this time as an adventure few girls your age get to experience."

"I suppose so. Good night, Mrs. Gaunt." As they reached the top of the stairs, Catherine turned toward her room, dragging her feet.

"Good night and be of good cheer, Catherine. You will like Mrs. Ursini if you give her a chance. You will see."

The girl didn't bother to answer, although she nodded her head before opening the door to the room she now shared with her unwanted companion. Pru watched until she closed the door and was firmly in the charge of her chaperone, before she went to her own chamber.

The day had been long and exhausting, though they had done very little. Even after having a nap that afternoon, Pru now felt drained. She washed her hands and face in the tepid water from the ewer left on the washstand in their room, and had barely changed into her nightgown and white cap when she heard heavy footsteps running.

The sound seemed to come from the floor below. What on earth was the matter, now? She grasped the doorknob and paused when she heard a barrage of clattering steps coming up the staircase.

Wrenching open the door, she peered out into the dim hallway. No one stood in the corridor. The emptiness seemed hushed, almost expectant.

Where had the runner gone?

Perhaps the noises had come from the first floor.

The haunted room? The floor beneath her bare feet creaked. A shiver went through her. She had yet to uncover a true haunting, but her heart raced nonetheless. The story about the inn was a ridiculous tale—sheer fiction—except she couldn't help glancing around nervously. When she had come upstairs with Catherine, it had already been after midnight, the time when spirits might appear. She returned to her room to pull on her favorite coat, a dark green redingote *à la Hussar* with a lavish trim of rows of golden braid, and she wriggled her toes into a slender pair of brocade slippers. After a moment's thought, she picked up a candle.

Some impulse made her walk to the window and glance outside. Her room was not on the same side of the building as Lieutenant Fisher's, so she knew she couldn't possibly see anything related to the haunted room. But she couldn't help herself. She opened the window and leaned over the sill.

Her gaze was drawn to her left and strayed to the corner of the building. The small, enclosed kitchen garden looked silvery gray in the starlight, and beyond the ordered rows stretched a patch of rocky ground. A thick fringe of trees marked the distant edge of the pasture.

Silence, and shadows, interspersed with pale patches of light, obscured the landscape. What had she expected to see?

She started to pull back inside the window when a wisp of white caught her attention. It hovered at the corner of the inn and then seemed to solidify into a man-sized shape. The figure ran parallel to the low garden wall, skimming over the uneven terrain as if flying. Tattered streamers of filmy white fluttered in its wake, blending with the silvery light like curls of icy mist.

The creature disappeared into the black line of trees before Pru could do anything more than suck in one sharp breath.

A spirit? Her icy hands gripped the sill as horror stiffened her arms.

Slowly, her rational mind reasserted itself, and the warm of her blood, returning to her limbs, relieved her cramping fingers.

If that mysterious shape was a ghost, it was the first one shed ever seen. Nonetheless, she rubbed her arms, aware of a deep chill that cascaded through the window and pooled around her. A shiver went through her as she searched the black line of trees for the form she had seen. Part of her refused to believe it could be a spirit, and yet she could not deny the prickle of her skin and thudding of her heart.

She *had* seen it. It was not an illusion. Her hands gripped the windowsill. Beneath the thin soles of her shoes, she could feel the roughness of the uneven floorboards and the wash of cold air over her ankles. She slammed the window shut.

If she felt cold, the mundane explanation of a chilly October breeze was the obvious answer, in combination with her own overwrought nerves.

She tried to smile at her own silliness. What would Knighton say if she told him? A dream or curl of mist she had mistaken for a spirit. However, she had not even gone to bed yet, and what she had seen moved too purposefully to be fog. And yet, she had a difficult time believing that strange shape had been entirely human.

Then she remembered the running footsteps.

Had something happened to Lieutenant Fisher? She hurried out the door.

By the time she descended one flight, she could hear several men's voices raised in an urgent conversation. Lamplight flickered along the corridor, throwing up wild, dancing shadows, but the eerie cold was gone. She hurried forward and saw that the door to Fisher's room stood open. A group of men, including Knighton, clustered half in and half out of the chamber.

"Is something wrong?" she called as she walked the last few feet toward the group.

"Pru! What are you doing awake?" Knighton edged around Mr. Hethering and approached her, his face drawn with concern.

"I heard noises—running footsteps. Is Lieutenant Fisher all right? Did something happen?"

"We are trying to ascertain that. Lieutenant Fisher—" He broke off with a partially confused, and partially skeptical, grimace. "Well, we don't precisely know what happened. He seems to have had a shock of some sort."

"A shock?" Domenica repeated the question as she came up behind Pru, moving with almost unnatural quiet.

"Yes." Knighton nodded, waving in the direction of the cluster of men near the doorway to Fisher's room. Someone had dragged a chair into the hallway, and Fisher sat in it, stiff and pallid, as he sipped from a silver flask. "I am sorry if we disturbed the contessa."

"The noise—it awakened her. What is this shock?"

Knighton hesitated and glanced at Pru as if searching her face for some indication of the proper response. Unfortunately, she had no answers, either, and could offer him nothing except a small shake of her head.

"Fisher claims he was asleep when something awakened him. The room was ice cold, and he thought one of the windows might have been left open. Although he remained in bed, he could clearly see both of them. He had neglected to draw the curtains when he went to bed, and the moonlight made it clear that the windows were both closed. At that moment, he claims that a white apparition appeared, glowing eerily in the darkness at the foot of his bed."

"Are you sure he did not have a nightmare?" Pru couldn't quite believe that she could truly say those words after her own fear that her husband would say them to her, but they tripped easily from her lips.

"He says not."

Domenica clasped her hands in front of her, a small, satisfied smile on her full lips. "You see? Buonfiglio warned you, did he not? That room is haunted. And so now he must be moved, or he will surely suffer some terrible fate."

"Moved?" Pru asked in surprise. "To where? He is wounded and should not be put to the effort of changing beds in the middle of the night."

"Ask him if he wishes to stay here," Domenica recommended, her smile growing crueler as a malicious gleam flickered in her dark eyes.

"Even if he wished to go, to where could we move him?" Pru moved to confront the maid, suppressing a strong desire to box the woman's sleek little ears for her callous suggestion. Lieutenant Fisher was clearly frightened and in pain, and the situation was not one for sarcastic amusement.

"The fourth room. The contessa offered the use of four chambers. You use only three."

Pru had to acknowledge that despite her spiteful attitude, Domenica had offered an eminently practical and useful suggestion. She glanced at her husband.

He nodded. "I will help Lieutenant Fisher. Why don't you return to our room, Pru? There is no point in exhausting yourself. I should be there shortly."

"So I will inform the contessa." The maid nodded and turned on her heel. As she walked down the hallway, Pru noted that she was still fully and warmly dressed. Apparently, the contessa kept late hours.

Or the maid did.

"I should tell you..." Her words trailed off as she stared into her Knighton's mildly curious eyes.

She'd sound like a foolish, hysterical woman if she told him what she had seen. But what about Lieutenant Fisher? Didn't it lend credence to his experience? Wouldn't it be cruel to remain silent and let the others believe the wounded man was suffering from delusions?

Perhaps it had only been swirl of mist rising over the warm earth as the cold night air cascaded down from the hills, or perhaps she had caught a glimpse of the apparition Lieutenant Fisher had seen in his bedchamber. Fairness insisted that she admit what she had witnessed.

"What is it?" Knighton prompted her, already distracted by thoughts of moving Fisher and turning back to the wounded man's room.

"I heard the noise—footsteps running down here— and I saw something, too. Lieutenant Fisher wasn't the only one." Her grip on his hands tightened. "I thought I saw a specter."

"A ghost? Not you, too." His lips twitched, but when she did not smile, his expression grew serious. "What precisely did you see?"

"A strange white form. It ran around the corner of the inn and disappeared into the woods."

"A man? Woman?"

"I could not tell. It was wispy, insubstantial, and only vaguely shaped like a man. Or a woman. It didn't look human. You don't suppose that was the same creature Lieutenant Fisher saw, do you?"

"Difficult to say." He chuckled and looped his arm over her shoulders to give her a brief, warm hug. "However, I should say that this is just the sort of affair you and your father used to investigate, is it not? Perhaps you can use your skills to discover the truth and put an end to these tales of vengeful ghosts. Poor Buonfiglio would undoubtedly be grateful to have a more wholesome room to rent."

"And what if, just this once, the tales prove to be true?" she answered sharply.

While she was not precisely ashamed of her father's researches into tales of mysterious happenings, she had often felt it necessary to defend him, and herself. She knew Knighton was only teasing her, but at the moment, she was not able to take his words as lightly as they were meant.

While she didn't entirely believe that spirits could remain at certain locations to haunt the living, she didn't precisely disbelieve it, either. There had been times in the darkest, coldest hours of the night when she pulled the bedclothes more tightly over her shoulders, fearing that such phenomena might just be possible.

And her father had honestly believed the incorporeal world existed.

"If the chamber is truly haunted, then you will have discovered your first specter," he said gently. "If you wish, we can both explore Fisher's room after I have taken him upstairs."

"Very well." She wrapped her arms around herself. "I will never be able to sleep now, anyway."

"Then wait here. I shall return immediately." He strode down the hallway to where Fisher was sitting and spoke to him briefly. Captain Marshall and Mr. Hethering assisted the lieutenant to stand. Knighton gently nudged Hethering aside and stepped in to take his place.

The men spoke for a moment. Lieutenant Fisher shook his head and seemed to resist, twisting his arms to shake off Knighton and Captain Marshall. In the end, he sagged, his face gray with his efforts, and finally allowed the two men to escort him past Pru and up the stairs.

Pru waited in the hallway, reluctant to enter the supposedly haunted room alone. The notion that she was not behaving with her usual spirit pestered her like a buzzing fly. Nonetheless, she did not venture into the shifting shadows at the end of the corridor. Her husband would return soon enough, and they could explore together.

To her relief, he joined her before her shame over her own cowardice forced her into Fisher's room without him.

"What do you think truly happened?" she asked, raising her candle above her head to survey the empty room.

"I haven't the slightest notion."

"He didn't say anything to you when you took him upstairs?"

"No." Knighton stood in the center of the room and raised the lamp he carried.

The covers on the narrow bed had been tossed back. A crumpled pillow lay on the floor, partially covering part of the blankets that lay half on the mattress and half on the wooden floor. The left curtain on one of the windows had been draw back, but the right curtain still covered the greasy-looking glass. The other window was also half hidden behind the heavy draperies.

However, as Fisher had said, enough light came through the dull panes to reveal that the windows were closed.

"Perhaps there was a draft because he neglected to pull the curtains together." Pru gestured at one window and then the other. "A draft could have caused the draperies to move and frighten him, particularly if he was awakened from a deep sleep."

Knighton fingered one of the heavy curtains. "The hangings are dark, not white. And he indicated whatever it was, it stood at the foot of his bed, looking down at him."

What an awful thought—an apparition staring at you while you lay helpless, fast asleep. On impulse, she went back to the doorway and reached out to set her candle on the seat of the chair in the hallway where Lieutenant Fisher had been sitting.

"Would you mind blowing out your lamp?" She shut the door behind her. "I would like to see the room as Lieutenant Fisher saw it when he was awakened."

Without comment, Knighton did as she asked.

The room was intensely dark and cold at first. However, her eyes soon grew accustomed to the gloom, and a weak, silvery thread of moonlight slipped in through the partially uncurtained windows. She examined the room, imagining how it would look if she was wounded and abed.

Nearly helpless and at the mercy of whoever—or whatever—had entered the chamber.

Almost without thinking, she pulled the coverlet and blanket back over the bed and absently smoothed the wrinkles. There was precious little to see in the tiny, barren room. Two windows, a bed, and a small table in the corner that looked forlorn without its accompanying chair, which the men had dragged into the corridor. She sighed in frustration and rubbed her icy fingers together. Well, what had she expected?

When she had accompanied her father and assisted in his research into the realm of spirits, she had spent countless days poking and prying, measuring and noting her findings. This was no different. If she wished to discover the truth, only patience would be rewarded.

She took a step toward the door, intending to retrieve her candle to light Knighton's lamp when he stopped her.

"Do you see that?" He was bending over the foot of the bed, his hands clasped behind his back, as if to prevent him from touching anything.

She walked to the bed and leaned over the foot of it. A faint trace of luminescence, as thin as a snail's trial, streaked the bedpost. A shiver skittered down her back. "What is that? Paint?"

"I'm not sure." He pulled a handkerchief out of his pocket and gently wiped at the glowing streak.

Pru strode over to the curtain that had been drawn back from the window closest to the door and examined the heavy linen. At a spot roughly level with her elbow, she found another faint trace of something that glowed eerily, shifting in intensity as she moved the fabric out of the moonlight into the relative darkness of the room.

"There is more here." A low, sad laugh escaped her. "Regrettably, it seems that I am doomed to disappointment yet again in my search for a true haunting. I have never heard of an apparition leaving behind a substance such as this. Have you?"

"No." Knighton sniffed at his handkerchief and then scraped up a small amount with his fingernail and rubbed it between his fingers. "I believe this may be a small sample of Vicenzo Cascariolo's *lapis solaris*—the Stone of Bologna." He glanced up as Pru went to the doorway to get her candle. "I read about the material once in a journal. It is from a stone that has the ability to accumulate the sun's light and then emit it in the dark. Curious. I believe the substance is actually barium sulfide, if I remember the article correctly."

"Could someone have created a powder from it and sprinkled it over their clothing?"

"Yes. And it would then glow if the wearer had had the foresight to leave the garments out in the sunshine before wearing them."

"Then the only questions that remain are how he—or she—got in, and why."

"Given you found the *lapis solaris* on the draperies, I would hazard a guess that the *apparition* climbed in through the window."

Pru angled her candle to light her husband's lamp before she went back to the window and looked out. "I cannot see how he could have managed it. The room is not on ground level, and there does not appear to be a trellis, or other convenient apparatus, to use as a ladder."

"However, this is one of the few rooms that has a fireplace. And it is opposite the bed." Knighton faced the brick hearth.

No wood had been provided, nor was any laid on the black iron andirons that stood behind a simple screen. The fireplace did not appear to have been used in quite a while. Although since it was only October, that might be reasonably explained by the fact it had not been required during the warm, summer months. Or Buonfiglio really had been afraid to the rent the room to anyone.

She studied the blackened bricks and small pile of ashes at the back of the fireplace and then looked at the wooden floor between the bed and the hearth.

Although the floor wasn't the cleanest one she'd ever seen, there were no tracks of ash. Surely there would be, if there was a secret entryway through the fireplace? And there were no streaks of luminescence anywhere that she could see, either. Wouldn't there be some of the glowing powder on the bricks or the fire screen?

Her husband poked and pried at the bricks while the frown creasing his face gradually deepened. All he succeeded in doing was to get a coating of gray ash all over his sleeves and hair.

"I don't think he came through the fireplace," she said at last. "There is no sign of it." She turned slowly as her husband brushed the gray powder off his clothing and out of his hair. "There must be some other answer."

He caught her gaze and shook his head, his mouth twisting into the lopsided grin that always made her warm to him and smile back. "It must be late, dear heart. Go to bed. I will join you in a few minutes."

"Don't be too long." She laughed teasingly. "This room will still be here tomorrow. It may be even easier to find what you're looking for with sunlight and a well-rested mind."

"No doubt you are right, as always. I won't be long." His dark eyes twinkled in the lamplight as she smothered a yawn behind one hand. "Go on before you fall asleep where you stand."

"Don't be absurd," she replied from the doorway. "You know very well it requires four feet to sleep standing up."

Knighton laughed. "Go to bed."

Even her thin shoes felt heavy and her calves ached as she walked softly down the hallway. Her candle flickered in her hand when odd swirls of cold, damp night air curled around her, lifting loose strands of hair from her neck and tickling her ears.

The inn was silent, almost abnormally so, as if she walked through a deserted graveyard instead of an old hostelry. Even the knowledge that others slumbered and snored in the rooms above failed to comfort her. She buttoned the top button of her redingote and walked faster until she came to the staircase.

Half-way up, she heard the rapid patter of footsteps coming up behind her as if in pursuit. For some reason, the sound made her shiver and take another, hurried step before she stopped. She turned resolutely and holding her candle aloft, she faced whoever was approaching.

"Mrs. Gaunt—thank goodness," the maid, Celestina, exclaimed as she came to a halt three steps down from Pru. Celestina's left hand clutched at her apron as her dark eyes glanced nervously up at her and then past her shoulder in a way that made Pru's neck stiffen in an effort to keep from looking up into the blackness at the top of the staircase.

"What is it?" The candle in Pru's hand shook. She took a deep breath and willed her hand to remain steady.

"Come—you must come." Without waiting for a reply, Celestina pirouetted and ran down the stairs.

"Wait!" Pru hesitated and then followed reluctantly. "What is it?"

The maid paused at the foot of the staircase, partially hidden in the shifting shadows. The light from Pru's candle glowed golden over the curve of her hand and illuminated Celestina's forearm as she waved urgently for her to follow. Before she could catch up with the maid, the woman rushed toward the back of the inn, stopping every few yards to gesture for Pru to follow.

Heart thudding, Pru's reluctant feet dragged even more slowly. Her senses prickled with a breath-stealing sense of danger. "Wait!"

Celestina jerked around, her face ghostly white in the poor light. "Come—quickly."

"Where are you going?"

Celestina ran on ahead, navigating through the corridor and gloomy kitchen, apparently knowing her way so well that she did not need a light.

Something was wrong. Pru's chest tightened, making it hard to breathe. She should have ignored the maid and gone to bed. Why had she stupidly followed her?

If there were some emergency, why didn't the girl awaken Buonfiglio or Fiorella, instead?

Pru stumbled as her hip hit the corner of the large, wooden table in the center of the kitchen.

Catherine! Had something had happened to the girl? That would explain the maid's choice of Pru. Catherine might have asked for her.

The pounding of her heart was deafening. Hethering had been awake and wandering around the inn. Had he decided to force Catherine to go with him after all? To make her marry him? Pru's step quickened.

Ahead of her several yards, Celestine flitted through the back door. She caught the edged of the door before it slammed shut and glanced over her thin shoulder at Pru. "Come—quickly!" she repeated in an urgent whisper.

"Is it Catherine?" Pru caught up and grasped the doorknob. "Did something happen to her?"

The maid let go of the edge of the door, picked up her skirts, and ran down the pale gray path leading through what appeared to be the neat geometry of the kitchen garden.

Sucking in a deep breath of frustration, liberally laced with tension, Pru stepped onto the pebble path. She immediately regretted her footwear. Sharp stones bit through the thin soles of her flimsy slippers, and she wrapped her arms around her waist, glad for the warmth of her heavy wool coat.

She had not gone more than a dozen steps when something gray swooped forward on her right. She caught the movement in the corner of her eye before her view of the garden and starry sky was cut off.

A sharp pain flashed like a shower of sparks in her head. Her candle tumbled from her hand.

Then complete darkness swallowed her.

Chapter Sixteen

Pru was jolted awake in a claustrophobic world of impenetrable blackness. Her head ached abominably. She blinked, trying to clear her vision, but nothing helped. Sharp bolts of pain sparkled against her eyelids and beyond was blackness.

She was blind! She took a deep breath, trying not to scream in panic.

The dusty air contained the strange smell of flour. She licked her lips and felt a fine powder coat her tongue and dry her mouth. She coughed and struggled to breath, but the air was as thick and dry as if she had shoved her head into a flour bin.

Wheezing, she jerked and jolted against something warm. A horse! She was riding a horse. The animal's heated flanks warmed her legs. She tried to bring her hands up to rub her eyes only to find her wrists bound with a harsh rope. She coughed again, tears running down her face. The air felt overheated and thick—too thick to breathe. She choked and gasped as another cloud of dust entered her nose and throat.

Calm—stay calm. Breathe slowly. Her heart thudded in her chest, despite her efforts, and her body tensed with the need for clean, cool air.

Before she could make sense of her surroundings, the horse swayed to a stop. Someone gripped her waist and dragged her down. She stumbled on the rocky ground, and a strong hand on her shoulder steadied her.

A second later, the bag over her head was removed. An old flour sack. The caress of cold night air on her cheek felt blessedly fresh. She took a long breath, only to cough again. The flour tickled her throat, and before she could do aught to control her reaction, she bent over and was horribly sick. Her throat strained and her mouth burned, but she finally straightened, aching and wishing for nothing more than to be lying in bed with her husband's comforting, warm bulk next to her.

"You remain ill?" a familiar voice asked.

She blinked and turned slowly to see Captain Nacchio holding the reins of a large horse in one gloved hand. He grinned insolently.

"What is the meaning of this?" She winced at the resulting throbbing in her head. When she touched her temple awkwardly with her bound hands, her fingertips came away white with flour.

"I wish to talk to signora."

"Release me at once."

Captain Nacchio threw his head back and laughed until tears ran over his round, tanned cheeks, glittering in the pale moonlight. "Not right away. Come." He waved at the dark entrance of a gloomy path running between a tumbled mound of boulders and a black line of gnarled evergreen trees.

"I will not." Pru raised her chin, although it was more in defiance of her own fear than to prove to him that he did not have the power to terrify her.

The ruffian chuckled as he picked up the now-soiled flour bag with two fingers and shook it off. "You wish to wear this again?"

"Of course not." The acrid smell of the vomit that had splashed onto it made her stomach clench. Her gorge rose again. She swallowed hastily.

"Then come."

"I will come with you, but only if you unbind my wrists." She held out her hands resolutely, proud to see that she did not tremble.

She could not escape on foot, not when he still held the reins of a horse he could easily mount. However, obtaining the freedom of her hands would improve her ability to elude him if the opportunity arose. She glanced around, trying to gauge how long she had been unconscious.

Surely it had been more than a few minutes. The night seemed colder, perhaps a sign that she had been unconscious for quite some time.

That meant that Knighton might have already discovered she was missing. He would find tracks—surely Captain Nacchio had left signs of his trespass—and he would follow them. He would find her.

Nonetheless, fear trickled through her. If her husband did follow, it might only make matters worse. The bandit might shoot him. And what about the rest of the ruffians? Knighton couldn't fight them all. He could be hurt—or killed—trying to rescue her.

No. Far better to try to escape on her own.

Smiling blandly, the bandit examined her face. After a long moment, he shrugged and pulled a knife out of his leather belt. The gleam of moonlight along the sharp edge made her limbs feel as useful as overcooked asparagus, but she held her wrists out. He slipped the blade under the rough rope. Her arms shook at the touch of the icy metal. She squeezed her eyes shut and uttered a soft, but fervent, prayer.

Free at last, she rubbed her hands over her face and brushed at her hair, which she had braided in preparation for bed. Although she couldn't see clearly, she felt as if she had shaken loose a cloud of flour. Grains floated and swirled around her like fairy dust, illuminated by the light of the moon.

"Now, go." Captain Nacchio pointed at the path with his knife.

"Lead on." She folded her arms tightly against her waist.

He gave her a push, not hard, but forceful enough to show his impatience. Something in the gesture made her aware that he could easily turn cruel, and that her well-being didn't signify to him in the least.

"I follow," he said briefly. "Go."

Pru edged into the darkness, pausing only briefly to allow her eyes to adjust to the shadows and dappled moonlight. The path rose at a mild incline and bent to the right. Behind her, she could hear the steady clip-clop of the plodding horse and the bandit's firm tread. Every once in a while, the animal whiffled and sniffed as if nuzzling the neck of Nacchio as he led it along.

"Why did you kidnap me?" She asked over her shoulder after walking for several minutes in silence.

"Kidnap? Is that what you fear, signora?" He sounded amused and even the horse whinnied and snorted in a sound suspiciously like cold, human laugher.

The callous sounds were more frightening than any threat.

"I fear you have made a mistake." Pru was proud of how calm she sounded, despite her deafening heartbeat.

When a glance ahead revealed the sharp vertical edge of a building, she stumbled and caught the thin trunk of a tree growing near the path. The edifice looked like the remains of an ancient stone fortress or castle that rose from the hillside, as if it had thrust itself up from the bones of the mountain. The windowless wall towered above the tops of the trees, blocking out the stars and moon and casting an even darker gloom over the narrow path. She rubbed her upper arms, freezing in spite of the heavy wool of her redingote.

She didn't want to die, not here, not at the hands of the laughing devil behind her.

"Nearly there. First the stables, then we talk." Captain Nacchio pushed her forward.

A small, wooden stable emerged from the blackness, and he thrust her again in its direction. The building was tacked on to the base of the stone edifice, and the sagging roof and rough-hewn supports leaned against the stone for support.

To her surprise, a young boy ran out at the sound of the horse's hooves on the flagstone courtyard. Nacchio handed the reins to him, ruffled the raggedy, dark hair on the child's head, and held a brief, whispered conversation with the boy, who flicked continual, curious glances at Pru.

Should she run? She looked at the thick tree trunks—the shadows might hide her. Her muscles tensed, but before she could move, Nacchio patted the horse on the neck and strolled back to her.

"So. Now we enjoy a glass of wine and talk."

"I don't understand—why are you doing this?"

"First the wine. Then we talk."

Wine was the last thing she wanted. She glanced around more frantically, but the boy had disappeared with the horse. In her thin shoes, outrunning Nacchio seemed impossible. She could see no alternative but to do as he asked.

Nacchio nodded and brushed past her to push open a heavy, iron-studded door. The hallway beyond yawned cavernously and inky black, except for a wavering golden light on the left. He studied her as he stood aside to bow her inside with all the aplomb of a well-trained butler.

"In there, if you please." He held up a lantern and gestured with it to the first door on their left.

A flickering, reddish-gold light poured from that doorway, drawing her toward the room and the warmth indicated by the glow. It promised safety after the misty chill of the woods, even if that safety was only an illusion.

"Where are your men?" she asked as she walked into the chamber. Without hesitation, she moved toward the huge stone fireplace where a large pile of wood was burning merrily.

"Here." He shrugged. "But elsewhere."

The fire was the only source of light in the room other than the lantern in Nacchio's hand. Despite the lack of light, Pru had the impression of a large chamber, although the corners and walls and whatever else filled the room were hidden by thick shadows. The stone floor felt cold under the thin soles of Pru's slippers, and she quickly stepped onto a braided rug, worn and unraveling at one edge, in front of the hearth. Heat from the fire warmed the front of her coat. She stretched out her hands and rubbed her stiff fingers, wincing at the chafed, reddened circles around her wrists.

"Sit." He waited for her to perch on the edge of one of the chairs near the fire before he strolled over to a highboy in the shadows to the right of the fireplace. He placed the lantern on top of it and pulled out a bottle of wine and two glasses.

After depositing those on a table near her, he returned to the highboy. When he came back, he carried a wicker basket containing a ball of cheese and a brown loaf of bread in one hand and a shallow dish of dried figs and nuts in the other. He placed them on the table, sat opposite her, and cut the cheese and bread with his knife.

"Eat." He poured the wine and handed her a glass. "Drink. We talk."

She nodded. There seemed little point in refusing.

She sipped her glass, glad to wash away the acrid taste that had remained in her mouth. At his urging, she accepted a small piece of bread laden by a lovely, white cheese. Her stomach gurgled, and she hoped the food would settle the queasiness that seemed to come and go without warning.

Finally, he leaned back in his chair and fixed his dark eyes on her face. "Why, you ask?"

"Indeed." She swallowed a mouthful of bread and cheese. "If you wish for ransom, you will be terribly disappointed."

His white teeth flashed in the firelight as he grinned. "Perhaps. Perhaps not." When she opened her mouth to disabuse him of the notion that he had captured a good prospect for ransom, he held up his hand. "That is not my purpose."

"And why should I believe you? You assaulted me, brought me here. Celestina—"

"Please signora, forgive me and little Celestina. These things—they were necessary, and Celestina has a difficult enough life. Forget her." He tilted his head to one side, reminding her of the particularly cocky wren that had once stolen bits of bread from her plates on a picnic with her husband. Without warning, his face hardened. "Maggiore Lupino made it necessary."

"Maggiore Lupino?" she echoed in surprise. What did the major have to do with her?

He refilled his glass of wine and held it up to study the flickering firelight through the red depths. "This dead woman of yours—I am innocent."

So he knew about Mrs. Ruberry's death. Pru took another sip of wine, wishing that that knowledge didn't frighten her so much that her glass clinked with a sharp ting against her front teeth. Her palms felt damp and her fingers stiffened with cold, despite the warmth radiating from the leaping flames in front of her.

His protestation of innocence did not impress her. What else would he say? He was a bandit, a ruffian who kidnapped, robbed, and murdered for gain. How could he expect her to believe him?

But then—why on earth would he kidnap her, just to tell her that he was innocent? The entire notion was ridiculous.

Her thoughts flitted to her husband. Would he believe this bandit? If not, what would he do, what would he expect her to do?

"Why do you believe anyone is dead?" she asked cautiously, hoping to flush out an understanding of the extent of his knowledge. From there, perhaps she could determine his guilt. Or innocence.

He grinned again, cut himself another slice of bread, and helped himself to a handful of dried figs and nuts. "Do not believe I am a fool. I know this woman is dead. And I know Maggiore Lupino, and why he is here. He believes I murdered the woman, does he not?"

"You should ask him."

"Have a care." He slammed his palm against the armrest of his chair. His brows snapped down over the bridge of his nose, exposing a sudden and unpredictable temper. "I took you for an intelligent woman. Do not make me regret this, signora."

Amy Corwin

"I am sorry, Capitano Nacchio." She stilled, hardly daring to breathe. "However, you must realize, you kidnapped me, and I am confused. How am I supposed to believe anything you say under these conditions?"

"You must believe the truth. That is all." Although he sat in a relaxed posture, she could see the tension in his hands and the tight muscles in his jaw. He was clearly trying not to lose control over his temper again. Oddly, it was this, and the intense flame of emotion in his eyes, that deepened her confusion.

He clearly had a temper, but was he telling the truth about Mrs. Ruberry?

He must have done other, equally terrible things, given his occupation. Indeed, he had tried to do terrible things to their party when their carriage became disabled. So what was the point in denying his part in Mrs. Ruberry's death? Unless he was actually speaking the truth.

She moved in her chair, wishing Knighton were there. They had been married just over three months, and while she was not precisely dependent upon him, he seemed to have become another part of her that she sorely missed when he was absent. He could untangle Nacchio's words and find the truth. And then, he would present some logical argument that the bandit could not refute and thereby obtain her freedom. She struggled to clear her mind and consider her situation dispassionately, the way Knighton might.

Before she could respond, something wet and cold nudged her hand. "What—" A huge, gray dog pushed its massive head into her lap, staring up at her with limpid eyes. Without thinking, she stroked its wrinkled brow and massaged the silky, warm ears. In the flickering light, the dog had an extraordinary color. The animal glowed silver, almost blue. "Aren't you a sweet dog?"

"Cabò! Come!" Capitano Nacchio called sharply. He snapped his fingers.

The dog's ears twitched, and it gave a soft huff, blowing air out of its broad nose. Instead of going to its master, it leaned closer to Pru and sat resolutely on her foot. Its thick tail thumped the floor a few times, and it moved its head again to force Pru to continue to rub its ears.

Pru glanced at the captain, slightly embarrassed that the dog continued to ignore him in favor of her attention. "I am sorry, Capitano. He is remarkably friendly."

"He is ridiculous! Of what use is a guard dog like that?"

"Well, perhaps he felt I was not an intruder, since you are sitting here with me."

The dog sniffed at her hands once more, pushing its nose under her right palm. For one terrifying moment, she thought it was considering climbing up into her lap. Finally, it shook its head, blinked sleepily, flopped down to the floor with a grunt, and trapped her feet under one huge paw and its massive, wrinkled head.

At least her toes were no longer cold. In fact, after a few seconds, she couldn't feel any sensation in her feet at all.

"He is useless." The exasperation on Nacchio's face competed with amusement as his lips twisted, and he shifted restlessly in his chair.

Somehow, she found the dog's presence, and Nacchio's frustration with the animal, reassuring.

"He is sweet." She managed to slip her right foot out and used it to rub the heavy folds of skin around the mastiff's neck. With the feeling that she was grabbing a bull by the horns, she said, "You say you are innocent of murder. If so, do you not think that kidnapping me will prejudice your case? Maggiore Lupino will see this as proof that you are indeed guilty."

"Lupino! That fool. You may blame him for your presence here." At the harsh note in its master's voice, Cabò lifted his head and glanced at him. "Oh, yes, even Cabò agrees. He does not like your Maggiore Lupino any more than I do. He is pleased to believe I am guilty because it pleases him. That is all." He emptied his wine glass and refilled it, staring at her with hard eyes. "That woman, she was found on the hill—my hill—to place her death at my door. What other reason was there to leave her there?"

"Whoever was responsible may have hoped that her body would not be found."

"No. You are wrong. It was to accuse me. I have done many things, but murder? No. This I have never done."

"I beg your pardon, but I believe Lieutenant Fisher may wish to argue the point."

Nacchio smiled grimly. "Is he dead?"

"No, but—"

"No, signora. It was but an error—on *his* part."

His argument seemed a bit disingenuous, however she was ill-inclined to argue the matter with him upon remembering his swift temper. "Once more, I must ask why you believe my presence here will help you prove your innocence." If that was truly what he wanted to do.

"Your husband—he will prove I am innocent. Until he does so, you will be my guest."

"Then we may be at an impasse. Maggiore Lupino is in charge of this case. My husband and I are simply visitors to the region. He cannot do as you ask."

"You are mistaken. I have heard that your husband has experience in these matters. He will do this and convince Lupino. You understand?" He stood and dusted his hands off on his thighs. "You will be safe here. Cabò will remain with you. Company, *si*?"

Pru stood and swayed, her left foot still trapped under Cabò's head. "You cannot do this!"

"It is done." He shrugged and picked up a lantern from the top of the cabinet that had held their food. After lighting the lamp sitting on the wooden mantle above the fireplace, he walked to the left side of the room and held the lantern up to reveal the long, wooden shutters. "In the morning, you will have light." He grabbed a shutter and shook it, proving that it could not be opened. "And you will be safe here."

Then he walked to the other side of the room. In the corner stood an ancient bed, draped with heavy brocade curtains. He pulled one of the curtains back to reveal a mound of pillows and heavy blanket. At least they looked clean and free of dust, even if they were a little threadbare. He set the lantern on the bedside table.

Her heart sank as she watched him. She didn't want to stay here, even with Cabò for company. She wanted to return to the inn, or better yet, return to England.

"My husband will not perjure himself—he will not lie."

"Even for you?"

"I would not want, or expect, him to. If you are guilty, he will not be able to prove otherwise."

"Have you not heard me?" He tensed and leaned toward her with such intensity that Cabò growled deeply in his throat. "I did not kill that woman. If your husband does not lie, then he cannot prove otherwise. So you see, you are safe. Now, I must bid you good night. It is late." He strode to the door, but stopped at the threshold and waved toward one of the still-dark corners. "There is water, as well. You will be comfortable, and Cabò will guard you." He chuckled. "If he wishes."

"Wait—" Suddenly, she feared being left alone in the huge, drafty room more than she feared Captain Nacchio and his temper. She said the first thing to come to mind, to delay the moment when the door would be shut, and presumably locked, by her captor. "Who will walk Cabò? Surely he must go out, at least in the morning."

"Never fear, signora. I will return in the morning. And we may take Cabò for his walk together." With that, he slammed the door shut.

The loud, hollow sound of a plank of wood dropping into place to bar the door made her last hope of escape fade.

She was trapped. There was no escape, unless her husband solved Mrs. Ruberry's murder and proved Nacchio's innocence.

Assuming that Nacchio hadn't lied.

Chapter Seventeen

Their room was empty. Knighton glanced around, but nothing appeared to be missing except his wife. The cold edge of worry slid between his shoulder blades.

Where was she? She should be here. The last time he'd seen her, she was heading for the stairs. Had she gone downstairs for something to eat? Certainly understandable. She had been sick so often recently that she had to be hungry. A half-smile curved his mouth at the reason.

A baby. He could hardly believe it.

But that knowledge only sharpened his worries. She should be in bed, resting, not dashing up and down the stairs in the dark. He strode to the staircase and descended, his back aching with tension when he saw the paucity of lights. The ground floor appeared to be deserted. The only light came from the red embers in the fireplace.

"Buonfiglio!" he yelled, slamming a fist down on the bar. "Buonfiglio, you scoundrel, wake up!"

It took almost five minutes to rouse the innkeeper. Buonfiglio finally stumbled out, drawing a heavy robe around his paunch. "What is it, signore?"

"My wife is missing, have you seen her?"

"Your wife?" Buonfiglio appeared confused. He rubbed his face and looked around as if he expected to spot Pru standing next to him. "Where is she?"

"That is what I am asking you. Have you seen her?"

"Seen her?" he repeated with a slack mouth. "How could I see her? She is in her room."

"No, she is not. She is missing, I tell you."

"Ah, then perhaps she visits the contessa. *Si?*"

Of course, that had to be the answer. He nodded and turned, only to stop as a sharp, icy breeze touched him. "Is there a window open?"

"A window? At night? Who would do such a thing?" Buonfiglio wrung his hands and glanced around uneasily. "No one would open a window. There can be no window

197

open." He studied Knighton, as if searching for reassurance. Apparently, whatever he saw in his face did not reassure him. "We will all be ill. This is terrible. We must find the window and shut it."

Ignoring the man's fretful complaints, Knighton pushed past him and strode into the kitchen. The rear door stood partially open. As he watched, the night air pushed it further open and then pulled it back until it nearly shut. Something white fluttered with the movement of the door.

At first, he thought it was simply a curtain. When he raised his lamp, he felt his stomach cramp. A knife had been driven through an object—a piece of paper or cloth—affixing it to the heavy wood of the door.

It might have nothing to do with Pru. No need for alarm.

Except that she was missing. It would be a wild coincidence if it did not.

He moved forward and grabbed the hilt of the knife, yanking it free. Paper. Heavy, expensive paper with bold, black writing. He held it near the lamp and tried to read it, but the words jumbled together. After a deep breath, he pushed his emotions aside and stared at the paper again.

Signor Gaunt:

As you no doubt have realized, your wife is now my guest. While she is safe and perfectly comfortable, she will remain my guest until you have resolved this issue of murder. Maggiore Lupino is incorrect, as always. He believes I am responsible. This is not true. I had no reason to kill any member of your party and would certainly never kill a lady. Look elsewhere. You will certainly find the one responsible at the inn.

Your humble servant,

Capitano Pasquino Nacchio

Knighton swore under his breath and read the note through again, making sure he did not translate the Italian incorrectly. The contents did not change upon review.

Pru was gone.

The inn felt empty and cold, as if all life had deserted the building. What should he do? He had to find her, protect her. If anything happened to her, or their baby, he would kill him.

The thought of life without Pru was unbearable. He shook it off and turned back, only to stop. He couldn't just return to their room and go to sleep as if nothing had happened. Sleep would be impossible without her lying next to him, even if she did have the uncomfortable habit of pressing her cold feet against his calves at night.

His hand clamped around the note, crumpling the crisp paper. A man who could kidnap a pregnant woman could easily kill. Nacchio must realize that his actions only served to make him appear even guiltier.

How dare he demand that Knighton prove him innocent after attacking Pru? Knighton stabbed the knife he held into the scarred surface of the kitchen table. The thud echoed hollowly as the hilt vibrated in his hand. What made him think he could possibly prove Nacchio did not murder Mrs. Ruberry? That arrogant idiot, Maggiore Lupino, had already decided the matter. He was the authority in charge. Men like Lupino did not like to change their minds, even when presented with a plethora of facts proving something completely different.

And there wasn't a plethora of facts. The few he'd collected hardly proved, or disproved, Lupino's hasty conclusion.

He stared at the knife, teeth clenched and his chest burning until he forced his unconstructive emotions. He had to remain calm. Detached. It was the only way to approach the truth.

He raised his head and caught sight of Buonfiglio standing a few feet away. The innkeeper eyed him with a worried frown creasing his broad face.

Knighton wrested the knife out of the table and pointed it at him. "Where can I find this Capitano Nacchio?"

"*Il* capitano?" He shook his head and took a step back, wiping a droplet of sweat off his temple with his wrist. His small eyes glanced to the left and then to the right, as if seeking escape. "I know no capitano."

"I am in no mood for trifling—where can I find him?"

His chin wobbled. He wiped his temple again, his skin glistening sickly in the wavering lamplight. "I—I—no. I cannot. He will kill me. I swear to you, I cannot help you."

"Do not be inhospitable, Buonfiglio. I am sure you can help our guest," Maggiore Lupino's silky voice came from the hallway.

When Knighton lifted his lamp, he saw the major leaning one shoulder against the kitchen doorway, his arms crossed over his medal-encrusted chest.

"I cannot!" Buonfiglio squeaked, gazing at Lupino and then back to Knighton. He was sweating so much that Knighton wondered if he would be ill right in the middle of the kitchen.

"If you cannot help your guest, Buonfiglio, then perhaps I may offer my assistance?"

Knighton hesitated, not entirely trusting the suave major's motives. He needed to find Nacchio and make sure that Pru was alive and unharmed, and yet... He hesitated.

The major might use this opportunity to flush Nacchio into the open and arrest him. The action might very well result in a fight and destroy any chance Knighton had of getting his wife back. And then there was Nacchio, himself. He would not be pleased if Knighton brought Lupino. Matters could go badly—very badly—for Pru in either case.

"I am surprised to see you here so late," Knighton temporized.

"Ah. You see, our good host insisted I stay, so here I am. Naturally, when I heard the noise, I must come to investigate. Now it is good, is it not? I will guide you to Capitano Nacchio."

"While I appreciate the offer, I cannot accept it. I will not risk my wife's life," Knighton said at last.

"Signora Gaunt?" Lupino's mustache twitched above a broad, knowing smile. "You see? I warned you." He shrugged, looking like a smug cat stretching and rubbing its back against the doorframe. "Nacchio is a bandit and a murderer. An innocent man would not do such a thing."

Knighton's hand tightened around the hilt of the knife. When he realized it, he forced his fingers to relax and threw the weapon onto the table.

An innocent man faced with an official as intransigent as Lupino might feel he had no other choice. Knighton didn't like either Lupino or Nacchio, but he was starting to get an inkling of why Nacchio acted as he had.

"Perhaps. Nonetheless, I must see him—alone. Will you tell me how to find him?"

"*Si.* I take you." Lupino help up his palm when Knighton started to refuse. "I only go partway. Enough to show you the path."

"Do I have your word of honor that you will not try to follow me, once you indicate the path?"

Lupino waved his hand in front of his face as if Knighton's words annoyed him. "*Si, si.* We go." He straightened and stepped forward.

Before they left, Knighton returned to his room. Best to be prepared for the worst. He grimly loaded both of his dueling pistols and tucked them into the pockets of his greatcoat. Then he glanced around their chamber and, remembering Pru's state of undress when he'd last seen her, he hurriedly picked up his leather portmanteau and filled it with her traveling dress, a stout pair of walking shoes, and a few other items she might desire. The action had the odd effect of lifting some of the oppression from his heart. If she were dead or badly injured, she wouldn't need such things. Irrational though it was, packing the items seemed to promise that she was alive and would want them.

He threw her brush and small hand mirror on top of the clothing and closed the case.

He would get her back—he had to.

Downstairs, he found Maggiore Lupino waiting for him in the kitchen. As soon as Knighton walked through the doorway, Lupino strode outside. He took the lead, and Knighton was content to let him do so.

"Nacchio will use you, if he can," Lupino said as they walked up the road. "You must see this."

"I understand." Knighton remained silent for a minute before he said, "It is possible, however, that Mrs. Ruberry's death was more complicated than it initially appeared."

"Complicated? How so? It is only complicated if you allow this man to dupe you. You cannot believe him. His words are lies."

"I will suspend judgment. Perhaps we can discuss this and review the evidence when we return to the inn?" The last thing he wanted was to get into a heated discussion about the guilt or innocence of Nacchio. He needed to focus his attention on Pru and not jeopardize her wellbeing by angering Lupino. What he needed from him was his cooperation.

They had walked two hundred yards or more past the spot where the carriage had broken down when Lupino suddenly stopped. There was nothing to be seen, nothing unusual about the area. It was simply a plain stretch of dirt road with a thick stand of woods on their right and the sharp downward slope of the hill on their left. Above, the moon shone clear and cold, and the stars twinkled uncaringly.

Silence and darkness. No owls called, nothing rustled in the shadows. The night was still, as if all life had paused to watch what the major would do.

"What is it?" Knighton slipped one hand into his pocket to clasp the curved grip of his pistol.

"The path is there." Maggiore Lupino pointed to a gloomy gap between a cluster of boulders and the trees. He smiled. "Nacchio still has friends in high places—my superiors would not approve of my intrusion. Yet. But if he steps off his land," he shrugged, his grin widening, "all things are fair. And he is guilty, now, of murder. He cannot escape this time."

"We can discuss it when I return. Where does this path lead?"

"It will take you to the house of Capitano Nacchio. Stay on the path. You will be safe enough."

The tension aching between his shoulder blades eased a fraction. He glanced at Lupino, but his arrogant face remained bland. "You will stay here?"

"*Si.*" He pressed his palm against his chest. "Upon my honor, I will remain on the road."

Knighton nodded and removed his hand from his pocket. "I should return shortly. And thank you."

"*Prego!*"

The path was not difficult to follow, despite the intermittent moonlight. The trail wended its way through the woods, following a gentle uphill incline until it disappeared around the thick bole of an ancient tree. As he plodded along, he almost wished he'd allowed Lupino to accompany him. The path felt both lonely and dangerous, with pines and vegetation hanging over him and providing deep shadows for anyone to hide within. With each step, he expected a shot to ring out or one of the *banditi* to slip out from between the trees to confront him. His neck itched. A trickle of sweat slid icily between his shoulder blades.

He could feel eyes fastened upon him, watching him.

The slender branches on his left suddenly rattled. He froze. Nothing moved. A breeze, then, nothing more. He let out the breath he was holding and glanced ahead.

A sharp edge of stone blocked the sky. He'd reached Nacchio's dwelling. Heart pounding, Knighton made his way around the side of the building to the heavy, iron-studded front door. A large, bronze knocker in the form of a lion's head hung in the center. He gripped the device and slammed it against its plate several times, listening to the clanging sound echoing dimly through the wooden door.

The building sounded empty. Deserted.

Had Lupino deliberately led him astray?

Looking more closely, he saw heavy vines covering good portions of the walls. Heavy metal bars covered the window on his left, and long streaks of rust ran over the stones beneath it. Signs of nature's insistent encroachment were everywhere. The building looked abandoned and in ruins.

So Lupino had sent him on a wild goose chase. He probably stood on the road below, gasping for air as he laughed. If he were still there at all and hadn't already returned to the inn.

Burning with frustrated anger, Knighton was about to return to the road when he heard the creak of the door. Slowly, with a rough grating noise, the wooden panel opened. A lamp was thrust out, and a moment later, a low chuckle flowed out of the darkness of the hall beyond.

"So. Who stands outside my door?" Another brief laugh followed the question.

Whoever stood in the darkness knew very well who stood outside his door and found it amusing.

"Capitano Nacchio? You know who I am—I want to see my wife."

The door opened a fraction wider and while the lamp showed part of a hallway and what appeared to be a marble floor. The person holding the light remained in darkness, partially behind and obscured by the heavy door.

"Wife? Why should your wife, or any wife, be here, my friend?"

"I am no friend of yours, as you shall find out if I do not see my wife in the next five minutes."

"Strong words for a man who is apparently so careless that he has mislaid his wife."

Losing patience, Knighton shouted, "Pru! PRU! Are you here?"

A muffled response came from a room nearby, followed surprisingly by the loud, bass notes of a dog's bark. A very large dog's bark. Knighton pushed past the man and strode a few yards down the gloomy hallway, his leather heels clacking on the marble floor.

"Pru?"

A loud banging and another rumble of barking, thrumming like distant thunder, sounded nearby. He moved forward another yard and in the Stygian gloom saw a door barred with a broad plank of wood. He wrenched away the beam, threw it down, and yanked open the door.

Before he could glance around, Pru flung herself into his arms. "Thank God! I am so glad to see you."

He tightened his grip. Thank God! She felt warm and whole in his arms. "Are you unharmed?"

"Yes. I am well." She tilted her head back to stare into his face with anxious eyes. "Did you solve the case already, then? How long has it been? It seems like only an hour or two."

"It is, and no. I have solved nothing. Maggiore Lupino is convinced he knows who is responsible, and he is the official in charge." He kissed her forehead and then, in a burst of relief, shifted his grip on her and pressed a long kiss on her mouth. When he lifted his head, he felt unready to let her go. He kept his arm around her shoulders, holding her against his chest where she was safe.

He pressed his cheek against her soft hair and took a deep breath. A cloud of irritating dust—flour?—flew up his nose. *Flour?* His nose tickled. He turned his head and sneezed violently.

"I am sorry," Pru whispered ruefully when he caught her gaze, after rubbing his nose with a handkerchief. She shook her head, and one hand touched her hair. "Don't ask, please."

"You see?" Capitano Nacchio placed his lamp on a nearby table and faced them, his thumbs hooked in his wide, leather belt. "She has come to no harm, and will not, if you do this thing I ask of you."

"You cannot expect me to stay here," Pru said. "I will not!"

As her voice rose sharply, a massive beast rose into view behind her.

Knighton's grip tightened around her shoulders at the sight of the huge, gray dog. He pulled her away and shifted to stand between her and the animal. The dog stared at him. Despite its fearsome aspect, the massive beast was a beautiful animal, with smooth silver-blue fur and an enormous head with drooping jowls. It was only when the dog padded into the flickering light that Knighton saw several scars on the animal's haunches. A slight limp betrayed a stiff left rear leg.

"You will stay!" Nacchio suddenly lost his smiling good humor and stepped closer. "I am innocent. You will stay until your husband proves the truth."

As if sensing the tension, the dog growled low in its throat and loped around Knighton and Pru to face its master. Or at least Knighton assumed Nacchio was the animal's master, although the dog, bristling at the anger in Nacchio's voice, seemed more protective of Pru than obedient to the bandit.

"Sit—be a good dog," Pru commanded.

The dog sat, his rump covering both of their sets of feet.

Immediately countermanding her, Nacchio ordered, "Cabò! Come!" He snapped his fingers, frowning. When the dog only emitted another deep growl, an ugly red color suffused Nacchio's face. He snapped his fingers again before exploding, "Useless animal! What good are you? You eat and eat and eat, and this is how you thank me? I can hardly afford to feed myself. Ungrateful beast. I, who rescue you when you are bleeding in the street, am treated this way? This?" His anger finally descended into a series of inventive curses that made Knighton hope his wife's Italian was not good enough to translate.

The dog, after the first few insults, eased over and lay on the marble floor with a thud that made Knighton wince. The animal gazed at Nacchio as if the torrent of words were nothing new and didn't interest him in the slightest. After a minute, Cabò yawned and closed his eyes, resting his massive head on equally large paws in seeming contempt of his master's chastisements.

"We are leaving." Knighton interrupted the flow of abuse aimed at the dog.

He felt almost sorry for the beast, but in some strange way, the animal's presence was a relief. Pru seemed to have found a protector of sorts, even if it did have four legs and apparently, the devil's own appetite. And oddly enough, it made Knighton consider—really consider—that Nacchio might actually be innocent. At least of murder. A man who could be so angry and frustrated at a disobedient dog and not physically abuse the animal—for it seemed the scars were not caused by Nacchio, but by a previous owner or accident—didn't seem like a man who would murder a woman, regardless of provocation.

"No! You are not." Nacchio's chest expanded as he took a deep breath, clearly trying to bring his emotions under control He pointed at Pru. "She is staying."

Cabò flicked one ear and opened one eye.

"She is not staying."

"I am innocent! She must stay."

"Kidnapping my wife only compounds your guilt—"

"I tell you, I have done nothing!" Nacchio spat on the floor and gesticulated wildly. "That Lupino, the swine! He curried favor with the French," he swore roundly, his dark eyes glittering with rage, before continuing, "and now thinks he can continue to take from us. Well, the French, they are gone, and I—I still have this land, and I will bring this place back to its former glory. He will see. He cannot cut all our heads off as Napoleon did in France. *Si*, he will discover this."

Clearly, the bourgeoisie Maggiore Lupino and the apparently aristocratic Capitano Nacchio had a long and unpleasant history of competition and antagonism.

"I understand, however, you must realize that he is the authority in charge. I have no official standing." Knighton raised his hand to stop Nacchio when the man's face grew red again and his chest puffed out, preparatory to more futile arguments. "I understand your position, and I will do this much for you. I will investigate this matter, as far as I am able. But I will only do so if my wife is allowed to return to the inn with me."

"You will do so *and* she will stay here. Cabò will keep her company. On my honor, she will be safe."

"I will not leave here without her."

"Do not be foolish. It does me no good to harm either you or her. But if that idiot, Lupino, accuses me of murder, it will make no difference if it is one or three English who die. One can only hang once. You go—alone— or I will shoot you where you stand." Nacchio leveled a pistol at Knighton and grinned. "*Si*, you have pistols. But your wife may be hurt if either of us uses them. Let us be friends. Do as I ask. It is a small favor, and you will free your beloved wife. The matter is in your hands."

He stared at the pistol in Nacchio's hand with chagrin. He should have pulled his out as soon as the door was open. But then what? Both of them might have been injured, or died.

"I will not leave her."

Pru moved restlessly in his arms. "Please don't fight. It will be far worse if you are injured." She touched his face with cool fingers. "I will be all right for a day or two. Please, do as he asks and find the answers."

He studied her wan face, feeling as if he were about to let go of the rope keeping him from falling over the edge of a cliff. "What if I discover he is not innocent?"

"Would I do these things if I were guilty?" Nacchio asked.

"You and Lupino have a score to settle between you, and you have pulled us into the middle of it." Knighton bit off the words coldly. "I believe you would do whatever is necessary to win your argument."

"I am an honorable man. Have I harmed your wife?"

"You were responsible for Lieutenant Fisher's injuries—"

"He drew his weapon first. No, I will not argue. No more of this. I am a man of honor, unlike that despicable bore, Lupino. You will do this. Now go." He edged closer to the wall and jerked his pistol toward the open door. "Find the one without honor, the one who kills women, and your wife will remain unharmed."

Knighton hugged Pru once more, pressing her against his chest and feeling the softness of her hair against his chin before she gently pushed him away.

"I will be fine." When she moved, the dog lumbered to its feet and pressed against her, staring up at her adoringly. She smiled and stroked the dog's head. "You see? He will stay with me until you return."

"See that he does." He stared at the dog. "You— guard the nice lady."

As if it could understand, the dog wagged its tail and pressed even closer to Pru, nearly pushing her over. She caught at Knighton's sleeve with a laugh and pushed the dog's massive head away enough to straighten. Before Knighton could say anything, she leaned forward, pressed a kiss against his cheek, and slipped through the doors of her prison with Cabò padding along behind her.

With the small satisfaction of knowing that he would be discommoding Nacchio at least a little, Knighton walked away. He refused to shut Pru's door. If Nacchio wanted to keep Pru locked up, he'd have to do it himself and bear the wrath of Cabò.

Chapter Eighteen

True to his word, Maggiore Lupino remained on the road, waiting for Knighton. "So?"

Too tired to initiate the argument that he knew would ensue if he told Lupino about Pru's kidnapping by Capitano Nacchio, Knighton merely said, "Nacchio is interested in the progress of our investigation. That is all." He rubbed his eyes wearily, wishing that information really was the sum of Nacchio's ransom.

In the distance, faint, rosy streaks stretched over the shadowed hillsides. The air felt cold and damp against his face, refreshing after the dusty air of Nacchio's decaying mansion. A surge of anger, mixed with fear, almost made him turn back and demand his wife's release. How could he trust Nacchio to keep his word? Anything might happen to her.

"No doubt he is curious." Lupino smiled with a predatory gleam in his eyes. He stroked his mustache thoughtfully as they turned to walk back to the inn. "We should lure him out to the road—I could arrest him then, you know. Ah, well. Soon enough he will discover he is not above the law as he believes. He is no better than the rest of us, mansion or no mansion. I believe in equality—we do not require the French to insist on this. Do you not agree, signor?"

"I believe we should pursue the truth." Knighton adroitly avoided the issue and increased his pace. Dawn was not the best time for discussions of liberty and equality.

Although the French no longer occupied the region, and the Papal State had returned to many of its old traditions, some of Napoleon's ideals had apparently left their mark on men such as Maggiore Lupino. On the whole, the ideas were not without some merit. If nothing else, the enforcement of law, initiated by Napoleon's management of the area, had curbed a few of the *eye for an eye, tooth for a tooth* vendettas.

At least it had until Lupino had recognized his opportunity to take Nacchio down a notch.

"The truth?" Lupino chuckled. "The truth is that Nacchio at last will hang." His hand went to the sword hanging at his side and rested on the pommel. "Unless he wishes to resist. Almost I wish he would."

The higgledy-piggledy jumble of the inn's roofline appeared around the bend in the road, and Knighton fixed his gaze on the chimneys in relief. "Perhaps we should go over the evidence again tomorrow. Or rather, later today."

"If it reassures you, certainly," Lupino agreed magnanimously. "We do this, have the funeral, then you English go, *si*?"

"I—"

"Oh—after the arrest of Nacchio and return of your dear wife, *si*?"

"A great deal to accomplish for a mere twenty-four hours."

Lupino shrugged. "A day—two days—what does it matter?" He reached the inn's door first and opened it with a flourish, holding it for Knighton. "You will soon be gone."

"I suppose we will," Knighton agreed in a dry voice. "However, not until we get at least a few hours of sleep."

His desire for rest was at least partially granted. He managed two hours of sleep before his anxiety about Pru's welfare gave him such a fearful nightmare of terrible, dark loneliness and grief that he forced himself to wake up. After dressing, his first thought was Fisher and his ghost. Perhaps it had nothing to do with the mystery at hand, but it gave him an excuse to question Mrs. Ruberry's first—and legal—husband again.

Fisher had more reason than anyone to do away with her, and Knighton had the unshakable feeling that he knew more than he had said thus far.

When he arrived at Fisher's door, he knocked softly, not wanting to awaken the injured man if he was still sleeping.

"Come in!" Fisher called, sounding irritable.

Knighton entered and gently shut the door behind him. "How are you this morning?"

A tray with empty breakfast dishes sat on a small wooden table next to the bed, indicating that Fisher was at least well enough to enjoy what appeared to be a generous breakfast. Yellow streaks and crumbs on one plate indicated he'd at least had an egg and bread, and the rich, smoky aroma of bacon hung in the air. Knighton's stomach grumbled, but he ignored its demands for nourishment.

"Well enough." Fisher's hands plucked at the coverlet restlessly. He kept flicking glances at the window, apparently unable to resist the pull of the sunshine streaming through the half-open draperies.

"The funeral is today. Will you attend?" Knighton asked by way of easing into conversation.

Fisher stared at him, and although Knighton couldn't be sure, he thought he caught the hard gleam of anger in his cold blue eyes. "Yes. And I am sure that scoundrel, Henry Savage, will be there as well, gloating."

"Why should he gloat?"

"Oh-ho, so he did not tell you after all, the weasel. Well, Violet always said her Cousin Henry would find a way to inherit, one way or the other. I suppose he has managed it, now." His hands plucked at his covers more frantically until he was twisting the materials into small ridges and mountains.

Knighton eyed Fisher's pale, angry face with sympathy, not unmixed with suspicion. He must have loved her at some point to have contacted her cousin to assist him in his search. But there was also the fact that Fisher had known about the possibility that Violet would inherit some money. He was not as ignorant of her affairs as he had originally stated, and any money she inherited would come to him after her death.

"Inherit?" Knighton asked, hoping that hiding the details of his discussion with Henry Savage might provoke a lengthy—and revealing—response.

"Go question him if you wish. I will say no more about it—it is none of my concern." Fisher clamped his mouth shut and stared at the window.

"I will do so. However, I did come here for another reason. Last night, you seemed to believe you had seen something unusual in your previous room. Have you any thoughts on the matter, now that you have had time to consider it?"

Fisher barked a harsh laugh and then groaned, paled, and pressed a hand against his side, apparently regretting his reaction. A white ring encircled his mouth as he said, "No doubt you mean reconsidered. Well, I have thought about it, and nothing has changed. Last night, I saw a specter standing at the foot of my bed, glowing in the darkness. The room was ice cold. It was the most terrifying moment of my life. I shall never forget it."

"Is it possible that it was a man? Or woman?"

"No, it was not! I am not a fool, Mr. Gaunt. No living man would appear like that out of the shadows."

"Did you notice anything else? Anything peculiar?"

"*Peculiar?*" He stared at Knighton as if he thought he'd gone mad. "The entire episode was peculiar. My God, the bloody thing *glowed* with a hellish light that is impossible to describe. It would have killed me if I had not cried out."

"I understand. Well, you were fortunate, then. If you remember anything else, would you let me know?"

"There was nothing else, I tell you." He lay back against his pillows and closed his eyes, before wiping the beads of sweat off his brow with the linen sleeve of his nightshirt.

"Thank you. I appreciate your patience, Lieutenant Fisher. I hope I have not tired you too much."

"No. Just get out."

Knighton complied, humming with tension. Neither Fisher nor Savage had been particularly forthcoming. Time to get the wily Mr. Savage to do some talking.

He found him in his usual comfortable chair in front of the fire. As he had with Lieutenant Fisher, Knighton decided to begin with the innocuous question about attendance at Violet Ruberry's funeral.

"I suppose so," Savage answered in a bored voice. "If the weather holds. I cannot abide funerals in the rain."

"You indicated before that you would inherit from your uncle if your cousin predeceased him. Is that not true?"

"I believe that is tolerably close to my original statement."

"Just how ill was your uncle when you left England?"

"The doctors gave him two weeks. Or so he claimed." Savage smiled. "But he was always known for his contrary nature, and he could very well decide to live quite a while longer out of sheer malice."

"So you really have no way of knowing if your uncle is still alive, or if he died before Violet?"

"Precisely. And as you may imagine, it has been a great deal longer than two weeks since the start of my travels."

Knighton considered this, sure that Savage was still not being entirely honest with him. "Did it occur to you that because of her refusal to grant Fisher a divorce, it is Lieutenant Fisher who may inherit your uncle's estate? Assuming he died before Violet."

Savage's smile broadened. "Naturally."

"Was Fisher aware of your uncle's condition?"

"I can hardly be expected to comment on what Fisher may, or may not, have known. However, I may have mentioned something of that nature when we meet again at the start of this journey."

"But Fisher wanted a divorce."

"So he claimed." Savage nodded. Nothing seemed to shake his annoying air of superiority and deep satisfaction with himself. He studied one nail on his delicate hand. "One, of course, wonders. He would gain nothing if he divorced her. But if my uncle lived up to his physician's prediction, then Cousin Violet inherited. And now, Lieutenant Fisher will profit, since he is still her legal husband, despite her whimsical change of name." He looked up at Knighton. "And I remain an innocent traveler on his way to view the cascades."

"I find it odd you did not recognize your own cousin," Knighton commented.

"It may strike you as odd, but as I mentioned before, I had never met her. Our families were not close. Our parents argued." He frowned with distaste. "Families are not always agreeable, are they?"

"No, I suppose not. However now, if anything were to happen to Fisher—"

"The inheritance would go to his heirs, whoever they may be," Savage finished blandly. "So you see, I cannot profit from my cousin's death. Even if I had recognized who she was."

"Perhaps. It all depends upon whether your uncle remains alive."

"Naturally. However, as there is no immediate way to discover this, we can only trust in the accuracy of his doctors. I believe Lieutenant Fisher is the one who profits." His smile turned malicious. "Perhaps that is why he finds his rest disturbed by ghosts."

"Perhaps so." If guilt over the death of Violet were oppressing Fisher, wouldn't he have recognized the spirit of a woman when he saw it at the foot of his bed? And would she really leave behind the traces of powder that glowed in the dark? "Thank you for your time. I hope the weather remains clear for the funeral."

"I am sure I cannot claim to care one way or the other." Savage shrugged and turned back to contemplate the dying flames of the fire smoldering in front of him.

Thinking through his conversations with Fisher and Savage, Knighton left the parlor and nearly ran into Hethering as he was coming down the stairs.

"What ho!" Hethering called, looking well-rested and in a remarkably good mood. "I don't suppose anyone thought to order breakfast?"

"If they did, it has already been eaten, and the dishes cleared away."

"Well then, order another. 'Tis a fine day, and this autumn air enlarges a man's appetite, does it not?" He strolled over to the bar and knocked briskly enough to bring Fiorella hurrying out of the depths of the inn, wiping her hands on her wrinkled apron.

"What is it?" She scowled at Hethering's smiling face.

"Breakfast, my good woman! And I heard the others stirring, so make it a large one. Miss Demaretti and our darling Captain Marshall shall be down soon, if I am not mistaken. I left Marshall struggling into his boots not less than a minute ago."

"It is nearly the time for the dinner," Fiorella's frown deepened as she glanced first at the staircase and then at Knighton.

"Then bring us dinner. Food, my good woman, of whatever variety, is what we require."

Muttering under her breath and casting black looks over her shoulder at Hethering, Fiorella walked back into the shadows from whence she had come.

"One assumes she will return with our viands," Hethering commented. "Shall we retire to our elegant dining room?"

"You are in a good mood this morning." Knighton waved him forward.

"Why not? It is a beautiful day, and with the good major here to investigate, we shall soon be on our way."

"In a few days. Mrs. Ruberry's funeral is today, and there is still the matter of her death to be investigated."

"But that is resolved, is it not? Maggiore Lupino indicated last night that he anticipated an arrest soon. That ruffian who attacked us on the road—terrible, of course—but these things happen."

216

"It seems that conclusion may be a trifle hasty."

"Hasty? No, no. I am sure he is correct. The matter is resolved, and as soon as Charron manages to get the carriage wheel replaced, we shall be on our way. You will see."

"No doubt I will." Knighton had pulled out the wooden chair at the head of the table in preparation to sit, when a woman called his name. He glanced at the doorway.

"Mr. Gaunt?" Domenica asked. "The Contessa wishes to speak with your wife, if you please."

Unwilling to publicize his wife's kidnapping, he strode to the door and gently eased Domenica into the hallway. "She is not here."

"Not here?" Her brows rose in a surprisingly haughty expression for a maid. "Then where is she?"

"As I said, she is not here."

"This is not right." She bit her lip, hesitating before giving one sharp nod to herself. "Then you will come. Follow, please."

So much for breakfast. Knighton cast one last, longing glance at the parlor before climbing the stairs, his eyes fixed on Domenica's rigid back. When they reached the contessa's room, the maid knocked once and then pushed the door open. She stood to the side to allow Knighton to enter first.

The contessa sat in an ornate chair in the center of the room, her sharp black eyes fixed on the door. When she saw Knighton, her gaze went past him briefly and then focused sharply on his face.

"What is she? Where is Mrs. Gaunt?"

"I am afraid she is unavailable at the moment."

"Unavailable?" The contessa rapped her ebony cane on the floor once in a gesture of frustration. "Where is she?"

"May I assist you in her stead?"

"No you may not! Where is your wife? I will see her. Now."

"I am sorry, but she is not here."

"You make no sense. Where else would she be? I must speak to her. She will tell me the truth." She waved at her maid, who stood silently by the door. The contessa's black eyes were hard with anger, and the lines of her face deepened around her mouth and eyes. "That one lies."

"I did not lie." Domenica stepped forward. "I only say what I hear. That Maggiore Lupino, he says he shot the English lady and will hang—I swear it!"

"How could he? Why should Pasquino shoot this English person? It is incomprehensible." She studied Knighton before raising her cane and pointing it at him. "You—you will tell me the truth. Who does that fool Lupino accuse?"

"He believes a local bandito was involved—" As he glanced from the maid to the contessa, he began to get some very peculiar notions.

"Bandito? Ha!" the contessa interrupted. "He is an idiot—this bandito exists only in his imagination. He is a fool to believe so. Your wife—she would know this. She is not such a fool. I wish to speak to her—now!"

He struggled with the strong desire to tell the contessa that the bandito did exist and in fact had kidnapped his wife. "He has reasons for believing as he does. We were stopped by a bandito along the road, and he shot one of our party."

"I heard of this." A cruel smile curved her mouth. "It is not as you paint it, however. Your wife—" She stopped suddenly and examined his face before looking quickly at Domenica. "I see. I ask, and tell me the truth, where is your wife?"

"The bandito kidnapped her."

"Kidnapped? Why? Why would he do this thing?"

"He wishes me to prove his innocence."

"Ha! You see? Lupino is an idiot, and Pasquino knows better than to do such a thing."

"Pasquino?" Knighton asked, although he believed he knew the answer already.

"Capitano Pasquino Nacchio." She placed both of her hands over the silver knob of her cane and stared past Knighton's shoulder, a thoughtful expression on her ancient, but compelling, face. "Of course. What else? But he should never have done such a thing. He knows this. We will go. Domenica, my cape." She stared at Knighton. "You will arrange the carriage and my chair. We go."

"Go? I will assist you in any way I can, but I don't understand. Where do you wish to go?"

"Why, to get your wife. Where else would we go?"

"How?" He glanced from the contessa's implacable face to Domenica. The maid shook her head. "Why would he agree to release her? I have not completed my investigation."

"No matter. He will do as I say. Arrange the wagon and my chair. You will need another man to assist you. It is not far from the road to the estate, but you and one other must carry my chair. Do you understand?"

Surprisingly, he did. "I will have the wagon ready. Do you need assistance on the stairs?"

"No. Domenica will do. Go." She rose from her chair, her back still straight despite her age. Although her hands shook, she held her chin high as she watched Knighton go to do her bidding.

Downstairs, he gave orders to prepare the wagon and the contessa's sedan chair, grabbed a lukewarm cup of milky coffee, which he gulped down in between cutting open a few buns and filling them with cheese. He managed to wrap the filled buns in napkins and place them in his pocket as he convinced Hethering to accompany him on a brief expedition.

"Where?" Hethering asked again as Knighton shoved a paper-thin piece of prosciutto into his mouth.

He chewed and swallowed before answering, "We are going to take the contessa to visit Capitano Nacchio."

"Why on earth should we do that?" Hethering looked aghast at the notion. His eyes widened. One nervous hand ran through the lock of white hair above his left brow.

"I have not got the slightest notion," Knighton said blithely. He wasn't going to explain his odd ideas to Hethering and find that he was completely wrong. "However, it may prove to be interesting and will give us both something to do until the funeral this afternoon."

"Very well. At least it is a pleasant day for an excursion."

The rattling sound of the wagon caught Knighton's attention just as he heard the hesitant steps of the contessa on the stairs. He hurried out of the parlor and climbed partway up the staircase to assist. The contessa frowned at him and continually shook off his hand when he tried to help her descend. All he could do was stay ahead of her and hope he could catch her if she fell.

Within a few minutes, they stood next to the vehicle, with the contessa's sedan chair wedged into the wagon's bed behind the seat. The litter was not much more than a chair mounted between two poles, so there was room for the others, although they might find it uncomfortable as the sedan chair's poles made it difficult to find a place to sit.

The contessa nodded at Hethering, obviously approving of him as the second man, and with Domenica's strong arm, she climbed unsteadily into the wagon's bench. Knighton climbed up beside her and picked up the reins, leaving Hethering and Domenica to scramble into the back and arrange themselves as best they could between the chair's poles.

The trip to the narrow path was brief, and the contessa seemed ill-inclined to talk as they rattled over the rutted road. She wore an abstracted expression, although a slight frown of worry deepened the wrinkles of her forehead beneath the brim of her surprisingly fashionable bonnet. When they reached the path, Knighton and Domenica assisted the contessa to dismount from the wagon and seat herself in the sedan chair. Knighton went to the front of the litter to stand between the poles and waited for Hethering to position himself in the rear.

The contessa did not weigh much, but the sedan chair was awkward. Several times, they had to back up and move forward in a series of spurts to ease the long poles around bends in the path. Both men were sweating and slightly out of breath when they finally arrived at the bleak, iron-studded door. In broad daylight, the stone building appeared even more derelict, with thick vines running up the walls and grass-like plants growing here and there in cracks between the stones.

The contessa did not wait for one of the men to knock. She walked determinedly to the front door and beat on it with the silver knob of her cane. A deep baying answered, and although Hethering stepped back a yard at the noise, it did not appear to trouble the contessa in the least.

After a minute, Nacchio flung open the door with a curse. When he saw the contessa, her cane raised in readiness to batter the door again, his eyes widened.

"Mother! What are you doing here?" He glanced from her to Knighton and Hethering. The look of stupefaction on his face deepened.

Knighton stared at Nacchio and then the contessa. *Son?* A great many odd facts suddenly seemed to make sense. It certainly explained why the contessa was staying at such a poor and uninviting inn.

"What are *we* doing here? You may well ask, Pasquino." She pushed past her son. "Where is Mrs. Gaunt?"

"Mrs. Gaunt?" Nacchio repeated, apparently still staggered by his mother's abrupt arrival. "Uh..." He flicked a quick glance at Knighton.

Knighton smiled blandly. He heard the soft scrap of a footstep behind him and out of the corner of his eye, he noticed Domenica entering. Nacchio's gaze went to the maid and lingered for a moment, his expression unreadable.

The contessa whirled around. *"Cretino*! Where is she? You disgrace us all with the nonsense—why have you done this thing?"

Nacchio flicked another uncomfortable glance at Knighton and strode forward to place a hand on his mother's forearm. "Mama, *per favore*, this is business—"

"Business? What business? Are you now to be a kidnapper? Is this to be your business now? How can you dishonor your mother this way? Your family? Does our name mean nothing to you?"

"It was necessary. I have been accused of the English woman's murder—"

"And this will prove you innocent? *Cretino!* This will prove nothing but that you are a fool. A man who would kidnap a woman would not stop at murder—you make yourself look guilty, no matter the truth." She shook off his hand and lifted her cane to prod his chest with the knob for emphasis. "You will release her. Now. And no more of this foolishness. Do you understand?"

"*Si.*" Nacchio rubbed his face wearily and walked over to the locked door. With a long suffering sigh, he removed the heavy wooden bar.

"Pru?" Knighton called when she did not immediately step into the hallway. His pulse quickened. Had something happened to her? The baby?

There was a whine and snuffling noise before she finally walked into view. She had changed into the blue dress he had brought, but her hair was still hanging down her back in a long dark braid. The gray mastiff pressed against her side, and when the beast saw the contessa, it wagged its tail.

"You and your dogs," the contessa remarked in a chiding voice, although she reached out and stroked the dog's massive, square head.

Before her son could respond, the front door creaked open wider. "Ah, so you have come to rescue your wife, Mr. Gaunt," Maggiore Lupino said. "And so perhaps you will now agree. I do not wait on the road any longer or seek permission. Capitano Nacchio, I am here to arrest you—"

"Arrest? You will do nothing of the sort, Maggiore Lupino." The contessa confronted him. "It is absurd. You have no reason to arrest my son, and I will not have it. The feud between the two of you grows old. It must end. We still have some influence, and you are trespassing. Do you wish to lose your position? You cannot do such a ridiculous thing—what grounds do you have?"

Lupino nodded at Knighton. "Signor Gaunt must agree and will support me. There is the murder of the English lady and now, Capitano Nacchio has kidnapped this lady. That is surely enough."

"Kidnapped?" The contessa's chin rose. She leaned forward, bracing both hands on the end of her cane. "There has been no kidnapping."

"No? I am sure Signor Gaunt and his wife may have another opinion on this matter. Well, Signor Gaunt? What is your answer?" Lupino faced him, a confident gleam in his eyes.

Knighton caught the contessa's glance. In the depths of her dark eyes, he thought he detected pleading and a terrible fear. "I beg differ with you, Maggiore Lupino. I am afraid you have mistaken my wife's impulsive," he flicked an apologetic look at his wife, "visit. We have been hoping to find a dog—a mastiff—and Capitano Nacchio kindly invited my wife here to see this one."

"Ah, then you like the creature," the contessa said quickly. "This is good. You will take him. He is a good animal, he will protect your wife."

"But—" Nacchio stared at his mother, blinked, and eyed Pru before falling silent.

Pru's mouth opened and shut in astonishment. She looked at Nacchio and then Knighton. "But surely, I mean, Capitano Nacchio would never wish to lose such a valuable dog. We cannot possibly take him."

The contessa shrugged elaborately as if she had no interest in the matter. A slightly malicious smile flickered over her thin lips, however, as she looked at her son and then Pru, before she caressed the mastiff's wide head again. "My son has many dogs, and will have many more. You will take this one as a gift." Apparently, she thought that the loss of his dog was his just deserts after forcing her to take a hand in matters and prevent the possibility of his arrest and the ensuing scandal.

"But—" Pru glanced at Knighton.

Feeling almost as overwhelmed as his wife looked, he nodded. He was the one who mentioned dogs, so he could hardly blame the contessa for leaping upon his suggestion so readily. "We are grateful, Contessa. Thank you."

"*Prego*. It is settled." The contessa stared at Lupino as if daring him to argue. "You see? There is no reason for you to speak of arresting anyone. And you trespass. We may see *you* arrested, instead." She let out a long, wheezing breath and seemed to sag slightly.

Her son quickly put an arm around her waist. "You are tired. You should not have come. The trip was too long." He glanced around distractedly, a frown burrowing between his eyebrows. "You will stay the night here."

"No." She touched her son's cheek in a loving gesture and smiled. "Another time, perhaps, when the house is more as it was. For now, we must go." Her son bent closer, and they had a brief, whispered conversation.

When Nacchio straightened, he wore a resigned look that emphasized the dark circles under his eyes and general air of weariness. However, he had enough energy to give them all a charming smile as he gently ushered them down the hallway.

Domenica waited silently next to the contessa and took her arm to assist when the elderly lady moved, her heels and cane clicking unevenly over the marble floor. As they walked forward, Domenica cast a surprisingly coy glance at Nacchio over the contessa's head. Nacchio smiled at her, his eyes sparkling.

Knighton observed the interplay, wondering. Nacchio did not seem to be the sort of man to seduce his mother's maid, but then, how well did he know either of them?

"There is still the murder," Lupino objected as the contessa brushed past him. "Nacchio is responsible for the death of the English lady."

Nacchio took a step forward, hands fisted.

Knighton stepped between the two men and held up his hands. A fight now would help no one.

Smiling, he patted Lupino on the shoulder and gently encouraged him to move away from the door. "There may be evidence otherwise. You are too wise to act so precipitously, Maggiore Lupino. If you could spare some of your time when we return to the inn, I would be honored to offer what little I have discovered. If, after you have considered everything, you wish to take Capitano Nacchio into custody, you may do so tomorrow."

"Today—" Lupino frowned as they walked down the path.

"Tomorrow. Come, you may ride in the wagon."

"I have a horse," Lupino said with an air of superiority as he eyed their conveyance.

"We should make haste. I wish to change, and there is the funeral," Pru reminded him as she waited next to the wagon. "We cannot be late."

Hethering, who had remained silent during the entire episode, dusted his hands off after carrying the contessa's sedan chair back to the vehicle and stepped aside. "I believe I will walk." He eyed the dog uneasily and kept well away from the animal.

"Perhaps you would be good enough to drive the wagon back to the inn? My wife and I shall follow with, uh, Cabò." Knighton suggested. He wasn't quite sure he really wanted the mastiff, currently dampening his wife's skirts by drooling on her as it stared up at her with adoring eyes. But he wasn't entirely averse to the notion of having a dog.

At least the animal seemed willing to protect her when Knighton wasn't present.

The notion made his jaw tighten in frustration. He should have been protected her instead of allowing an elderly lady obtain her release.

Hethering dithered a few minutes as he watched Lupino mount the horse he had left in the shade of one of the trees near the path. He finally nodded. "Very well. Have a pleasant walk."

The wagon rattled off, the sedan chair swaying in the back, and Domenica holding onto the chair as if she feared the entire thing would topple over the side of the wagon and take her with it. The plodding horses did not move swiftly, and Hethering kept them at a sedate walk, ensuring that they stayed within sight of Knighton and Pru whether he intended it or not. Lupino, on the other hand, kicked the sides of his sleek brown horse and rode ahead, passing the conveyance with a frown marring his face.

"Are you really unharmed?" Knighton asked after they had walked for a while.

Pru laughed. "Yes, indeed. Cabò made sure of that." She flung a searching glance at him, the corners of her mouth turned down. "Are you—are you terribly angry about the dog?"

"Angry?" He faltered, tripping over a loose rock in the road. "Why should I be angry?"

"Well, he is a terribly big dog, and it may make traveling a bit difficult."

"Nonsense. I have no objection to him if you do not. Are you pleased with him?"

"Oh, yes," she replied warmly, her hold on his arm tightening. "He was splendid company and is so gentle. Really, I am rather glad to keep him."

"Then we shall." He paused to reach around her and pet the dog.

The animal suffered his caress and gave one, brief wag of the tail, but it was clear the dog thought of itself as Pru's companion. Despite a twinge of jealousy, Knighton was glad to see the mastiff's devotion. As an inquiry agent, Knighton was frequently forced to travel, and he hated to think of leaving his wife alone. He had been brooding about it during the course of their honeymoon and had not been able to come up with a satisfactory solution. If she had Cabò at her side, he need not worry so much about her safety.

And he liked the dog.

The fact was, he had always liked dogs, but had been disinclined to have one when he was away from home so frequently. So Pru simply served as an excuse to obtain the dog he had always wanted.

"Do you really think Capitano Nacchio is innocent?" she asked as the wagon up ahead disappeared around the last bend in the road, where the church stood.

"Yes, I do." A sense of surprise at the certainty of his words hit him. He truly did believe Nacchio was innocent of Mrs. Ruberry's murder.

Sadly, he felt the murderer would be a member of their small group. He had a notion, still as nebulous as a shape seen through the smoke of a smoldering fire, as to whom it might be.

"It is one of us, is it not?" Pru sounded as unhappy about the idea as he felt.

"I am afraid it might be."

"Do you know who?"

"Perhaps."

"Oh, don't tell me," she replied in a rush. "I don't want to go to Mrs. Ruberry's funeral thinking that one of us murdered her." She gazed up at him, a pleading look in her dark gray eyes.

He pressed his hand over hers where it lay in the crook of his arm. "Never fear. I do not plan on accusing anyone, yet."

By the time they arrived at the inn, the occupants of the wagon had already disappeared inside, and the stable boy was busy leading the horses through the arch into the stable yard. The Gaunts had to hurry to change into clothes suitable for a funeral, and by the time they descended from their room, the others were waiting for them in their allotted parlor.

The funeral was long and depressing. Their small party occupied only a few stalls in the tiny church, and the echoing space behind them seemed to emphasize the fact that Mrs. Ruberry was far from home and not a particularly beloved woman. No one displayed any grief at her passing. In fact, the best that could be said was that no one actually yawned during the service, although many of those who attended were clearly bored and had to sit rigidly to avoid betraying their restlessness.

The circumstances were so sad that at the end of the services, Pru was dabbing the corner of her eye with her handkerchief. Knighton pressed her hand silently, strangely glad to see the evidence of her tender heart. No one else might mourn the English lady who had died so far from home but Pru, at least, showed understanding and sympathy. It reminded him forcefully of why he had married her. She truly was the heart of their marriage.

By the time they returned to the inn, the sun was setting, and Knighton was once again running through the clues in his mind.

A bit of paper used as wadding, a spent and deformed lead ball, a borrowed cloak, and a body moved from the churchyard to the hillside. They didn't amount to much, and yet they pointed to one of them as a murderer.

Knighton had a handful of suspects with motives, and though he was loathe to point at the one he felt had committed the act without more proof, he could feel time running short.

Someone would have to pay. And soon.

Chapter Nineteen

Despite the cheerful weather of the morning, by the time they left the churchyard, the skies had darkened. A chill wind swirled around the corners of the church and tossed brown, dead leaves into the air. A crack of thunder and the following lance of lightning gave them only a few seconds of warning. They quickened their pace, but the black sky opened up. A deluge of icy water sluiced down upon their hurrying party.

Water trickled down Knighton's neck and quickly saturated his coat. Pru was no better off, and her dark bonnet wilted soggily over her head. The road rapidly turned to mud and splashed over their shoes and stockings. Pru's sodden hem slapped Knighton's shins with every step.

Hethering reached the inn's door first and held it open for the others, smiling cheerfully, despite the water dripping off his eyelashes and nose. Catherine and Marshall arrived next. The two men tussled briefly over holding the door for the young woman. Displaying his magnanimity with a flourish, Hethering slapped Marshall on the back, only to have Marshall shove him with his elbow.

Despite Marshall's maneuver, Hethering entered the inn in front of him, leaving the younger man to hold the door while Hethering escorted Catherine to the warmth of the fire in the parlor. Marshall watched the two disappear together with a frown of aggravation wrinkling his brow and water dripping off his eyebrows.

By the time the rest of them dashed past him into the inn, they were thoroughly miserable and hunched over from the chilly weight of their drenched clothing. Steam from the heat of their bodies condensing in the icy air rose from their shoulders, and the room soon smelled unpleasantly of wet wool and earthy mud.

Buonfiglio took one look and danced around them, trying to keep them from dripping water and mud on any of his worn rugs. He called the maid, Celestina, sharply,

Amy Corwin

"Towels! Celestina, come at once. Take these wet jackets—gentlemen and ladies—please give Celestina your coats." He mopped ineffectually with an old rag at the entryway where a small river was rapidly forming.

"*Si, si.*" Celestina began collecting sopping wet cloaks and jackets, clucking like a worried hen as she did so. When she reached Pru, she flushed and fixed her gaze on the floor.

Pru shook her head and handed her cloak to the maid in silence.

Divested of his coat, Knighton escorted Pru upstairs to change, considering how best to convince Lupino to abandon his persecution of Nacchio. Despite the villain's recent actions, Knighton was convinced he had not been involved in Mrs. Ruberry's death. There was no reason for him to both shoot her and throw her down the hillside. That action could only be explained one way: someone had tried to shift the blame to Nacchio. Or possibly hoped the body would never be found. In either event, Nacchio would not have bothered to move her. If he had met her in the churchyard and murdered her, she would have been found there.

Nacchio was intelligent enough to realize that moving the body to the hillside would make him appear guilty.

Once or twice, Lupino almost made Knighton wonder if the major would kill someone simply to be able to accuse Nacchio of murder. The notion was ridiculous as Lupino had only arrived after the unfortunate incident, but it remained strangely appealing. The fact that the idea even occurred to Knighton was proof of his concern that Lupino was not as uninterested and fair as he should have been. The major's prejudice made Knighton's task more difficult. He had to prove who had done the foul deed in a way that would leave no doubts.

He was surprised when Pru refrained from asking him about the progress of the inquiry, however it did not take him long to realize that she was preoccupied with other things. At one point, he caught her gaze and almost brought up the subject of children. The thought that he should wait for her to bring it up of her own accord stayed him. She would raise the issue when she was ready. He just hoped the notion filled her with as much joy as it had him.

Knighton and Pru were among the last to arrive in the parlor, and he was happy to see that Celestina had set a huge tureen on the table. The dish contained a thick, savory soup with hearty chunks of meat and green kale. They each took bowls and went to sit at the table, which someone had moved closer to the fire.

Despite the excellent food and two hearty loaves of bread, a somber mood settled over the group. Hethering tried to enliven the group by bringing out a deck of cards. Neither Pru nor Catherine were interested in playing. The men indulged in a few hands of commerce, but the play was uneven, and no one seemed particularly riveted by the game.

By ten o'clock, several people were stifling yawns and glancing at the clock on the mantle every few minutes.

"I believe I will retire." Pru stood and gave Mrs. Ursini and Catherine a meaningful look.

Mrs. Ursini got to her feet quickly and tapped Catherine on the shoulder. "Come, signorina. We shall retire as well."

"But it is not even ten yet." Catherine's lower lip protruded. She glanced at Captain Marshall. "It is too early—I shall never sleep." A flicker of hope lit her eyes. "I would like to take a walk—it stopped raining an hour ago. Perhaps the captain will escort me?"

"No, signorina. It is too cold and damp. You will certainly become ill if you go walking now. We will go, and you will sleep, I assure you." Mrs. Ursini rested a plump hand on the girl's shoulder, despite Catherine's frown and attempt to twitch away from her touch. "You may walk with your capitano tomorrow."

Captain Marshall bowed and smiled good-humoredly. "Indeed, tomorrow will be much better."

"If you are still here," Maggiore Lupino interrupted. He had taken a seat in a shadowy corner after the funeral and had spent the hours since studying each of them with his usual air of arrogant cynicism. "I took the liberty of speaking with Signor Charron. The wheel has been repaired, and there is no reason to remain."

Catherine and Marshall exchanged glances that didn't seem particularly happy at the prospect of departing. Knighton studied them. Matters seemed to be slipping at a faster pace through his fingers. The only reason for Lupino to suggest they leave was to terminate Knighton's inquiry and arrest Nacchio, as he seemed so determined to do.

"I am glad the carriage is repaired," Pru said, sliding her hand around Knighton's elbow.

Before she could continue, Hethering rose, collected his playing cards, and tucked them into his pocket. "Indeed it is. You must have identified the villain, then."

"*Si.*" Lupino smiled grimly. "And tomorrow, he will be arrested."

"Good news, sir, very good news." Hethering rubbed his hands together in front of the fire. "A relief to everyone, I am sure."

"*Si*, a relief. Now you may continue with your travels. Everyone is pleased, *si?*"

"That is a terrible thing to say!" Pru rounded on him, pulling at Knighton's arm as she turned. Her pale face flushed with anger. "No one can possibly be *pleased* by the situation."

Mrs. Ursini also frowned at Lupino. In a spate of nearly unintelligible Italian, she let him know her opinion of men who had no sense of decorum or manners in the face of a terrible tragedy such as the one that had overtaken poor Mrs. Ruberry. Her virulent reprimands made even Lupino turn pale. He fixed his gaze on the toes of his boots and could barely glance at the small woman as she pointed out each and every one of his failings in luxurious detail.

"I apologize, *si*. I was, perhaps, hasty," Lupino mumbled as Mrs. Ursini began to wind down. "Of course, I shall ensure I do not arrest an innocent man—all things shall be done properly." He looked around, appearing a trifle helpless and overwhelmed. "And now I, too, shall retire." He nodded at the ladies and strode rapidly toward the door with the desperate air of a man escaping from an uncomfortable situation.

Unfortunately, he did not quite make it to the stairs. Celestina bumped into him as he dashed through the doorway. The pile of cloaks and coats she had in her arms, dried and freshly ironed, fell to the floor, blocking Lupino's path.

"Oh, signore, look what you have done!" Celestina exclaimed, her words rising in a shrill wail. "All my work..."

He swore impatiently and bent to assist her in picking up the garments that still smelled of the hot iron she had used to smooth out the wrinkles. When he straightened, he had Pru's cloak draped over his left arm and held Marshall's coat in his right hand.

Captain Marshall stepped forward to take his garment, but Lupino seemed to notice something and pulled his arm back. He frowned. Knighton caught a glimpse of the corner of a whitish piece of paper before Lupino extracted it from the pocket and held it up.

"A note—it falls from your pocket, *si*?" Lupino shifted both garments to his left hand to look at the scrap.

The paper was not very big, and one edge had been raggedly torn. A tingle went down the back of Knighton's neck. A few lines of smudged, dark writing scrawled across it, reminding him of something...

He'd seen the other half of that bit of paper. In fact, it was in his wallet.

The paper Lupino held was the other half of the wadding from the bullet that had killed Mrs. Ruberry.

Knighton caught Marshall's gaze. Mild confusion clouded the young man's blue eyes as he looked from the paper to Knighton.

Marshall didn't recognize the scrap of paper or understand its significance.

Or perhaps he simply didn't realize that Knighton had found the piece used as wadding when Mrs. Ruberry was shot. And yet, despite the evidence in Lupino's hand, Knighton could not believe that Marshall was guilty of that crime, even if Ruberry had tried to stand in the way of his courtship of Catherine.

"A bit of paper." Lupino turned the half-note over. "With writing. I have seen this before, have I not? Or the other half." He looked at Knighton. "You have the other half, *si*?"

Knighton extracted his wallet reluctantly. This was a mistake. He sighed. Perhaps Lupino would ultimately ignore the sheet. It would not help his case against Nacchio, after all. He almost handed the small piece of bloodied wadding to Lupino, but at the last minute, he twitched the note from Marshall's pocket out of his hand and walked over to the table. Placing both halves down there was no doubt they belonged together. The ragged edges matched up perfectly, as did the scrawled lines of writing.

The words were relatively unimportant, except to prove that the paper belonged to someone who had ridden in the hired carriage. It was a hasty record of the time and location of the coach's initial departure.

The note did serve to indicate, however, that someone who had ridden in the coach had committed the murder.

"What is it?" Captain Marshall leaned over Knighton's shoulder to peer curiously at the papers.

Knighton stretched out one long finger and placed it on the bloodied remnant. "I found this in Mrs. Ruberry's wound. It is the wadding from the gunshot that killed her."

"But the other piece matches it." Marshall stared at him, his face growing pale. "Maggiore Lupino said it was in my pocket. How is that possible?"

"One would suppose it is possible if you are the one who shot the poor English lady." Lupino grinned wolfishly at him, apparently pleased despite the fact that it proved that someone other than his nemesis, Capitano Nacchio, had committed murder.

Marshall gripped Knighton's sleeve. "That cannot be! How could that be in my pocket? I did not kill her—I swear it! It could not have been in my pocket, it simply could not have been there."

"And yet I, myself, removed it from there," Lupino replied softly. "You saw me do so, as did the rest of you."

"Mr. Gaunt, I beseech you! You know I did not do this thing. How could I? I love Miss Demaretti. I would never do anything to harm her, or her chaperone." Marshall's grip on his sleeve tightened.

When he glanced around, Knighton noted Savage studying them with a small, complaisant smile on his face.

Hethering watched them all with undisguised curiosity as he rubbed his hands together in front of the fire.

Knighton shook Marshall's hand off his arm and brushed his sleeve thoughtfully. "I understand your feelings, Captain Marshall. However, the presence of this scrap is awkward, to say the least. Have you any explanation for it?"

"I don't understand." Marshall threaded a shaking hand through his blond hair. "I have no explanation. How could I? I was not even aware that it was in my pocket."

Catherine ran to his side and wrapped her hands around his arm, holding him tightly as she flicked a haughty, angry glance at Knighton. "Any fool can see Fred—Captain Marshall—is innocent. He would never do such a thing, as you would know if you had the least bit of sense."

"Miss Demaretti!" Mrs. Ursini exclaimed in a shocked voice. "Do not say such things to Signor Gaunt. He only remarks upon what we can all see."

"Then you are a fool as well," Catherine berated her in a shrill voice. "He did not do it, I tell you. You must believe me." Tears suddenly welled up in her terrified eyes and cascaded over her plump cheeks as she looked at Knighton. "Please believe us. He is innocent. You must find someone else—someone else placed that piece of paper in his pocket. It is obvious. Someone intended him to be blamed for the murder." Her chin tilted up in pretend confidence, despite the quiver in her lower lip and her shaking voice.

"You are soft-hearted, signorina," Lupino said. He nodded at Mrs. Ursini and gestured toward the door. "Too innocent to be involved in such matters. Go with Mrs. Ursini and leave this to us. Be assured that you are young and shall soon forget your tears when you arrive in Rome. No one can remain sad in such a city, *si*? You will soon have many new suitors."

"No! I shall never forget him—never! And I will not leave his side until you admit Captain Marshall is innocent." She flung the words at him and stamped her foot. Her grip on Marshall's arm did not loosen, despite her response to Lupino. It was as if she feared that Marshall would disappear forever if she let go.

"Then I am sorry, but I must do what is necessary. I must most assuredly arrest Capitano Marshall for the murder of your English lady, Signora Ruberry."

Chapter Twenty

"Please, Mr. Gaunt, you must do something," Catherine pleaded, refusing to relinquish her hold on Captain Marshall's sleeve. "You cannot let him arrest Frederick—you simply cannot! He is innocent."

"Knighton?" Pru asked softly, gazing up at him with troubled eyes. She was clearly unconvinced that Marshall was guilty and upset by Lupino's decision.

As if sensing her distress, Cabò pushed his head under Pru's hand and leaned against her briefly before lying down with his head on her feet.

Knighton gave his wife a brief smile before stepping forward. "Are you sure you have never seen that paper before, Captain Marshall?"

"Absolutely certain. I have a digest containing the coach's timetable. I had no reason to make note of it." He seemed to struggle to maintain an air of calm confidence in the face of the accusation. He patted Catherine's hand and then pressed it against his forearm, unwilling, or unable, to release her. Perhaps her touch gave him courage.

Regardless, his words were logical. Most travelers owned such pocket guides because they included distances and places of interest along various roads. Knighton had one, himself.

"Maggiore Lupino, we would be remiss if we did not collect one more piece of evidence before making any accusations," Knighton said.

"What evidence is that, signore?" For once, Lupino did not seem to be in any rush to drag someone away to meet justice. Perhaps because he had no personal argument with Marshall.

How best to prove what he suspected was true without causing further subterfuge? Or worse, provoking some sort of violence that could very well harm one of the ladies.

That question had made him procrastinate for the last few hours, despite his conviction that he knew who was responsible for Mrs. Ruberry's death, and why.

Well, the time for delay was over.

"I would appreciate it if we could collect any weapons, as well as their cases, that the members of our party brought with them," Knighton said. "Simply to ensure the safety of the ladies."

"Ah, *si*." Lupino nodded. "A man who sees his doom on the horizon will take any risk. Very wise. Then we shall seek this additional evidence you mention, *si*?"

"Yes," Knighton agreed. "I will, of course, bring my own set of dueling pistols and case down."

The other men eyed him, most of them appearing more confused than concerned.

Captain Marshall, with the air of a man flinging off the last rope and casting his fate upon the waves, pried Catherine's hand off his arm. "I will bring my pair down." Without waiting for a reply, he strode through the parlor doorway, and they heard his loud footsteps as he began to climb the stairs.

Scowling, Fisher trudged to the stairs without comment and disappeared in search of his weapons. After a shrug, Hethering agreed and followed Fisher and Marshall.

"I hate to disappoint you, Mr. Gaunt, but I do not have any such weapons," Savage said. He remained in his cozy chair, sipping a glass of wine, and generally appearing cooperative, as long as that meant he need not exert himself unduly.

"Excuse me," Knighton said to Lupino. "I must get my own weapons. I will return shortly." He hesitated at the doorway. "You may wish to watch the doors—just to ensure no one decides to go for a walk."

Lupino grinned and stroked his luxurious mustache. "*Si*. Already I observe the doors. One never knows, *si*?"

"Yes. Indeed." Knighton laughed and ascended the staircase, the excitement of finally spotting the quarry, and beginning the chase in earnest, tightening the muscles in his shoulders and chest.

He picked up the case containing his pair of dueling pistols and returned to the parlor, arriving a few minutes after Hethering and Marshall, but before Fisher.

"I fail to see the point of this," Marshall complained as he placed his worn, battered box on the table. "You have my word that I did not harm anyone and will not. Why collect our pistols?"

Hethering placed his much more elegant, two-foot long case down next to Marshall's, a slight frown forming a V over the bridge of his nose. "Indeed. You would think our word is insufficient guarantee of good behavior. Surely you realize that none of us is quite so crude as to brandish a firearm and leap upon our delightful maggiore, no matter the provocation."

"I agree," Fisher interjected.

His face twisted in pain as he threw his box onto the table with one hand and staggered over to one of the chairs. He sat down heavily and stared angrily at Knighton. His gray skin and the white ring around his mouth indicated the effort it took for him to bring his weapons down the stairs.

Knighton shifted uncomfortably. There had been no better way to obtain the information he needed. Searching the individual rooms would have met with even more vehement protests and anger and would have left them open to deception.

"I apologize, gentlemen, but it was necessary." He glanced at Lupino.

The major quickly agreed, although there was curiosity and doubt in his brown eyes. He already had two men that he could comfortably arrest and no doubt, he felt this was sufficient choice.

"Would you open your case, Captain Marshall? I merely wish to ensure that both pistols are inside."

"Oh, very well." Marshall flung open the case abruptly.

Two much-used dueling pistols lay inside, along with all their accoutrements, including several screwdrivers, pliers, flask and mold to make bullets, and a handful of bullets. The pistols had plain brown, unadorned wooden grips, with no elegant scrollwork or decoration anywhere. They were utilitarian and deadly.

Knighton picked up one of the smooth, lead balls, turning it over in his fingers. The bullet was .52 caliber, slightly larger than the .50 caliber bullet he had discovered in the churchyard.

He dropped the ball back into the case and nodded to Fisher. "If you don't mind, Lieutenant, would you open your box as well?"

"Frankly, I would rather not. You may take my word for it, the entire set is there." His lip curled into a sneer. "I have not hidden one upon my person."

"I will open it for you," Maggiore Lupino offered with a slight bow. "You need not disturb yourself."

"You will do nothing of the sort!" Fisher started to rise. Halfway to his feet, he sucked in a sharp breath and sat down again abruptly. His face paled further as he pressed a hand against his side.

With a glance of dismay at Knighton, Pru rushed to Fisher's side with Cabò following at her heels. "Did you harm yourself? You have not reopened your wound, have you?"

Fisher shook her off with a black look. "Leave me in peace. My health is no business of yours, or your husband's." He stared past her. "And you will kindly keep your hands off of my belongings. I brought the case down and gave you my word that I am unarmed. That should be more than sufficient for you, particularly since it is obvious to all of us that it is Captain Marshall who murdered Violet. He had the paper in his pocket that matched the wadding. What more do you want?"

Maggiore Lupino grinned and laughed briefly. "It is sufficient for me, I think, but there is no harm in looking at these pistols, *si*?"

"If you are examining them to see if they have been fired recently then anyone but a fool would know that mine were fired. I shot at that blasted ruffian, and Gaunt knows it as well as I," Fisher said, his voice rising. His right hand gripped the arm of his chair, the knuckles standing out whitely. He was clearly insulted past bearing.

Or frightened.

Despite the lieutenant's vehement objections, Lupino calmly opened the case. As Fisher said, both pistols were present, along with all the paraphernalia required for their maintenance and use.

There were no spare bullets in the case. Knighton picked up the mold and examined its interior surfaces. "Have you any bullets?"

"I doubt it." Fisher shifted uncomfortably in his chair, pressing his hand against his side. He breathed in shallow gasps. "I believe I may have used the last one on the road."

The inside of the mold was clean and free of blemishes, but it appeared to be of the same caliber as the bullet that had killed Mrs. Ruberry. As Knighton was fitting the mold back into its compartment, something rattled in the box. He picked up one side and tilted it slightly. A lead ball tumbled into view.

He retrieved it and weighed it in the palm of his hand. It was a .50 caliber—the same as the bullet that had killed Mrs. Ruberry. He studied it for a minute and then placed it in the corner of the case's lid.

When he looked up, Lupino was opening Knighton's case. The pistols inside were nearly as plain as the ones in Marshall's case, but they had an elegant, well-crafted appearance that was hard to match. The weapons had never been fired, except in practice, and Knighton was unreasonably proud of the set fashioned by the famous

Durs Egg and given to him by his wife as an unexpected gift after their marriage.

Even Lupino seemed impressed. He let out a long, soft whistle and held one of the pistols in his hand, turning it this way and that to inspect it. "Very nice, Signor Gaunt. I would not mind such a pair." The weapon also used .50 caliber bullets, but was well-cleaned and had obviously not been fired recently.

"Yes, I am rather fond of them, myself." Knighton caught Pru's gaze and winked.

The tension in the room was palpable, although it seemed to emanate mostly from Fisher. Savage watched them all with a disinterested expression from his comfortable chair while Marshall, standing near Catherine with his hand pressed lightly against her back, simply appeared puzzled. Hethering stood near the table, watching Lupino and Knighton with an affable and mildly curious expression on his face.

"Mr. Hethering, would you care to open your case?" Knighton asked.

"Certainly, though I cannot help but wonder why." Hethering pulled out a gold chain from a waistcoat pocket and produced a key. He fumbled with the lock, but eventually lifted the lid on the case.

A beautiful set of dueling pistols, some of Manton's most elegant work, lay within.

Seeing the weapons, Lupino almost threw Knighton's pistol back into its compartment and picked up one of Hethering's. "Magnificent!" He held the weapon at arm's length toward the window as if aiming it. "Not, of course, as beautiful as one of our Italian dueling pistols, but still—magnificent. *Si?*"

Knighton picked up the bullet mold and examined it before selecting one of the bullets.

After a moment, he faced Hethering. "Do you always keep your case locked?"

"Yes." Hethering smiled. "It can be awkward if one needs a weapon, but I prefer to keep temptation out of the way of others." He shrugged and held his hands palm upwards. "As it is not precisely a work of the moment to load a flintlock, the delay in unlocking the case hardly matters." He glanced from Knighton to Lupino and then back. Some of the easy good humor seeped out of his face, making him appear older and much harder. His mouth compressed into a thin line. "Say, what is the meaning of this display? I don't believe you did this to ensure no one lost his head and shot one of our companions accidentally."

"You are very astute, Mr. Hethering." Knighton extracted the deformed, spent bullet from his pocket and placed it on the table. "I found this in the churchyard, where Mrs. Ruberry was murdered."

"So she died at the church instead of on the road. What does it matter? Marshall killed her, that is the important point. Why do you not let Maggiore Lupino arrest him and be done with it?" Fisher asked. He ran a shaking hand through his sweat-dampened hair.

If anyone looked guilty, he did.

Marshall scowled and stepped toward him with fisted hands. At the last moment, he seemed to remember that Fisher was already injured, and he stopped. When he glanced around the room, he flushed as if ashamed of his brief loss of control.

"It matters. Whoever moved her, hoped she would either not be found, or that the bandits would be blamed for her death." Knighton picked up the bullet and held it between his index finger and his thumb. "And this bullet is .50 caliber, not the larger .52 caliber used by Captain Marshall's pistols."

"He could shoot a .50 caliber in that gun—that means nothing," Fisher asserted.

Hethering bent closer to study the deformed ball in Knighton's hand. "And you cannot be sure of the caliber. A fragment may have broken off. It may well have been a .52 caliber originally."

"Both of those facts are true," Knighton agreed. "However, one side of the ball is not destroyed, and it presents a curious imperfection. If you look more closely, you will see a small dimple created during the manufacture of the bullet. One of the molds here has such an imperfection, as do the extra bullets made from it." His gaze held Hethering's cold blue eyes. "I am afraid you murdered Mrs. Ruberry, Mr. Hethering."

Hethering blinked and then threw back his head and laughed. "Me? You must be mad. That fragment you hold is no proof of anything, except a vivid imagination. You might just as easily accuse Mr. Savage. He, at least, had ample motive."

Instead of anger, Savage chuckled and shook his head when everyone turned to stare at him. Truth be told, Knighton wouldn't have minded discovering that Mr. Savage had indeed murdered Violet Ruberry. There was something about his complacency that set Knighton's teeth on edge.

"Unfortunately, or rather fortunately for Mr. Savage, he had very little motive to murder Mrs. Ruberry," Knighton pointed out gently.

"What?" Hethering appeared astounded. "Why I daresay everyone is aware by now that Mr. Savage hoped to inherit his uncle's estate, which could only happen if Mrs. Ruberry was dead."

"If she predeceased their uncle," Knighton corrected. "And the illness of their uncle made that highly unlikely."

"Unless he murdered her as soon as possible," Hethering persisted.

Knighton shook his head. "The risk would not be worth it. He had no way of determining if his uncle remained alive. In fact, there was every possibility that their uncle was already dead when Mr. Savage joined the list of passengers. He could not know for certain unless he received word, and the only communication he would be likely to receive would be a notice of his uncle's death. Did you receive such a notice, Mr. Savage?"

"I am sorry to say I have received no word one way or the other. I do not know if my uncle still lives, or if he has succumbed to his illness." Savage studied Knighton with eyes that seemed to hold a grudging respect. "Mr. Gaunt is correct. It would have been foolish of me to risk murdering my cousin, even if I were so inclined after traveling with her for two days. I have no desire to hang, and in the end, I suspect Lieutenant Fisher may be the one to benefit. There is every probability that my uncle may have passed away well before I met my cousin." He took a deep breath. "It appears to be the time for confiding, and I am not so callous that I do not realize how traveling now, when my uncle may be dead or dying, appears. He is the one who insisted I go and attempt to find Violet. He wanted her to know that he remembered her, despite her mother's somewhat unfortunate marriage and Violet's previous life. When I discovered that she was traveling with Miss Demaretti, I joined the group. It seemed best, for Miss Demaretti's sake, to wait until they reached Rome to introduce myself to her. Violet would then have been free to return to England and visit our uncle. That is the sum of it. I have my own legacy from our Uncle. I have no need of hers, which now goes to Lieutenant Fisher."

"That story proves nothing," Hethering flung at them. "And that fragment of lead cannot possibly assist you. It is too deformed for any use."

"Not so. If Maggiore Lupino wished to do so, he could use your mold to produce more bullets. He would find that they, too, have this small dimple in the side, just as these spare balls from your case do."

"And what does that prove? Why, either the captain or Lieutenant Fisher could have swapped molds. Or even you, Mr. Gaunt. There are three of us with smaller caliber weapons. Who is to say?"

"Your case was locked, Mr. Hethering," Knighton pointed out. "You kept the key upon your person."

He shrugged. "Anyone could have stolen the key as I slept. It was Captain Marshall who had the scrap of wadding in his pocket, lest you forget. We shared a room. He could have used my pistols."

"Why would he when he had a set of his own? He had no way of knowing about the imperfection in your bullet mold. And I noticed your little *contretemps* with Marshall at the inn door after the funeral. Your hand slipped into his pocket. You placed that paper in his coat at that time," Knighton said. "You must have hoped by doing so that you could shift the blame to your rival, leaving your way clear to court Miss Demaretti."

"Court?" Catherine's voice rose shrilly as she stepped in front of Marshall to confront Hethering. "You tried to force me to marry you! I will have you know that I would never have married you—never!"

Frowning, Mrs. Ursini put her plump arm around Catherine's shoulders to draw her back. The girl shook her off and stood, almost vibrating with rage, between Marshall and the rest of them.

Hethering studied her flushed face, a slow, patronizing smile curving his mouth, although his eyes remained hard. "You are overwrought, my dear. I should think your chaperone would have the decency to remove you from such an awkward and unutterably crass situation."

"You say this Hethering murdered the English lady?" Lupino picked up the mold from Hethering's box and opened it to examine the inside.

"Yes. I believe he tried to lure Miss Demaretti to the churchyard that night, in an attempt to compromise her and thereby gain access to her fortune." He faced Hethering. "Anyone who has played cards with you is sadly familiar with your lack of ready funds and your promises to pay any debts incurred once you reach Rome. Presumably, you hoped to have secured Miss Demaretti's fortune by that time. In any event, Mrs. Ruberry intercepted the message you sent to Miss Demaretti and borrowed the young lady's cloak to go in her stead. When you realized you had been tricked, you lost your temper and shot her. You must have reasoned that without a chaperone, Miss Demaretti would be vulnerable and easily seduced. Then you moved the body, as already stated, in an attempt to hide it. Failing that, you hoped Capitano Nacchio would be blamed," Knighton explained, watching Hethering closely.

The man seemed determined to brazen it out, despite the proof against him. He stared into space, rocking back onto his heels, forward, and then back again.

"You already know the rest." Knighton closed his dueling pistol case and flipped the lids shut on all the other boxes except for Hethering's. "I heard Marshall remark that you had borrowed his guide. You would only have done that if you did not have a guide or index of roads. So you were the one who needed the coach's information recorded on that note. If you obtain a sample of his handwriting, Maggiore Lupino, I am confident that you will find that it matches the scrawl on the paper used for wadding. Hethering slipped it into Marshall's pocket to deflect attention away from himself and condemn his rival."

"Mr. Hethering, what say you?" Lupino asked, his dark eyes glittering with the promise of an enjoyable fight should Hethering's reply merit it.

"I admit nothing." Hethering's words sounded confident, but the drooping line of his wide shoulders and dull, hopeless expression in his eyes told their own story.

"No matter. Come." Lupino glanced at Knighton. "This time, no one will object, I think, to the arrest." He shoved Hethering toward the door and paused at the threshold. "You will collect these things. I will take them with the prisoner in Buonfiglio's wagon." A quick smile made his white teeth flash. "He will, I am sure, not mind, *sì?*"

Knighton nodded, already collecting the bits and pieces and placing them all together in Hethering's case.

"My God," Fisher said, again threading his fingers through his hair. "I never—what a dreadful thing."

"Dreadful, yes, but at least it is over," Knighton said, feeling the sudden exhaustion—and sadness—that the end of a case often brought with it.

Chapter Twenty-One

It seemed as if they had barely retired before Pru was awakened by loud pounding on the door.

"What is it?" Knighton asked sleepily, rolling over to face her.

"I don't know." She glanced at the window. Dawn had only threaded a few pale strands of rose through the velvety blue sky. "It is early—"

Another sharp series of knocks rattled the door. Pru swung her legs out of bed, flinching at the cold rush of air brushing her bare ankles. Before she could stand, Knighton grabbed her wrist.

"Stay," he mumbled. "I will see who it is."

With a grateful smile, she tucked her icy feet back into the warm depths of the bed and drew the covers up. Knighton stood and reached for his robe, but before he could open the door, it flew open.

"She is gone!" Mrs. Ursini rushed into the room, wringing her hands.

Her graying, black hair hung in a thick braid down her back, and her nightcap was askew, hanging over her right ear. She had obviously rushed out of her room without thinking, for her feet were bare, and she clutched an old, gray knitted shawl over her nightdress. A certain slackness in her face and her puffy eyes made Pru think that Mrs. Ursini had only awakened a few minutes ago and had almost immediately came to their door.

"Gone? Who is gone?" Knighton asked, tying his robe and slipping his feet into a pair of slippers.

"Catherine! Miss Demaretti! She has disappeared!" Mrs. Ursini grabbed the lapels of Knighton's robe and shook him, letting her shawl fall around her chubby little feet. "That man—that *murderer*—must have escaped. He has kidnapped her!"

Pru got out of bed and pulled her cloak over her shoulders. The morning air was frigid, and the room was drafty. Cold air seemed to seep through the very walls and flow over the plain, wooden floor in thick waves that rolled over her feet.

"Maggiore Lupino left last night with Mr. Hethering in the wagon. He could not have kidnapped her," Pru pointed out, rubbing one cold foot over the other as she searched for her slippers.

"Then where is she? Where has she gone?" Mrs. Ursini turned to face her when Knighton gently removed her hands from his robe.

"I don't know." After a glance at her husband, Pru caught the frantic woman's hands and chafed them. "However, we shall find her, I promise you. Perhaps she simply could not sleep and went outside for some air."

"Air?" Mrs. Ursini stared at her as if Pru had suddenly started raving. Her expression was so similar to Mrs. Ruberry's when they had opened the windows in the coach that Pru almost laughed. "Who would want the air at night? It can only make you ill. Oh, where can she be?" She pulled her hands away from Pru and twisted them together.

"Have you searched your room for a note?" Knighton's voice was patient and eminently reasonable.

"Note? What is this note?"

"I don't know if there is a note, but perhaps you should search for one," he said. "In the meantime, we shall dress and alert the others. We shall find her, never fear."

While Knighton tried to calm down the excited woman and gently pushed her through the door, Pru dressed hurriedly in her blue traveling dress. It was beginning to look a little less than fresh after their unexpected adventures. She rubbed at a few of the dust marks on the skirts to get rid of them before pulling on her pelisse and a pair of stout walking shoes, all the while worrying about Catherine.

Where could she have gone? Had something happened to her? Had they misjudged Capitano Nacchio's honesty? The fact that he was the son of the contessa made him seem slightly more acceptable and trustworthy, but in truth, they lacked any evidence to support that belief. True, he had not harmed her when he held her captive. However, he would have gained nothing but Knighton's enmity if he had done so.

And given the state of Nacchio's estate, it was clear that he was almost as desperate for funds as Hethering was. A sick feeling made her sit briefly on the edge of the bed, her hands cold with fear. Nacchio may have succeeded where Hethering failed. She took a deep breath and pushed the terrible thought away.

"Are you ready?" Knighton stretched out a hand to help her to her feet. While she had mulled over the situation, he had dressed.

One look into his worried eyes told her that he experienced the same concerns that she did.

"Yes." She pulled on a bonnet and tied the wide, deep blue ribbons under her chin. Cabò lumbered over and sniffed at her pelisse before pushing his head under her hand. She stroked his head absentmindedly. "I... Do you think Capitano Nacchio kidnapped her?"

"I would not think so."

"Then where could she be?"

Knighton reached around her to open the door and held it as she and Cabò stepped into the dim hallway. Dark, shifting shadows and the musty smell of old wood greeted her. The other guests apparently still slept, and the only sound was the occasional creaking of the building's floors and walls.

"Oh dear, do bring a lamp," she said, her hand involuntarily playing with the top button on her pelisse in a nervous gesture. "It is still mostly dark. I don't even know where to look."

A movement in the corner of her eye caught her attention. At the end of the hallway, a glowing, ghostly figure stood, watching her. A cold chill ran down her back. She sucked in a sharp, startled gasp.

"Knighton." She could hardly force the name through her stiff lips. "Knighton!"

"What is it?" Behind her, she heard the soft tread of her husband's booted feet as he collected a lamp.

She gripped the edge of the door and searched for the reassuring silhouette of her husband. "Ghost—I saw it!"

"Where?" He strode back to her, carrying the lamp.

"There." She pointed down the hallway toward the Contessa's door, only to realize that the specter had disappeared. "I saw it—it was standing right there." Even as she spoke, she remembered—and realized—what she had seen. That pale face and dark eyes...

"I don't see anything. Did you see it disappear?" He walked a few steps away and held up the lamp.

"No." She brushed past him and walked softly down the corridor until she reached the door adjacent to the contessa's. Domenica's door. When Knighton followed her with the lamp, she waved him away. She needed the darkness to see what she expected to find.

Soft, luminescent streaks of silver touched the doorframe about a foot from the floor. Another glimmer highlighted the doorknob. She raised her hand and knocked.

"Who is there?" Domenica asked through the closed door.

"Mrs. Gaunt. Domenica, I must speak with you."

"Not now. Later."

Pru knocked again. "There is no need to worry. I will not tell the contessa."

Silence. Then the doorknob turned and the door opened a crack. Domenica peered at her through the slit. "What do you want?"

"You and Capitano Nacchio are the ghosts, aren't you?"

"Why would you say such a thing?"

"I saw you, just now."

Domenica shut the door. A second later, she threw it open and stood in front of Pru, wearing a long white dress and white veil liberally dusted with luminescent powder. "So? So you see. You know nothing."

"I promise I won't tell anyone your secret, I just want to know why the two of you masquerade as ghosts."

Domenica jerked her head in the direction of the contessa's door. "She does not approve. And there is Maggiore Lupino, always waiting for Pasquino to leave his estate. He wants to arrest him." Her chin went up and her dark eyes flashed. "We will not allow this, *si*?"

"And so you made up the story of ghosts so that you could meet in the small bedroom on the second floor."

"*Si*. There is a way—under the bed." She studied Pru. "We do nothing wrong."

"Thank you for trusting me. I won't give your secret away."

Domenica shrugged. "It does not matter so much to me." She smiled grimly. "Soon—I think Pasquino must marry me."

"I see. Well, good luck, and I wish you both happiness."

"*Si*. Now, I must go. Before *la contessa* awakens." Domenica gently closed the door.

Satisfied, Pru strode back to her husband.

"What did you find?" he asked when she joined him.

"Traces of our ghost, or ghosts. The figure I saw was Domenica."

Knighton chuckled. "Indeed. I thought there was something between her and Capitano Nacchio. In fact, I suspect both of them have acted the part of ghost as needed in order to meet. I doubt the contessa would approve."

"Must you always be correct?" She shook her head in mock disgust. "I wonder, though, if Domenica might also be the cause of the feud between Captain Nacchio and Maggiore Lupino? In any event, if we took another look at the haunted room, we would find an entrance beneath the bed. It explains why Lieutenant Fisher claimed the figure appeared at the foot of his bed, and that is the one place we did not search."

"No doubt." He placed a warm hand against her back. "However, at the moment, we need to locate the girl. We should awaken the others so they can assist in the search. If we cannot find her, then perhaps we should visit Capitano Nacchio one more time. I would like to believe that he will be as surprised as we are at her absence, but it is possible that he, too, remains interested in her fortune."

"If he had an assignation with Domenica, I don't see how he could also have kidnapped Catherine. Unless Domenica was involved." Pru frowned, hoping she was wrong. Despite everything, she rather liked the contessa and Domenica. In her heart, she hoped that the maid and Capitano Nacchio would make a match of it, despite any opposition—if there was any—on the part of the contessa.

"There is no point in speculation," Knighton said. "We shall only know the truth when we find Catherine Demaretti."

On their way down the stairs, Knighton knocked on Mr. Savage's door and quietly explained to him that his assistance was required. When he got to the room shared by Hethering and Marshall, there was no answer to his tapping.

"Perhaps the captain is a sound sleeper," Knighton said, hand on the doorknob. He glanced at Pru.

She nodded, and he tried the door. It was unlocked. Holding the lamp above his head, Knighton stepped into the room. No one was inside. The covers on the bed closest to the door were rumpled, and there was a dent in the pillow, indicating that someone, presumably Captain Marshall, had slept there. Knighton walked over to the bed and pressed his hand on the pillow and then slid it under the covers.

"The bed is cold." He straightened and took Pru's elbow to guide her through the door. "He left at least fifteen or twenty minutes ago."

"Do you think he is with Catherine?"

Knighton smiled and hurried her toward the staircase. "I would not doubt it. Although it may be that Mrs. Ursini roused him first and for some reason delayed knocking on our door."

"I should not admit this, but I would feel better if she was with him, even if it meant she is compromised. He seems to be a decent man and to care for her."

"Perhaps. But she would lead him, or any man, in a merry dance. She is one of the most capricious young ladies I have been privileged to meet." Knighton scarcely stepped off the last step when the sound of voices and laughter interrupted them.

The sounds came from the parlor.

Pru exchanged a chagrined glance with her husband. They walked into the gloomy room to find a roaring fire crackling in the fireplace and Catherine standing in front of it. She was fully dressed in an elegant, velvet pelisse and silk bonnet with large plumes nodding above the brim. One hand held the fur muff that had matched her ermine-trimmed red cloak, and her other hand clutched Captain Marshall's forearm.

Her cheeks were flushed, and when she caught sight of Pru, Knighton, and the dog in the doorway, she laughed again, her dark eyes gleaming. She flicked a coquettish glance at the captain. He also flushed, but it was clearly with agonized embarrassment. He looked at Pru, flushed more deeply, and then returned his gaze to Mrs. Ursini, who stood in front of the pair.

Mrs. Ursini, dressed in her usual black gown, faced the two with her fists on her hips and a frown marring her usually cheerful, plump face. "You behave with no thought—it is beyond my comprehension how a young lady could do what you have done!" she berated the couple, her voice rising and her words coming faster and faster.

"What has happened?" Pru asked, interrupting the flow of Mrs. Ursini's increasingly incomprehensible tirade.

"The most exciting thing." Catherine's grip on Captain Marshall's arm tightened. "We are married!"

"Married?" Pru echoed, bewildered. "How could you get married?"

"Captain Marshall was so wonderful," Catherine gushed while Captain Marshall shifted from one foot to the other and stuck one finger into his collar to loosen the neckcloth. "He arranged everything with the priest."

"But a license—how did you obtain a license?" Bewilderment made Pru feel as if someone had pushed her down a rabbit hole. She gripped her own husband's arm with one hand and rested the palm of her other hand on Cabò's warm, silky head. Her husband and her dog steadied her and made the room seem less like it was spinning around her.

Catherine waved the fur muff with supreme unconcern. "We are married, that is all that matters." Her nose rose as she assumed an extremely haughty expression. "And I shall not need your services, Mrs. Ursini." When Captain Marshall shifted and cleared his throat, she added, "Although I will pay you for the week, of course."

"Pay? Why should you pay? *Mio Dio*." Mrs. Ursini flung her hands into the air. "That I should ever hear such words."

"Well, now if you will excuse us, we shall retire." Catherine glanced up at her husband and flashed a dimpled smile.

Captain Marshall appeared to be choking. His already flushed face became alarmingly red, and after one appalled glance at his wife, he stared at the floor as if wishing the floorboards would peel back and allow him to fall to a quick and merciful death.

Even Catherine blushed as she seemed to hear her words echoed back to her, but she straightened her shoulders and led her husband out of the room.

"Well," Knighton said, gazing after them. "At least she is not lost."

"Or kidnapped," Pru couldn't help but add. Then she sighed tiredly. The pale, gray light streaming through the windows said it was too late to return to bed, no matter how much she wanted to.

She caught Mrs. Ursini's glance. The older woman shook her head and shrugged her ample shoulders. "So. That is all." A wistful expression passed over her face. "So I shall not go to Rome."

Pru looked at her husband. She had not had the chance to speak to him about their plans, although to be honest, she had put it off. She was with child, and the thought both thrilled and terrified her. She desperately wanted a baby to cradle in her arms, and yet she did not know if Knighton truly felt the same way. Oh, he had told her that he wished for a family and seemed pleased that she might be pregnant, but he had never seemed particularly anxious about it. That could either mean he did not really want children, or he simply did not care.

And she wanted him to care. Desperately.

Because that might help her overcome her more private fear at the thought of bearing children. So many women died in childbirth. So much pain, so many difficulties. What if it happened to her?

Her hand went of its own accord to cover her belly protectively. She wanted this baby, wanted to see it laugh and grow up and to hold it in her arms.

"I think," she paused once again to look into her husband's dark eyes, "I would like it very much if you would consent to accompany us, instead, Mrs. Ursini. Would you consider it?"

"*Si!*" Mrs. Ursini clapped her hands and ran over to embrace Pru. "I would like this this very much."

"There is something..." Pru flushed. He had mentioned the notion to her, but they had not discussed it. Did he have second thoughts?

Mrs. Ursini laughed and looked up at Knighton, a wide smile on her lips. "I shall care for your child, *si?*"

"My child?" Pru studied her husband's dear face and saw knowledge and joy in equal measures glimmering in his eyes. "*Our* child."

"*Si*. And you will have many children, and I will care for all of them. You will see." Mrs. Ursini said.

"I have been meaning to discuss the matter with you for days," he said. "But we have had regrettably little time alone."

"Regrettably little time!" Her voice rose. She hit his arm lightly with one fist. "I am appalled to hear such excuses." She paused and then said in a low, quiet voice, "Are you pleased?"

"Very pleased." He grinned and flung a heavy arm across her shoulders, dragging her against him. With his mouth against her cheek, he murmured, "And I shall prove it when we are alone, my love."

Giggling, she flushed and glanced self-consciously at Mrs. Ursini.

The signora clucked her tongue, flung her hands up in amusement, and headed for the door. "I shall pack. Signor Charron will have the carriage ready, and we will go. Today. *Si?*"

"Undoubtedly," Knighton agreed, watching her bustle through the door and head for the stairs.

When they heard the sounds of her quick footsteps on the staircase, Pru looked up at her husband, turning aside her face with a laugh when he tried to kiss her. "Behave yourself, you brute. Are you really pleased?"

"Yes, I am. And you?"

She nodded, the knot in her throat preventing her from speaking.

"Do you still wish to continue to Terni and Rome? Perhaps we should return to England?" he asked, concern wrinkling his brow.

"Oh, please, we cannot come this far and not see Rome. Mrs. Ursini would never forgive us."

"And you?"

"I—can we still go to the cascade, first?"

He laughed. "You certainly have an *idée fixe* concerning that particular destination."

She felt her cheeks burn even more warmly. "You will think me foolish—"

"Never."

"My father proposed to my mother at the *Cascata delle Marmore,* and they were so in love and so happy that... Well, I always hoped..." Her voice trailed off as she searched his face for understanding.

All she had ever wanted was the same joy as her parents had experienced. Their time together had been short, Pru barely remembered her mother, but she had seen the soft glow of love in her father's face when he spoke of her before he died.

"My love," Knighton kissed her forehead and smiled down at her, the intentness in his eyes making the excitement build within her to an almost unbearable level. "I would be honored and delighted to accompany you there. Your happiness is my happiness, and I cannot think of a better destination. I only wish I could have met your father. He seems to have been a most estimable gentleman."

"He was. I miss him terribly, and only wish I had known my mother."

"Well, our child shall know both of us and will undoubtedly be spoiled even worse than Miss Demaretti."

Pru pressed her fingers against his warm lips and laughed. "Oh, do not tempt fate by saying such things."

"Ah, there you are," Charron wandered into the room, his misshapen hat twisted between his hands. "The carriage is ready—we must go to reach Terni today."

"Oh, dear." Pru's stomach twisted and gurgled. The memory of the close confines of the coach, and the incessant swaying and jolting intensified her queasiness. With all the resolution she possessed, she straightened her shoulders. "We shall be ready in twenty minutes."

"Bravo, my love. The falls at the river Velino await us, and I promise you will not be disappointed."

"And I shall keep you to that promise," she replied tartly before heading up the stairs.

THE END

Other Titles by Amy Corwin
ARC Program

If you enjoyed this book and are interested in receiving a free copy of my next book in exchange for writing a review on Amazon.com, let me know!

Send an email to contact@amycorwin.com with the following information:

- If you want a paperback or ebook version
- Your address (snail mail) if you want a paperback copy
- The email to use for sending you an ebook (if you want an ebook version)

Note: Your information will be considered private and will *not* be shared. I will always send an email first with the summary of any new book before the book is sent to ensure that you are still interested.

Thank you!

The Archer Family Series

The **Archer Family series** are traditional Regency romances spiced with a mystery, and *The Earl's Masquerade* is the latest in the series. The books all offer at least a glimpse of John Archer, the instigator of many a fateful adventure. He can't seem to keep from dragging his nieces, nephews, and other unfortunate relatives, with him on escapades that invariably uncover a murder or two. Thankfully, Mr. Knighton Gaunt, of the Second Sons Inquiry Agency is often on hand to help the Archers out of the worst of their troubles, when he's allowed to do so.

While these books do not need to be read in order, the list below presents them in chronological order. Reading them in the listed order may be best to gain a true understanding of the mischief John Archer can create amongst his young, unattached family members.

The Necklace ~ A young woman, a scoundrel, and a family heirloom that might possibly be cursed.

The Necklace introduces John Archer and his exasperated niece, Oriana Archer, who is fed up trying to keep her uncle out of trouble. When Uncle John drags home yet another disreputable, wounded associate for her to nurse, she's at her wit's end. But there's no rest for the weary, and Oriana soon discovers another of her uncle's acquaintances, murdered in a way that points suspicion directly at her!

The Unwanted Heiress ~ An American heiress nobody wants; a duke every woman desires; and a murder no one expects.

In *I Bid One American,* Nathaniel Archer, Oriana's brother, no sooner inherits a dukedom than he's accused of murder. And his Uncle John's schemes don't help. Uncle John is the guardian to an American heiress he's anxious to unload on the first, unwary, English peer, and Nathaniel looks as good as any, despite the shadow of a noose hanging above his head.

But Nathaniel is made of sterner stuff, or so he thinks, and he's got more to worry about than romancing a singularly unromantic heiress when a dead debutante is found in his carriage.

The Bricklayer's Helper ~ A masquerade turns deadly when a murderer discovers one of his victims survived.

The Bricklayer's Helper features Sarah Sanderson, an orphaned girl disguised as a man and working as a bricklayer. She's the sole surviving member of her family, murdered thirteen years ago in a terrible fire. She may, or may not, be the niece of John Archer, and John is determined to bring her back into the family by hiring one of the newest agents at the **Second** Sons Inquiry Agency. Unfortunately, when the killer realizes Sarah escaped, her life is threatened despite the efforts of the attractive inquiry agent and her matchmaking uncle.

The Earl's Masquerade ~ A sabotaged boat forces an earl to investigate murder and discover that love may ultimately be what he's searching for.

Everyone believes Hugh drowned with his brother after their boat is sabotaged, and Hugh fosters that belief trick the elusive killer into revealing himself. But he doesn't count on running into two others also desperate to escape notice behind the comforting anonymity of false identities. Helen Archer lost the fabled Peckham necklace at a ball given at Hugh's home and is desperate to get it back. Young Edward Brown only wants to run away to sea like his hero, Admiral Nelson. When the three meet, Helen and Hugh hatch the perfect plan. By masquerading as servants, they can accomplish their goals in secret. However, Edward objects for purely practical reasons. He wants to go to sea, and he definitely doesn't want to spend his days polishing boots as a pretend servant. But the young boy is overruled and their adventure begins.

Second Sons Inquiry Agency Series

The **Second Sons Inquiry Agency series** are traditional historical mysteries spiced with a romance. The books all feature Second Sons, but do not necessarily focus on the found of the agency, Mr. Knighton Gaunt. Many of the stories feature other inquiry agents, or investigators, as the agency grows and flourishes. Mr. Gaunt is often called to the aid of the Archers, who seem to be inordinately fond of trouble.

While these books do not need to be read in order, the list below presents them in chronological order.

The Vital Principle ~ Gaunt is called to a séance to uncover a fraud, only to stumble upon a murder. **Book 1**

The Vital Principle is the first in the **Second Sons Inquiry Agency** historical mystery series and features coolly intellectual Mr. Knighton Gaunt, the agency's founder. Once accused of murder, himself, Knighton is driven to uncover the truth behind the complex, often mysterious murders that cross his path.

In *The Vital Principle,* Knighton Gaunt meets Prudence Barnard, a spiritualist accused of murder. While those involved are happy to accuse her as the stranger in their midst, Knighton is not so sure and sets out once again to discover the truth.

The two meet again in *The Dead Man's View*.

A Rose Before Dying ~ An earl is enmeshed in a deadly game to prove his uncle didn't murder his mistress. **Book 2**

In *A Rose Before Dying,* Charles Vance impulsively decides to pluck the role of inquiry agent out of Knighton's hands and discover the real killer. Charles is determined to exonerate his irascible uncle, Sir Edward, the only real father he has ever known. Unfortunately, Sir Edward doesn't make it easy for his nephew, and the only clues Charles has are sprays of roses left at the scene.

As **Second Sons Inquiry Agency** grows, you'll encounter other agents who run into odd mysteries and formidable murderers during the vibrant first half of the 19th century.

"Witty historical whodunits in the tradition of Bruce Alexander's *Blind Justice* and Victoria Holt's *The Mistress of Mellyn,* that will keep you guessing until the unexpected end." –A Reader

The Dead Man's View ~ Pru requests Knighton Gaunt's aid to help her prove the death of her cousin was not suicide, but murder.
Book 3

The Dead Man's View is the second mystery featuring Prudence Barnard and Knighton Gaunt, and the third in the **Second Sons Inquiry Agency** historical mystery series.

When Eric Knibbs invites Pru, his second cousin, to a house party, she's pleased to discover that she has a family, even if it is a distant one. Unfortunately, their reunion is cut short when Eric is found dead, hanging from a noose outside his bedroom window.

The authorities believe Eric hung himself, but Pru begs to differ. Eric was afraid of heights and could never have committed suicide in such a manner. After a quick examination of his room, Pru finds too many anomalies and can't help questioning the circumstance of Eric's supposed suicide.

So Pru does the only thing she can, she asks Knighton to help her prove that her cousin's death was murder.

The Illusion of Desire ~ A new inquiry agent, Captain Nicholas Ainsley, is enmeshed in a murder investigation where even the victim seems determined to obscure the truth behind a series of illusions.
Book 4

The Illusion of Desire features a new inquiry agent, Captain Nicholas Ainsley and is the fourth mystery in the **Second Sons Inquiry Agency** historical mystery series.

When Nicholas accepts employment as an inquiry agent, he is soon drawn into a complex murder investigation. Lord Taunton has been killed just a few weeks before he plans to marry a young debutante. The dead earl's closest friend claims Taunton's mistress, Kathryn, killed him in a jealous rage over his plans to marry another woman. Despite the evidence pointing to Kathryn, Nicholas believes she may be innocent. Others have equally strong motives and matters are complicated by the complex series of illusions Taunton cultivated to hide the details of his private life. Nicholas is sure that one of the carefully constructed veils may be hiding the face of the killer.

As he digs deeper, Nicholas discovers an older mystery left unresolved. Is the earl's death related to the seven-year-old tragedy, or was his murder committed for entirely different reasons? Nicholas is determined to rip away the illusions and reveal the face of the vicious killer, regardless of personal cost.

As **Second Sons Inquiry Agency** grows, you'll encounter other agents who run into odd mysteries and formidable murderers during the vibrant first half of the 19th century.

A Second Chance Paranormal Romances ~

The **Second Chance Romances** are paranormal romances spiced with mystery, danger and an "Urban Fantasy" feel that will keep readers enthralled. They do not have to be read in any particular order since each book stands alone.

Vampire Protector ~ *Vampires, a haunted house, and a lost relic, and Gwen's evening is just beginning.*

An anonymous note sends Gwen on a mission to uncover a dark family secret that may be hidden in her long abandoned childhood home. When she asks her handsome neighbor, John, to accompany her, she's not expecting much. Unfortunately, that's her first mistake. John is a vampire and her house is not exactly empty. Secrets—and the dead—won't always stay buried, and John's extraordinary strength and determination may be all that can withstand what awaits them in the shadows.

A Fall of Silver ~ *A woman bent on the destruction of all vampires discovers redemption in the arms of an ex-priest determined to save the undead.*

Their secrets are about to catch up with them.

The only good vampire is a dead vampire: that's Quicksilver's philosophy and she sees no reason to change it. In fact, she's about to kill one of the undead when Kethan Hilliard confronts her, promising redemption for both vampires and humans in exchange for an end to the slaughter.

But Quicksilver knows that's not going to happen.

Someone is killing humans and vampires, and sweet words aren't going to end the nightmare.

The events awaken terrible secrets from Quicksilver's past, and she's not about to repeat her previous mistakes by trusting the undead. This time, she's going to end the madness and silence the horror, forever.

Cozy Contemporary Mysteries

A new series of contemporary, cozy mysteries is underway, set in fictitious towns near the Outer Banks of North Carolina.

Whacked! ~ *Cassie's hopes for a quiet vacation go up in flames when she discovers her uncle sharing a smoke with a dead body.*

Love can make anyone crazy, but Cassie, a stressed-out computer expert, has always chosen logic over that uncomfortable emotion. This is, until in a weak moment, she agrees to housesit for her aunt and uncle. Within minutes of her arrival, she finds a murdered man. And her uncle is inexplicably determined to implicate himself. Cold logic suggests he's hiding something and Cassie isn't going to let him get arrested without a fight. Unfortunately, her past history with the sheriff makes him all too happy to accept her uncle's guilt.

But love is supposed to overcome all obstacles, not create them, and Cassie refuses to let a ridiculous emotion stand in the way of logic.

Too bad Cassie is about to discover just how far people will go for love.

About the Author

Amy Corwin is a charter member of the Romance Writers of America and recently joined Mystery Writers of America. She writes historical and cozy mysteries with a touch of romance, as well as paranormal romances. To be truthful, most of her books include a bit of murder and mayhem since she discovered that killing off at least one character is a highly effective way to make the remaining ones toe the plot line.

Join her and discover that every good mystery has a touch of romance.

Connect with Me Online

Website: http://www.amycorwin.com

Twitter: http://twitter.com/amycorwin

Facebook: http://www.facebook.com/AmyCorwinAuthor

Blog: http://amycorwin.blogspot.com

www.ingramcontent.com/pod-product-compliance
Lightning Source LLC
Chambersburg PA
CBHW061951170626
46813CB00006B/2608

* 9 7 8 1 9 4 0 9 2 6 0 8 7 *